all
SHOOK
UP

To: Laura

I hope you enjoy my book!

Happy reading!

♡ Chelsey

all SHOOK UP

Chelsey Krause

TRYST BOOKS

Tryst Books
720 Bathurst Street, Suite 303
Toronto, Ontario M5S 2R4

This is a work of fiction. Names, places, and incidents are either the product of the author's imagination or used fictitiously. Any resemblance to actual people, living or dead, events, or locations is entirely coincidental.

Cover design: Meghan Behse & Chelsey Krause
Front cover photo: licensed through Adobe Systems Inc.

Library and Archives Canada Cataloguing in Publication

Krause, Chelsey, 1987–, author.
        All Shook Up / Chelsey Krause

Issued in print and electronic formats.
ISBN 978-0-988387-04-8 (pbk)
ISBN 978-0-988387-05-5 (epub)
ISBN 978-0-988387-06-2 (kindle)

        I. Title

PS8621.R383A79 2019   C813'.6   C2016-904789-X
                                              C2016-904790-3

This is an original print edition of *All Shook Up*.

To Amber, my dear friend and neighbor, who would probably marry Casey if he were a real person. Thanks for believing in me.

CHAPTER 1

Return to Sender

"Ugh! What is that smell?" the new girl asks.

Three large green garbage bags are lined up beside each other on the sorting table.

"We'll find out in a minute."

I rip open the first bag. All clothes. The second bag: assorted cast-off toys. The third bag is full of household garbage. Old coffee grounds. Plastic wrappers. Half-eaten food.

"We have a winner."

"Who would donate garbage?" she asks.

"They probably just mixed up the bags."

"Does this happen a lot?"

"Not really," I say. "I've been here for about two years, and I've only seen it a couple of times."

I look over at the new girl, Millie. She has short black hair that's shaved on the sides, a nose ring, and bright red lipstick. The thrift store has been short on volunteers lately, so it's been nice having her around.

"Coming through," shouts Gladys. She's a round bundle of white hair, pointy elbows, and shrill squawks. Sometimes she reminds me of a seagull. She's volunteered here for the past thirty years and has a bad habit of bossing me around, even though technically – as of today – I'm kind of her boss.

I've worked at this thrift store, One Man's Treasure, for about two years now, and I help out at the local hospital when I can. Mostly with handing out breakfast trays and stuff. It's okay, but I prefer working here. I started out volunteering but slowly moved up the ranks. Today is my first day as manager.

To be honest, I'm a bit nervous. Don't get me wrong, I'm sure I can do the job. I've just never been "in charge" before. I know there was some talk about whether the quiet one would be a good leader. I almost feel like I have to prove myself or something. Here's hoping today goes well, with no surprises.

Gladys barges between Millie and me and plonks a few boxes on the sorting table. Stabbing a finger toward the mountain of clothes and toys in front of me, she says, "You're falling behind."

"Gladys, have you met Millie?"

Gladys waves an impatient, veiny hand in front of her face and yanks a box toward her. She starts randomly chucking items but doesn't seem to actually see what she's handling.

Save for the occasional strange surprise, like dead mice in old work boots, it's like Christmas every time I go to work. Or treasure hunting. If you dig long enough, you usually find something worth keeping. And I should know – I was thrifting way before Macklemore made it cool.

As soon as Millie and I are done with one pile, another load of boxes and lumpy plastic bags is dumped in front of us. An ocean of unwanted things.

My eyes land on a dusty, warped cardboard box that was set on the far end of the table by one of our newer volunteers.

"Just throw it out," Gladys says. "It's probably old junk."

I nod, placating her. As soon as her back is turned, I dive into it anyway. My fingers glide over some sort of silky material. I lift it out of the box and hold it up to the light.

"Oh my god…"

Millie cranes her neck. "What?"

I pull and pull until the dress is finally out, the fabric draping artfully as I hold it above me. It's navy blue, with a halter neck, a full skirt, and about twenty off-white buttons down the back. It reminds me of smiling pin-up girls with wide red lips and black garters. Pure 1950s glamor. Hands down, it's the most beautiful dress I've ever seen. This is so going home with me.

Millie smiles and returns to her pile, and I carefully set the dress aside and return to the cardboard box. A wrinkled photo album and a couple of hand-written letters rest at the bottom.

"Who would throw away pictures?" Millie asks.

I shrug. "This is nothing. I've seen people sell their photo albums on eBay."

Millie's eyes widen comically. "It's who's *buying* them that worries me."

I leisurely flip through the album, but stop cold a couple of pages in.

It looks like a picture of me, playing dress up.

What? That can't be right.

I bring the album closer, my eyes squinting.

It's a black and white portrait of a young woman with cat-eye glasses and a 1950s-style blouse. I'd guess that she's probably in her early twenties. Her dark hair hangs in loose waves over her shoulders.

She has my nose. The same long, hook-type nose that I was teased for in school. The one I've learned to cover up and reshape with contouring makeup. The one no one else in my family has.

At first glance, my family and I kind of blend together. But if you look a bit closer, you'll see that my hair is a little bit darker and my skin is more olive-toned. That my nose is definitely different from everyone else's.

I often wonder if outsiders think my mom nailed the mailman or something. But for all I know, the mailman *could* be my dad. When you're adopted, you wonder about the stranger at the restaurant who has your laugh or the cashier who has your smile. The world becomes one giant question mark.

I run my finger over the portrait of the young woman. We have the same nose. I wonder...

Millie playfully bumps her hip into me. "You all right?"

"What? Oh, I'm fine," I say. I close the album and set it aside. "I wish I knew who it belonged to."

There aren't any names written in the photo album. No captions, either. Just a few scattered dates confirming my guess that they were taken in the fifties and sixties.

Just then, my phone buzzes in my pocket. It's from my oldest brother, Matthew.

Tell Mom I can't make it to dinner tonight. Something's come up.

I bash a quick reply: Tell her yourself, you arse.

My brothers and I try to go home at least once a month for a big family dinner. Recently, Matthew has developed the habit of flaking out at the last minute. He's also developed the bad habit of getting me to do his dirty work.

Matthew: I'll try to make it next month.

I sigh and return my phone to my pocket. I chew on my thumbnail, and my eyes flick back to the cardboard box. What else is in there?

I pick up the pile of letters that was wedged under the photo album. They're tied neatly with string. I turn them over in my hands, noting the address on the tattered envelopes. They're addressed to someone named Nancy Carlyle.

Nancy.

Does that ring any bells? I pause for a moment, ready to be struck by lightning or something.

I wait.

Nothing.

My eyes scan the envelope. The address is only a few blocks from here. My heart pounds out an excited, hopeful rhythm. Wouldn't it be amazing if some blood relatives of mine lived close by? And they had donated this box by accident, and, by some miracle, I intercepted it?

Gladys flies into the back room and slams the door behind her. I look up from the sorting table, as do Millie and Cheryl, another lady who's been volunteering here for years.

"Disgusting," Gladys spits.

Millie frowns. "What?"

"There's a guy out there," Gladys says, pointing toward the main shopping area of the store. "He's got a snake wrapped around his neck."

So much for no surprises on my first day in my new role.

Cheryl laughs. "You're kidding."

"Nope," Gladys says. "A big, disgusting snake. It's got to be at least five feet long." She gives our table a focused stare. "He's creepy. We've gotta get this guy out of here."

Cheryl peeks out the door. After about two seconds, she ducks back in. "Oh hell no. I'm not talking to that guy."

"Why not?" I ask.

"He looks scary," Cheryl says. She sweeps an expectant gaze over to Millie. "You go."

Millie scrunches up her nose. "I'm scared of snakes."

"I'll go," I say.

Gladys lifts her wispy white eyebrows, her eyes scanning me head to toe. At last, she smirks. "Okay, missy. Have fun."

I supress an eye roll and walk out of the back room. It doesn't take me long to locate snake guy. And he isn't the three-hundred-pound bristling biker I expected.

He's young. Late teens, I'd guess. Greasy hair. Tattoos on his neck. A grubby coat with split seams.

He doesn't scare me. I know his type. And besides, the snake he has around his neck is maybe eighteen inches long, probably a baby corn snake. In other words, harmless.

"Hello," I say. "Can I help you find something?"

He shifts from side to side, never quite looking me in the eye.

"You got any cages around here?" he asks.

"What kind of cages?"

The sweet, stale smell of alcohol oozes from his pores. "Dunno. A fish tank would probably work."

I reach out a tentative hand and hover over the shiny scales. "May I?"

He briefly makes eye contact, but then looks away. "Suit yourself."

"He's nice," I say. Looking down, I see a dirty white sock poking through a hole in his left shoe.

"I had a cage, but someone stole it," he says.

"That sucks," I sympathize.

He shoves his hands in his pockets. "I had a cardboard box for him for a while, but someone took that too."

"Who would steal a cardboard box?" I ask.

A tiny grin peeks through his lips. "An asshole."

"We have an old fish tank in the storage room. Should I bring it out for you? Let you take a look?"

He runs a hand over the snake coiling over his shoulders. "Sure."

A little while later, the snake is slithering around his new tank. Snake Guy is beaming.

"Thanks," he says quietly while digging in his pockets. He brings out two dollars. "I don't have much…"

I discreetly rip off the price sticker and smile. "Would you believe it? We're having a pet sale. Two dollars for cat trees, fish bowls, you name it."

He smiles and hands me his money.

I spot a pair of men's running shoes on the rack nearby. They're about the right size. "Take these too," I say, making a mental note to pay for them later.

Snake Guy gives me a look, the kind of look that means he actually sees me and isn't looking through me, like most people. "Thanks."

I ask him to come back if he needs anything else. We often give quilts and winter jackets to people in need.

A few minutes later, Cheryl quietly sidles up to me. "You handled that well," she says.

"Thanks," I say. "You never know what a person might be going through."

She nods. "Indeed."

A few hours later, I finish my shift and hand over the keys to Cheryl so she can lock up later. She's my favorite person to work with here. Mid-sixties, wide smile, wears lots of chunky wood necklaces, and always smells of cinnamon. Being around her feels like being in a warm hug all day. She used to be manager, but after ten years she decided to take on a lesser role and passed the baton onto me.

Usually we're chatty during shift change. But today, I'm feeling distracted. My mind is still buzzing from that box. I really want to get out of here and process what I've found.

"You were really good with that guy today," she says.

"Hmm?" I say, thoughts elsewhere.

"The snake guy."

"No big deal."

She tilts her head to the side. "I never would've thought someone like you could relate to someone like him."

I feel myself bristling. I hate it when people reduce humans to an "us versus them" mentality. We're all people.

"He was a nice guy," I say.

"But you just seemed so...comfortable. Do you volunteer at homeless shelters? Or did you have a snake when you were a kid, or something?"

I feel my stomach clench. "Something like that." I pick up my coat and purse and head out the door. "See you tomorrow, Cheryl."

I walk out to my car, a dusty cardboard box and its contents tucked under my arm. On my way, I say a little prayer for Snake Guy. I wonder if he has anywhere warm to sleep tonight. I know what it's like to walk in his shoes.

I take out the envelopes, although I don't really need to. I've memorized the address already. I'm tempted to sit in my car and read the letters before I do anything else, but I'm feeling too jittery. I need to move.

I map out a route in my head and start driving.

CHAPTER 2

Brown Eyed Handsome Man

The drive takes about ten minutes. I'm kind of surprised that it's only a few streets away from where I work. As far as Canadian cities go, Edmonton isn't too hard to navigate. That is, unless you're looking for something on Kingsway. Then you're screwed.

It's a sloppy day in April, the roads coated with brown piles of gritty slush. Robins hop around on front lawns, hinting that spring has arrived. I pull up alongside a two-story house with sun-bleached blue siding, a U-shaped driveway, and a detached garage out back.

I stare up at it for a moment, my hands shaking on the steering wheel, wondering what I've got myself into. I do some breathing exercises to calm down, pick up the box, and get out of the car. I can barely stand, my legs are so wobbly.

Maybe I'm working myself up over nothing. So what if the woman in the picture looks like me? It could be a coincidence.

Or maybe, just maybe…

I walk slowly up the driveway and knock on the door, my heart racing. After a couple of minutes, I knock again. Maybe they aren't home? Maybe they didn't hear me? I try the doorbell.

After a minute, I hear heavy, muffled footsteps.

Oh god. I should have worn a better outfit. I quickly smooth my hair with my free hand and stand a bit taller. Am I going to meet my birth mother? Or, at the very least, an aunt or something? Or my grandmother? Although, if someone cared enough to take these pictures and put them in an album, why would they throw them away? Is that the sort of person I *want* to meet?

The door swings open. The person standing in front of me is most definitely not a granny.

"Can I help you?" he asks as he rubs his eyes.

"Oh, I, umm..."

My brain has stalled.

He shouldn't be the most beautiful man I've ever seen. But for some reason, he is. He looks like he's in his late twenties, maybe early thirties. He isn't wearing anything that spectacular, just a plain T-shirt and fleece pants. And his dark eyebrows are a bit thick for my liking.

But those lips...thin on top, full on the bottom, framed by a cleft chin and dark stubble. And those brown eyes fringed with black lashes...

He blinks. "Okay, then. Well, if that's all..." He starts to close the door.

"Does this belong to you?" I yelp. I shove the box into his chest. He takes a half step back and sneezes as the dust flies up around him.

He frowns. "Is this the crap I took to the thrift store?" With a confused look on his face, he hands the box back to me and crosses his arms. He leans on the door frame, making his biceps strain against his T-shirt. His entire left arm is covered in swirling blue and green tattoos. "How did you find where I live?" he asks cautiously. He has a hint of an accent. Scottish, maybe?

I roll my eyes. "Don't flatter yourself, I'm not stalking you."

He smirks. "Good. I've already got too many stalkers."

I'm momentarily disarmed, and then I remember why I'm here. Perhaps he knows the people who live here.

Oh god. He lives here, doesn't he? Have I been checking out a cousin or brother or something?

I take a step backward. "There were some letters inside addressed to this house. There was also a family photo album. I wondered if they were donated by mistake."

He rubs his eyes again. "No mistake. I just bought this place and found this box in the basement. So, off to the thrift store it went."

"You didn't look inside?"

He shrugs.

"You're unbelievable," I say.

He bows slightly. "Why, thank you."

"What if there'd been a million dollars inside?" I ask.

"What's it to you?"

I sigh. "Long story."

His face seems a bit frozen. "All right."

"I'm adopted," I say. "When I found this box today and looked at the photo album inside, I saw pictures of a young woman who looks like me. Until today, I've never seen anyone else with a nose like this."

I turn to display my profile.

He leans toward me, his dark eyebrows knitted together. "It looks fine to me."

"It's huge! And it's got this weird hook thing at the end…What?"

He shakes his head. "Nothing," he says, looking somewhere between amused and sleepy.

I feel my cheeks flush, and I wonder if dropping in unannounced was such a good idea.

"Anyway," I continue, "even if we aren't related, she and her family might want their pictures back." I dig through the box a bit and show him the letters. "Do you know anyone named Nancy Carlyle?"

He shakes his head. "Never heard of her."

I feel two distinct reactions to this news:

1)   Elation, because I haven't been checking out a brother or cousin.

2)   Disappointment, because he can't offer me any new information.

We're quiet for a moment, and he shifts his weight. "Listen, I'm sorry, but I don't know anything about…" he gestures to the cardboard box tucked under my arm "…all of that. I'm tired. I'm going to back to bed." He gives me a casual waving salute and says, "Good luck, Thrift Shop Girl."

I frown, feeling as though I've run into a brick wall. This isn't the way I thought this would play out. I imagined that by now I'd be seated in my grandma's kitchen eating fresh-baked biscuits and drinking tea. There'd be a teary reunion. She'd answer my burning questions. We'd laugh about our noses.

It would've been wonderful.

The door is halfway closed by the time I come back to the moment.

"Who's still in bed at three p.m. on a Tuesday?" I blurt.

He winks. "Someone who had fun the night before."

The door closes and I hear the click of the deadbolt. I trudge back to my car, limbs feeling heavy.

Okay. Let's put some perspective on this.

First, any number of people out there could have my nose, though I've never actually seen them. Second, what are the odds that my adoptive family and my birth family would live in the same city after all these years? And third, what if the letters and the photo album aren't connected at all? What if the person who lived there before was just storing the box for a friend?

My phone buzzes with a text. It's from my youngest brother, Patrick.

Mom is wondering: Are you still coming to dinner on Friday?

Me: Yes. Matthew isn't coming, btw.

Patrick: Good. I didn't want to see the nasty old grouch anyway. Come early. Mom wants you to peel potatoes.

I climb into the car and slam the door shut behind me.

Me: You're the official potato masher of the family.

Patrick: My delicate hands can't handle it.

Me: Delicate, my arse. You're a mechanic. See you on Friday.

I shove my phone into my purse and pull away from the curb. As I shoulder check, I glance at the house with the faded blue siding. A curtain from a side window on the upper floor is drawn slightly, and I see a pair of dark eyes looking down at me. I give a little wave.

He waves back, with an odd look on his face. So much for him going back to sleep. Maybe he's just making sure that his weirdo stalker actually leaves.

Hmm. I wonder who Mystery Man is. I didn't even get his name.

I try to concentrate on the road, but my mind keeps mulling the day over. Rational, logical thoughts are the loudest in my head, saying it was just a coincidence, my imagination running with a silly, childish fantasy.

But there's one small, quiet voice underneath it all telling me that it wasn't a coincidence, that it wasn't a mistake. It says that I was meant to find that photo album.

And above all, it says that I need to find out who Nancy Carlyle is.

CHAPTER 3

Que Sera Sera

"So where's Matthew?" my mom asks.

I pick up a potato and start peeling it. "Something came up."

Mom sniffs and tosses a potato into the pot.

"He said he'll try to come next time," I say, aiming for soothing tones.

She sighs and raises her eyebrows thoughtfully. "He's always kind of been an ass."

"Mom!"

She gives a stuttering laugh back. "Well, he is!"

I shake my head and return to peeling potatoes.

My brother Matthew is adopted too. Our parents, Doug and Mary Bishop, got him first when he was two years old, and then they added me to the mix about a year later, when I was a baby. And, as often happens when couples adopt, our parents got pregnant, and along came Patrick.

Matthew isn't a bad person, really. He's very type-A, all about fitness and self-improvement. He just says it like it is, which is a nice way of saying that he doesn't have a filter. Patrick is a redneck class clown. He's all about drinking beer, wearing camo, and spraying people with deer pee for fun. And I fit somewhere in the middle. The peacemaker, the quiet one, the dependable one.

Well, now I am, anyway.

I peel another potato and toss it into the pot.

"Maybe it's best he isn't here tonight anyway," she says after a dramatic sigh. "I imagine he would have had a few choice words about the potatoes."

"He wouldn't have said anything about the potatoes," I reply.

No. He wouldn't have said anything about them. But he would have eyed them suspiciously, calculating how many gallons of butter and milk were in every spoonful, and then lectured us throughout dinner about the benefits of "going paleo."

"We were at the accountant's office last week," Mom says casually as she tosses another potato into the pot. She has a home business and Dad runs his own landscaping company, so between the two, they see their accountant often. Especially this time of year, when they're doing taxes.

"Uh huh."

"Yes," she says, flicking the vegetable peeler faster and faster. "Martin's so wonderful with our accounts."

"Cool," I reply vaguely.

"We really like Martin. He's handsome, too," she adds. "I don't understand why he doesn't have a girlfriend."

Ah. There it is.

"Maybe Martin has a boyfriend," I suggest helpfully.

"You should meet him sometime," she says, ignoring my comment. "Maybe go on a date?"

A date with Martin the accountant.

"I think I'll pass," I say.

"Dad really likes him," she adds.

My dad has only two criteria for liking people, men in particular: their stance on manscaping (they must detest the idea) and the quality of their zombie apocalypse survival plan. I don't even want to know how Dad would've found those things out about his accountant.

"Just throwing options out there," Mom says. "You've been single for a while."

I can just see it now. Martin and my dad ridding the world of body trimmers and discussing whether adult diapers should be in their survival kit. You know, so they don't have to slow down to pee while running from the zombie hordes.

"Really, I'm good," I say.

Just as she's about to reply, a tapping sound comes from the front door. Relief floods my entire body.

My mom, now elbow-deep in dishwater, points her chin toward the front door. "Can you get that? I think it's my five o'clock fitting."

Mom is a tailor. Or seamstress. I don't know what the difference is. Either way, she works from home and sews people's stuff, bridesmaid dresses and wedding gowns, mostly. My favorite childhood memories are of lying on the floor in her office, raking my fingers through the soft carpet and looking up at the dresses that hung from the rack above. I'd watch as she tweaked and pulled, hemmed and darted her way around fabric, turning plain cloth into something extraordinary.

I'm a bit worried about her, actually. Over the past few years, her hands have become arthritic. She doesn't like to complain, but I know she can't do as much as she used to. I worry about her ability to keep sewing and make money, so sometimes I come over and help her work on the more finicky projects.

And now that she's getting older and more health problems are coming up, I keep wondering what's in store for me. What sort of genetic Pandora's box am I going to open up someday?

I dry my hands and open the door to a sight I've seen over and over again: a woman clutching a garment bag. "Come in, I'll show you to the office," I say.

I love to watch my mother work. I love the way she holds pins in her mouth and how her face screws up when she's concentrating. I love the spools of thread she has on the wall in dozens of colors. The office is always a mess. I don't think I'd recognize it if it were ever organized.

After the five o'clock fitting and dinner are over, Patrick and his wife and daughter go home and I bring the photo album in from the car. I lay it on the kitchen table and flip a few pages inward. I find the portrait and wave my hand over it. Like magic. Maybe if I wish for it enough, it'll come true.

"Remind you of anyone?" I ask.

Dad raises his eyebrows and Mom gasps. She turns to me. "Where did you find this?"

I feel overwhelming relief and sag into my chair. So it isn't just me. I'm not just seeing things.

"I found it at the thrift store this afternoon."

"This is incredible," my mom says while manically flipping pages. "I wonder who brought it in."

"I found him, actually." I explain the events of the day to my parents.

"You went to a stranger's house? Alone? What if he were a freaky axe murderer?" Dad asks.

"He wasn't a freaky axe murderer."

He huffs. "As far as you know."

"Does the name Nancy Carlyle ring any bells?" I ask.

Both Mom and Dad frown in concentration and purse their lips. It's funny how their expressions are so alike. I wonder if that's something they've always done or if it's something that happens when you've been with someone for decades.

"Sorry, kiddo," my dad says, shaking his head. "It was a closed adoption. We never learned her name."

Her. "Her" has become my birth mom's name. The ever-present, ever-vague term that is my past. "Her" is everywhere and nowhere at the same time.

I look across the table at the people I call Mom and Dad. I've been with them since I was five weeks old. I couldn't have asked for better parents.

But, I still have always wondered…

I twist my hair around my fingers, noticing the split ends. "So, what do you think I should do with this?" I ask, nodding to the photo album.

"You said there were letters too?" my mom asks.

"Yes."

"Have you read them?"

"Not yet."

"Maybe you should start there," she suggests.

"Yeah. And then what?"

They look thoughtfully at one another for a moment.

And then, to my relief, my mother smiles and says, "Whatever you want."

CHAPTER 4

Don't Be Cruel

Whatever I want.

Well, what I want right now is a cup of coffee.

Luckily, I'm sitting on the patio of my favorite café. It's a sunny spring day, the smell of early morning rain perfuming the air, and I'm meeting my best friend, Laura, for lunch before my afternoon shift at One Man's Treasure. It's Saturday, but spring is a busy time of year for us, so that means I'm working weekends too. People go into a spring cleaning frenzy and dump all of their crap – er, I mean treasures – onto us.

While I wait, I decide to read the letters.

There are three in total. Each is signed, *Love, Mom.*

There's no return address or stamp, so I wonder if they were hand delivered. But by whom?

From what I can tell, Nancy, whoever she was, had a falling-out with her family, but the details are vague. The letters all basically say the same thing. *Come back home. We miss you. We love you. It's never too late to mend fences. Papa is sorry for what he said.*

They're all dated twenty-seven years ago – 1989, the year I was born.

A thin, connecting detail. I'm trying not to cling to it.

I sip my coffee and look around for Laura. I wonder what she'll think of all this. She's my first proper "grown-up" friend.

Before I met her, I was pretty wild. My early twenties were a blur of vodka shots, flashing lights, and heavy eyeliner. It was fun, for a while. But chronic hangovers, relationship drama, and, well…other stuff gets old fast.

That "I'm such a rebel – just watch me destroy my life!" attitude is textbook behavior for adopted children, by the way. According to my counselor, at least. Even if they've never acted out before, even if they've always seemed well adjusted, the belief that they're unlovable and unwanted usually simmers just below the surface.

Or, on the other side of the spectrum, adopted kids often strive to be the "perfect" child. One who blends into the background. No one can reject you if you do everything right or don't attract attention. And it's common for kids to flip-flop between the two extremes.

I've worked really hard with counselors to put all of that behind me. And now I feel all that shit has been dredged up.

Laura was the first person who reached out to me when I started healing. I was determined to get in control of my life and be a healthier, better me, so I'd started yoga classes. I met her at my first class. Eventually she invited me to go for coffee, and that was that.

While I wait, I notice the woman sitting at the table next to me. She's very colorful: bright purple nails, unicorn hair, and patterned leggings. A few years ago, I would've rocked that look, but now my wardrobe is a thrilling palette of cream and oatmeal, all timeless neutrals that Pinterest style boards say I should have.

A sleek silver SUV screeches to a halt across the street. A woman in a slim-fit, bright white dress shirt and gray slacks slams the driver's side door and marches over to me.

"Hello," I say, smiling.

Laura plops down in the chair beside me. "Sorry I'm late," she says. "Our meeting ran into the lunch hour."

"Why are you working on a Saturday?" I ask, then sip my coffee.

She exhales. "We're hiring lots of people now. Doing interviews and orientation shifts…" After a moment, her eyes flicker to the woman at the table next to us. "I wonder what the office would think if I dyed my hair pink."

I look up at the rainbow woman. She's sitting alone in the sunshine, quietly flipping through a magazine. She looks completely content with her place in the world.

"Go for it," I say. "HR personnel are supposed to be hip."

She does a half snort that seems strangely at odds with her put-together perfection.

"How've you been?" I ask.

"Good," Laura says while peering at a menu. "I've just had a great cooking night with Elle."

I supress my grimace. "Sounds fun."

Elle is Laura's "foodie" friend, a purchaser for a terribly overpriced gourmet food store downtown. She and Laura met a year ago at a wine tasting at Red Piano, a dueling piano bar on the west side. They bonded over a mutual love for the movie *Julie and Julia* and a preference for homemade mayonnaise. They've been almost inseparable ever since.

Elle is okay, I guess. She seems nice enough. But she always has this plastered-on smile that reminds me of plastic.

"Cooking was fun," Laura enthuses. "She's really into teff lately."

I raise an eyebrow. "Teff?"

"It's this fabulous grain that's even better than quinoa," she gushes. "It's going to be the 'new' old grain. Oh, and Elle made me these appetizers with vegan nut-based cheese."

"Yummy," I say, supressing a groan. I glance at my phone to check the time. "We'll have to make lunch short. I'm due at the thrift store in half an hour."

"Still spending half of your paycheck on other people's old junk?"

"Not quite half," I say, smirking. "I get a great discount."

Being the manager of a charity doesn't pay me oodles of money, but it's enough to get by. And, with my discount, I can stretch my dollars a long way. My closet has quadrupled since I started working there. It's amazing how many precious things get thrown away every day.

Speaking of which…

I dig out the photo album, which is shoved into the side pocket of my favorite oversized tote. I flip it open and place it in front of her. I've already memorized the exact spot where the young woman's portrait is. My body is vibrating; I feel like I have to sit on my hands.

She stares at it for a minute before her eyebrows shoot up ever so slightly. I knew it! I knew she'd get it, that she'd see the resemblance.

She looks up at me. "What's this?"

I pause. "Don't you see it?"

She squints and leans in closer. "See what?"

"Doesn't she remind you of anyone?"

"Not really."

I blink. "She looks just like me," I say.

I tell Laura about finding the album and the letters. I don't tell her about going to the house because it was a dead end. It's not like I'm going to see that guy again.

Laura tilts her head to the side and taps the photo.

"So let me get this straight. You think that this woman who bears maybe a slight passing resemblance is somehow related to you."

I slowly exhale. "Basically, yes."

"And you think that Nancy Carlyle could be your mom."

I swallow hard and think about all the times I laid under racks of colorful dresses. I think about the severe allergic reaction I had to a bee sting when I was twelve, and my mother racing me to the hospital. I think about every music class she drove me to, every crappy piece of glitter-and-glue art she proudly displayed on the fridge. I think about the years when I was absolutely vile and she loved me anyway.

"Mary will always be my mother. But yes, I think Nancy might be my birth mom."

Laura is silent for a moment. "Natalie, I want to be supportive here, but what are you basing that on?"

I shrug. "Maybe if you read the letters…"

"Have you considered that you may have an overactive imagination?"

I'm suddenly aware that I'm holding my breath. "Well…"

She gives me full eye contact and places both of her arms on the table. Uh oh. Laura's officially in interview mode.

I laugh. "God, professional you is intimidating."

Her expression softens. "Okay. Let's think about this rationally. This is a coincidence. This isn't your grandmother. And Nancy isn't your mother. It's just a fantasy."

"You don't know that for sure," I say. "I could be right."

She bobs her head from side to side in a contemplative gesture. "Yes, you could be right. But you could be right about the mailman being your dad too. There are just way too many variables to consider here. What are you going to do next, start calling up anyone named Nancy Carlyle?"

I stir the ice in my drink. "No."

Actually, I was going to do a Facebook search first, but I won't bother telling her that.

She sighs. "I know you've always wondered about your birth family. I think it's natural, in some ways, to grieve for the family you think you never had. But Natalie, you have the best parents in the world."

She pins me with another one of her intense stares. It's a good thing I know that under that hard-ass professional is a woman who snorts when she laughs and freaks out over baby ducks.

"Anyway, the point is, you've been given a good life. You have a mom and dad who love you. You aren't a kid anymore; you're a full-grown woman. Is it really that important to start digging now?"

I look down at the album.

The woman's hair looks much coarser than mine. And her eyes are a different shape. Her mouth, too. And maybe her nose isn't quite that big after all. But then again, our noses are the same shape. And we have nearly identical smiles.

"I don't know. I feel so confused," I say, smiling weakly. "Maybe you have a point."

Perhaps she's right. Perhaps it was a silly idea, and I was seeing what I wanted to see.

But then, why do I have this niggling doubt? Why do I feel like I was meant to find this box?

At least I have tomorrow off. I feel like I need a day just to mentally process all of this.

CHAPTER 5

At the Hop

Ha. So much for having Sunday off.

The hospital called me at five thirty a.m. saying they were short on volunteers and asking if I could come in. The timing sucked, but the work wasn't hard: I folded towels, handed out breakfast trays, and fetched ice water for patients.

It was okay, for the most part. Though what was supposed to be a quick four-hour shift somehow turned into eight. Usually I don't mind, but I'm still feeling emotionally and mentally out of sorts. That, and there's this new patient on the long-term care unit who I'd much rather avoid.

He bawls his eyes out whenever he sees me. I have no idea why.

His name is Karl. I think he has dementia. I've heard that he understands English but only speaks Polish. There's a list of Polish words taped above his bed, with words like "Hungry?" and "Thank you" and "Pain?" beside them.

Karl just needs to look at me once and he starts crying, gesturing wildly with his thick, arthritic hands, his pale blue eyes and ruddy face twisting in some deep emotion. Even though I don't speak a word of Polish, I sometimes feel like he's begging me for something or trying to explain some sad story.

So yeah. Not really sure what I'm going to do about him. All I know is that I'm glad to be out of here for the day.

I walk out to my car and look down the empty street. Old houses with faded siding block out the setting sun. I climb into my car, my stomach grumbling impatiently.

I should just go home. Cook for myself. Save some money. I look at my phone, sitting black and silent in the seat beside me. It reminds me of the quiet, empty place I'm going home to.

Ah, fuck it. I'm going out.

I drive aimlessly for about twenty minutes, not really sure what I'm in the mood for. That is, until I come across a restaurant wedged in between a grimy pawn shop and an auto insurance place with boarded-up windows. The place is called Nifties, and posters tacked up outside of the restaurant shout in pink and black letters A MODERN TWIST ON VINTAGE TASTE AND LIVE MUSIC EVERY WEEKEND. A long line-up snakes out the door, and the inside is bright and pulsing. I immediately park my car and get in line.

It's a welcoming crowd, and it doesn't take long for me to make friends. I'm talking with a pleasant young man with a bushy beard and suspenders when someone taps my shoulder.

"Millie!" I say, turning to hug her. "What are you doing here?"

"I'm here most weekends," she says. "Have you ever been?"

"It's my first time."

I've finally make it to a window so I can peek inside. It looks like a 1950s ice-cream parlor meets gothic hideout.

"You look amazing," I tell Millie. She's wearing a stunning blood-red dress with a keyhole cut just below her breast bone. "I wish I could still wear stuff like that."

"What's stopping you?" she asks.

I think of the beige life I've built over the past two years. I clear my throat. "So, is the food any good?"

A new song starts up from inside and is greeted with raucous cheers. Millie smiles. "People don't come here for the food."

A gravelly voice breaks into our conversation. "Thrift Shop Girl? What are you doing here?" The voice has a vaguely Scottish lilt.

I turn around.

Oh. Dear. God. It's Mystery Man.

And what is up with his hair? He's shaved the sides, while the top is longer and slicked back. Surprisingly sexy.

"You *are* stalking me, aren't you?" he says.

I laugh. "You'd be so lucky." I notice a black guitar case slung over his shoulder. "Are you playing here tonight?"

He waves it off, like it's nothing. "Nah. Just helping my buddy set up. See you inside?"

"Yeah, sure," I say, willing my pulse to slow.

As soon as he disappears into the crowd, Millie bumps her shoulder into mine. "How do you know him?"

"I don't," I say.

"Well he sure seems to know you, *Thrift Shop Girl*," she says. "Is he a regular at the store or something? Please don't tell me he's weird like Guinea Pig Guy or Sock Lady."

We have a few regulars at One Man's Treasure. Most just like to browse and buy odds and ends. A shirt here, a zipper there. Maybe a picture frame one week and a couple of books the next.

And then there are the *other* regulars.

Guinea Pig Guy comes in every Monday. He carries a plush guinea pig in his pocket and calls it Bill. He doesn't buy anything. To be honest, I'm not sure that he has any money. He just likes to wander around and ask Bill what he thinks of this coffeemaker or that ball of yarn.

And then there's Sock Lady. I have no idea how old she is, but my guess is that she's in her early seventies. She doesn't like to buy the socks. She likes to stuff them in her sleeves and down her pants, and she tries to sneak out of the store without us noticing. One time she stuck a whole package of new socks under her shirt and told other customers that she was "expecting."

We usually just let her be. There isn't a big demand for second-hand socks, anyway.

"Nope, no guinea pigs that I know of," I laugh.

"Well, get to know him. Then you could introduce me."

"Is he a regular here?"

She smiles, her bright red lips a startling contrast to her pale skin. "You could say that."

The line moves slowly, but Millie keeps me very entertained with stories about Mystery Man. Rumor has it last week he had sex with a woman in the coat room after talking to her for about five minutes.

Hmm. Can't say that I'm surprised. He gives off that I'd-have-a-quickie-with-a-stranger sort of vibe.

Soon we pile into the narrow restaurant and sit as close to the band as possible.

The music mirrors the decor: 1950s with a dark twist. Some songs are bluesy and have a country twang. Others are distinctly fifties pop, but with a punk rock edge. I've never heard anything like it.

"What do you call this?" I ask Millie.

"Rockabilly," she replies.

"I kind of love it."

Mystery Man, whom I haven't seen since we met outside, flops down in the seat beside me and butts into our conversation. "What do you love?"

A breath catches in my chest, as if it's lodged in there and can't find its way out.

"All of this," I say, circling my hand through the air.

"So you'll be back next week, right?" he says.

Millie waves at the door. "I just saw some friends of mine come in," she says. "Be back in a minute."

She's leaving me alone? With *him*?

Okay. This is no big deal, right? He's just a person, after all. And a guy who I've met before. I can handle a normal, adult conversation with a man I've just met.

I look back at Mystery Man, and he gives me a small, lopsided smile that makes my pulse speed up and my breath catch.

Oh God. I'm so going to bomb this conversation. I'm sure he'll love awkward-around-hot-guys Natalie. And he's looking pretty hot tonight. He's wearing a tight black T-shirt, faded blue jeans rolled up at the hem, and scuffed-up leather boots. The black T-shirt contrasts beautifully with the colorful tattoo on his left arm. The skin looks a bit weird underneath. There are valleys and ridges and faint silvery splotches peeking between the swirls of blue and green ink.

He looks up and notices me staring. He runs his other hand over the arm, and for a second, his eyes look guarded. He quickly recovers, however.

"So, Thrift Shop Girl, are you planning to drop by my house later?"
I raise an eyebrow.

"To drop off more boxes of crap, I mean," he adds, with a flirty grin.

Ha! Yeah, right. He definitely *is* an I'd-have-a-quickie-with-a-stranger guy. At least he's consistent. Once upon a time, I might have taken him up on his offer. But, I know better now. Live and learn.

"I'm not that kind of girl," I reply.

Not anymore, anyway.

He sighs dramatically. "A guy can dream. So. What's your real name? Or am I going to have to keep calling you Thrift Shop Girl?"

"It's Natalie."

"Hmm. Natalie," he says, rolling my name around on his tongue in that delightful accent. He stretches his hand out to me. "Nice to meet you. I'm Casey."

He smiles a disarming smile, and I feel a familiar lurch in my stomach. This guy is way too smooth. I bet he never has to work hard to get anyone's attention.

I know his type. Stomach lurches be damned, I'm going to make him work for it.

I sip my drink. "Casey? That doesn't sound like a very tough guy name."

"No?"

"No. It's kind of girlie."

He shrugs. "Ever hear the song 'A Boy Named Sue' by Johnny Cash?"

"I don't think so," I say, trying to remember the songs on my dad's old country CDs.

"I bet you'd see my name differently after you heard it," he says, kindly. "Besides," he adds, "some of the best men in history had feminine names. Leslie Neilsen, for example. Or John Wayne. Did you know that John Wayne's real name was Marilyn?"

I laugh. "Actually, it was Marion."

He shakes his head, grinning. "You're fun."

Ever meet someone that you just immediately click with? And you can't explain why you like them – you simply do? Neither have I. That is, until tonight.

I don't think I've ever felt attraction on this level. To be honest, it's overwhelming. Pleasurably scary.

Casey orders another drink, asking if I want one too. I look at the clock.

It's midnight. How did it get that late? I should go home. By the time I get home, it'll be one, and I'm working tomorrow, and I have all sorts of crap to catch up on at home afterward.

Casey looks at me expectantly.

I throw up my hands. "Okay. Another iced tea for me."

He shoots me a puzzled look. "You don't drink?"

This is always a hard question to answer without opening a can of worms. I've stopped trying to explain it.

"Nope," I say simply.

Thankfully, he doesn't press the issue.

When our drinks arrive, I notice Millie standing by the door. She's waving at me and making crude gestures with her tongue, confusing some poor guy sitting at the next table.

I can't help but laugh. I try to shoot her a look that says, *Not interested at all; just having another drink.* It's kind of a hard look to pull off.

"Listen," Casey says, "I feel bad for being so rude with you the other day. I'd only had about two hours of sleep when you woke me up."

"I didn't think you were rude," I say. "Why were you sleeping so late on a Tuesday, anyway?"

"I'm a firefighter. I'd just got off night shift that morning. It had been a rough night."

A firefighter. Hot damn. I wonder what he looks like in his suspenders. *Only* his suspenders.

"Oh," I say. "Well, that's a bit more respectable than partying till the wee hours of the morning."

"Wee," he laughs. "Ah, you've just made me miss my mum. She's Irish, so everything is 'wee.'"

"So that's where it comes from. I thought Scottish at first, but…"

"You've been thinking of me?"

"No. Well…kind of. I've been thinking more about the house, and who lived there before."

"Uh huh." He smirks. "I sometimes have a bit of a Texas accent too, if you want to know. My dad worked there off and on for years, and I sort of just picked it up."

I feel like teasing him about being my very own international man of mystery but feel weird about it at the last moment. Instead, I simply nod and hide behind my drink.

"So," Casey continues, "Have you started looking for her?"

I swallow the last of my iced tea. "Who?"

"Nancy?" he says slowly.

"Oh. No," I say. "I've kind of given up on that venture."

"Just like that?"

"I'm a bit embarrassed by the whole thing, actually," I say. "I just pieced together some wild fantasy and ran with it."

He folds his arms across his chest. I can see the muscles in his forearms flex. The effect looks particularly cool under his swirling tattoos. Sort of like waves.

"So that's it? You're just going to give up?"

I shrug. "There's nothing to give up. There wasn't anything to start with."

He leans back in his chair. "Then you don't have anything to lose. Worst case scenario, you look for this Nancy woman, try to track her down, and don't find squat. Are you out anything?"

I stir the straw around in my drink. "Well, no. I guess not."

"You seemed pretty pumped up on Tuesday. So much so that you drove to a stranger's house and started poking around. Don't you think you'll regret it and always wonder 'What if?' if you don't at least try?"

"Why do you care so much?" I ask.

He shrugs. "Dunno. I like you. I want to help you out."

That same excitement I felt when I first saw the picture blooms in my chest again. Maybe...

"Thanks for the offer, but the whole idea was silly," I reply. "Besides, even if I did want to look, I wouldn't know where to start."

"I've got a friend who's a cop. He can search their databases for names," Casey says. "It's a start, anyway."

I chew on my lip. "So...you want to help me? Just like that? Who are you, the world's nicest guy?"

"Nah, I just really want to get into your pants."

We stare at each other for a moment before his face crumples into a smile, and we both laugh, breaking the tension.

I have a feeling that Casey is the type who likes to tease. Which, strangely, makes me feel more comfortable around him. It's almost like it pushes all the formality of making new friends away and gets right down to the good, fun stuff.

"I'm not quite that creepy," he says. "No, to be honest, I just really value family, and I, uh…"

He pauses for a moment, as if he's struggling to find the right words. "I guess I just know what it's like to miss a parent."

Our eyes meet, and for a moment the fun, easygoing Casey I've been getting to know has dimmed. Instead, I see old pain, dulled with time, in his expression.

I really, really want to do this.

Mostly because I might find whoever owns these photos. But also, the prospect of being around Casey makes me feel thirteen again, swooning over a first crush. I recognize what it feels like to be swept up in powerful, yet immature, emotions. Better to hold him at arms' length.

Damn this pragmatism. He looks rather fun.

"It's a closed adoption," I say. "And how do we even get the police involved? Even if it's your friend, surely there's some sort of red tape involved?"

He waves my comment away. "Details. Just hang out with me, and I'll help you look for whatsherface."

I laugh. "Nancy."

"Right," he says. "Come on, Thrift Shop Girl. This will be fun. Besides, I like adventure."

I'm trying to look serious. Casey gives me big puppy dog eyes, and I feel something inside me break. Like sunshine spilling through the cracks.

"Okay," I say, relenting.

He slams the rest of his beer and clinks the empty bottle onto the table. "Great. We start tomorrow."

CHAPTER 6

It's Now or Never

I can't believe I just did that.

I've just agreed to let a complete stranger help me find my...well, whoever she is.

The thought of finding this person, family or not, is kind of thrilling. Even if all we do is find the rightful owner of this photo album, I'll be happy. Better than it ending up in some landfill.

After another drink (and some sickeningly thick burgers), Casey and I leave the restaurant and he walks me to my car. We agree to meet at his place the next day so we can drive to the police station together and start our search. As good a place to start as any.

On the walk to my car, I keep stealing glances at him. I don't think I've ever seen shoulders that broad or biceps that huge before. I bet it would be fun to watch him work out.

Even though I try not to think about him, he keeps intruding in my thoughts. He's handsome, charming, and too smooth for his own good. He has a cool job and a sexy accent. He has tattoos and plays guitar.

He's exactly the sort of guy I'd normally go for. All the more reason to keep it "just friends."

The next morning, a bright, sunny day, I roll out of bed and shrug on a pair of cropped beige tights and a spring dress. By ten thirty, I'm waiting outside of Casey's house. I'm about to knock on the door when it swings open. Casey is standing there, a crooked smile showcasing one dimple.

And, oh dear God, he's shirtless.

"Morning, stranger," he says.

"Do you always answer the door half naked?"

"I just rolled out of bed. You're lucky I have pants on."

I feel a smile tugging on my lips. "Do you need a few minutes to get ready?"

He leans into the hallway and grabs a T-shirt and a set of keys off of a narrow table. "I'm good." He bounds out of the house, and walks down the driveway to the backyard.

I spot an orange cat with white stripes wandering through his front yard. I crouch down, and he arches his back into my hand, purring as if a motor has been switched on inside.

"Do you make friends everywhere you go?" Casey asks, looking amused.

I stand and brush loose orange fur off my hands. "I have a thing for orange cats," I say. "They've always been my favorite."

Casey turns and beckons me down the driveway. I follow him into a dark garage. Hmm. I sure hope he isn't a serial killer.

I decide to linger in the doorway. "So, how long have you lived in Canada?"

"Since I was thirteen," he says. "Why?"

"You still have an accent, so…"

He hits the garage door button, and an ancient motor and pulley system rattles to life. "We came over for Dad's work. But we were from County Kerry, originally," he says. "Very thick accents."

I'm about to blurt out, "I love your accent," but think better of it.

The garage door is finally up, and sunlight spills through the dusty air onto a very old, very sad looking blue truck.

"That's your truck?"

He nods. "Isn't she great?"

I examine the rust-bitten tailgate. It's barely hanging on. It doesn't even look road-worthy. "She's okay."

His eyes widen playfully and he places a hand on his chest. "You don't like Old Blue? But this is a '57 Chevy! It's a classic!"

I wrinkle my nose.

Casey pats the hood affectionately. "There, there," he stage-whispers. "She just needs to get to know you first. You have a great personality."

He walks over to the passenger side and opens the truck door for me, and I look into the cab. It isn't filthy, exactly. Everything just looks weathered. Cracked. Stained.

"I don't mind driving my car."

He sighs. "Just get in."

"Casey. There are holes in the floor."

Casey's mouth draws to the side and he looks around the garage. After a beat, he reaches over to a nearby bench and pulls out a piece of cardboard.

"There," he says, patting it onto the floor. "Good as new." He opens the door wider and bows gallantly.

I eye him warily. "All right. But if this truck gets my tights dirty, you're a dead man."

His eyes sharpen. "Don't worry. If your pants get dirty, you can take them off at my house when we get back."

My mouth drops open and I'm about to spout off some protest when he smiles impishly.

"What? Just so you can throw them in the wash. Geez. Dirty mind," he admonishes, and slams the door.

He climbs into the driver's side and looks over his shoulder as we back out of the driveway.

"Who likes wearing beige, anyway? Gets too dirty," he says. "Besides, it doesn't suit you."

I look down at my outfit. It's not fancy or anything, but I look decent. "Why would you say that?"

He looks over his shoulder as we back out onto the driveway. "Dunno. You just don't strike me as an oatmeal kind of person."

We pull onto the street, and we're quiet for a while. The hum of the engine is all we can hear. I press the photo album to my chest, trying not to think about what Casey just said. But my mind circles around the thought anyway.

I shouldn't worry about it. I doubt I'll see him again after today. He's just taking me to the police station, and after that, I imagine we'll part ways.

I wonder what we'll find today, if anything. I looked through the album for more names, and although the occasional date is written beneath a picture, most from the 1960s, no one is named. It's a simple family photo album. The woman who looks like me pops up throughout it. She had a husband and four daughters, from what I can tell.

"Thanks for doing this," I say. "It means a lot."

"You're welcome," Casey says.

I start picking at my nails and my knees bounce nervously. He glances over at me and then rummages in the large cardboard box on the seat between us. It's full of cassette tapes. The labels have worn off of most of them, so who knows what he's putting on.

"Here it is," he says, and he slaps a tape into the cassette player.

"I didn't think anyone used cassettes anymore."

"Only the best people do."

Roy Orbison's voice comes over the speakers, the song starting about halfway through. "Dream Baby." Casey sings along and taps a rhythm on the steering wheel.

"You've got a nice voice," I say.

He starts bobbing his head and sings a bit louder, making me smile.

"I love fifties music," I say.

"Me too."

I smile and relax back into my seat. After a second, I start singing along, my foot bobbing to the beat.

He reaches over and turns the volume down. "Natalie?"

I tap my fingers on the doorframe. "Yes?"

"Are you seeing anyone?"

My fingers stop tapping. "Why do you ask?"

"Just trying to be friendly."

I look out the window, feeling a bit queasy. It's not entirely unpleasant. It's been a long time since I liked someone and they've liked me back. It's just too bad that I always like people who are completely wrong for me.

"Not really looking for anyone, at the moment. What about you?" I ask, glancing over at Casey. "Do you have a girlfriend?"

He sucks a breath in through his teeth. "Just boyfriends."

My eyebrows shoot up. "Oh. Well, I…that's great."

I look around the dirty, nasty, old truck. Aren't gay guys supposed to be clean? Although his hair is a bit more quaffed than most of the rednecks around here. Hmm...

Casey cracks up laughing. "I'm not gay," he says. "I just don't do the girlfriend thing."

I purse my lips. "So are you asexual?" I ask, teasingly.

He glances at me. "Do I look asexual?"

No, you look like sex on legs.

I clear my throat, feeling a bit flustered. "Okay. So, you don't 'do' the girlfriend thing. Maybe you just 'do' girls," I joke.

"Wouldn't you like to know," he says, clearly amused at the turn the conversation has taken. "I like women. I *love* women, actually. I just don't see the point of being in a long-term relationship. I don't plan on getting married or having kids. So why be tied down to just one person? Besides," he adds, "I'd be a disappointing husband and an even worse father."

Hmm. Mini alarm bells start ringing in my head. It's definitely a good idea to keep this guy in the friend zone. But it doesn't stop me from wondering what it'd be like to...you know. Take him for a test drive. Speaking of which...

"So, you say you love women but don't want a relationship. Umm..."

Oh god. I can't believe I'm going to ask him this.

"Rumor has it that you banged some random woman at Nifties last week after knowing her for five minutes. Is that what you're looking for?"

Casey bursts out laughing.

"Is it true?"

"We were both adults and both there for one thing, so we decided to go for it," he says simply. After a moment, he adds, "Sex is fun. You don't have to make it complicated."

I angle my body toward him, feeling curiosity take over my good sense. "So what, you're just a big man slut?"

He signals into the police station parking lot. "You offend me, madam," he says, purposely making his accent thicker.

He turns the key and the engine turns off. My cheeks feel flushed. How did we get on this topic, exactly?

"I'm sorry. It's none of my business," I say, feeling embarrassed for trying to shame him.

"Is that what you're looking for? Husband, kids, the whole shebang?" he asks.

I consider this for a moment.

Do I want to get married someday? Have kids?

"I guess so. Down the road, anyway," I say.

"That's too bad," he says. "We could've had a lot of fun. Just friends for us then, eh?"

I nod. "Just friends."

We climb out of the rusty death trap and walk toward the station, my hand clutching my bag tight. It holds the photo album and letters to Nancy.

"This should be interesting," he says.

And even though I keep telling myself that Casey isn't the sort of guy I want to be with, I struggle to remember the last time I felt this happy.

CHAPTER 7

Crazy

"Well that was a bust," I say as Casey and I climb back into the truck.

Casey's friend, Constable Oakes, was nice. Indulgent even, which seemed odd. Maybe he was bored and just thankful for the distraction.

We didn't find anything on Nancy Carlyle. It's too generic a name to get any sort of real lead on without supporting information. He said that we'd be better off doing a Facebook search.

I instantly felt smug and wanted to shout, "Ha! I thought of that first."

But after the smugness faded, I only felt deflated. Who'd have thought that free social media could trump a police database?

Oakes explained to me that there were certain challenges to finding people. People pass away. Maybe they've never owned property or filed taxes. Some people have multiple aliases. Finding women can be particularly difficult if they've married several times or moved a lot.

This would've been so much easier if this were an open adoption.

"Thanks anyway," I say.

"No problem," Casey says. "I'm kind of surprised that Oakes went through with it, actually. Searching through police databases for personal use and all."

"Aren't there rules about that sort of thing?" I ask, panic rising up in me.

"There are," he says.

My stomach twists into ropes. Oh god. Maybe I've just committed some sort of federal offense.

"What if Oakes says something?"

"Trust me, he won't."

"Right," I say, trying to calm down. Maybe I'm freaking out over nothing. "And it's not like we found anything, so maybe it won't matter." After a pause, I add, "How do you know that he won't say anything?"

Casey doesn't respond.

I peek over at him.

"Casey?"

"I'm thinking," he says.

Casey turns the corner onto his street. It's funny that I hadn't been to this part of the city before. It's only a few blocks away from the thrift store. All this time, clues to who I am and where I came from were so close.

Well. Possible clues, anyway. I'm still just going on a hunch.

"I guess it was worth a try," I muse.

"What if I've come up with a brilliant plan?" Casey says.

"Brilliant plan?"

We pull into his driveway and he parks in the garage. As I close the passenger door, I feel something give way under my hands.

"Oh shit," I mutter. "Casey, the umm…the door handle broke off."

"Tsk tsk tsk," he says, taking it from me. He pats the truck box. "I'm sorry, old girl, but you're falling apart."

"You really love this old thing, don't you?"

He shrugs. "It was my dad's."

"He didn't want to keep this beauty all for himself, hmm?" I tease.

Casey looks me in the eye, and then looks away quickly. "He died," he says.

Embarrassment coils like a spring in my chest, winding tighter and tighter until I think I might explode. "Oh, Casey. I'm so sorry. If I'd known–"

He waves his hand. "No worries. It happened a long time ago. Had a massive heart attack. My mum sort of fell apart after it happened, so…" He trails off, looking a little lost. "Anyway, I keep it around because it reminds me of him. He used to take me riding in here when I was a kid."

I suddenly have an image of a little brown-haired, brown-eyed boy, full of mischief, bouncing around the truck cab.

"That's sweet," I say sincerely.

Casey tilts his head and rubs the back of his neck. "So, do you want to hear my brilliant plan?"

"Fire away," I say.

"Some of it involves paperwork, from the sale of my house. I'll have to go through my files. It could take a little while."

"Paperwork?"

"I figure whoever owned the house before might know who you're looking for."

I smile up at him. "Casey, that *is* brilliant."

He smiles right back. "Told ya. Do you want to come in? I'll make us some coffee."

Hmm. Is it a good idea to go into a strange man's house? Maybe he has some sort of creepy dungeon in his basement and he'll lock me up in there as his sex slave.

Although, considering how hot he is, that may not necessarily be a bad thing…

Oh god. What am I thinking!?

Okay. I've already spent time with this man in public places. It's not like he's a complete stranger. And he doesn't give off creepy vibes. In fact, he seems genuinely nice. Who goes out of their way to help a stranger these days?

And then, there's the possibility that he might walk around shirtless again.

"Sure, that'd be nice," I say, feigning nonchalance.

He leads me into a cramped entryway and kicks off his shoes. "Please ignore the mess."

The hall and living room are littered with half-opened boxes with black Sharpie marker labels.

"You really did just move in." I jump over a box in the entrance to the kitchen. It's an older house, with yellowed linoleum and dated paint colors on the wall. Whoever lived here before either was really behind the times or just didn't give a crap.

"It's lovely," I say.

"I know it looks like crap," he says as he turns the coffee pot on. I notice his back muscles shift under his tight gray T-shirt and can't help but wonder if he's ever posed in a firefighter calendar. "But," he continues, "the price was right, and I don't mind fixing it up. I plan to fix the truck up too."

"I could help you."

Casey looks over his shoulder at me. "With the house or the truck?"

I roll my eyes. "The house, obviously." I think the truck is beyond saving. I wonder how it ever passed inspection.

"What do you know about home renos?" he asks.

I shrug. "Well, I'm not going to be of much help if you want to knock down walls or redo the plumbing, but I could help with other stuff."

He takes a sip of coffee as he offers mine, the steam curling up around his face.

"Like what?"

"Like painting and decorating," I say.

He walks down the hall and motions for me to follow. "I don't give a rat's ass about paint colors," he says. "I just want to fix it up to the point that it looks presentable and isn't falling apart."

We walk up a short flight of stairs and into a small room furnished with a beat-up wood desk and a guitar propped up in the corner. Casey sets down his coffee and starts running his fingers over his files.

I look up at the bare white walls. Rusty picture hooks and yellow rectangle outlines of photos long forgotten stare down at me.

"Sorry, but this is just too sad," I say.

He glances up from the pile of papers in his lap. "What's that?"

"The state of this room. It's simply too depressing for words. You have to let me help you decorate, even if it's just this one room."

He laughs and returns to his papers. "Whatever makes you happy."

I sit cross-legged on the floor and lean against the wall with my coffee. "It would. I'm pretty good at this decorating stuff, you know. I'm good with do-it-yourself projects."

He nods but doesn't look up from whatever he's reading.

"I'm thinking maybe a grayish blue, with dark brown accents."

No response.

"And a proper guitar stand," I add.

Absolute quiet.

"Glitter would really liven up the space too," I say.

He lifts an eyebrow and seems to roll a comment around in his mouth before deciding it's better to choke it down. We're silent for a moment. I can't think of anything to say, so I sip on my coffee instead. Casey returns to his papers. A moment later, he hands me a folder.

"Here are my purchase agreements," he says. "Maybe this guy will know something. He sold me the house."

I flip through the file. "So, what's the plan? Just call this guy up and ask him stuff?"

"Sure. Why not?"

"It just seems a bit awkward, doesn't it?"

Casey leans toward the phone charging on the desk. "I'll call him up right now."

"No, not yet!" I say, leaping forward and spilling coffee onto the carpet. "Ah! I'm so sorry."

He crouches on the floor beside me. "No worries. It's not like the carpet could have gotten any worse," he says warmly.

I glance around. Stains of all colors, big and small, surround me.

"It's seen better days," I say.

"Makes you wonder what they did in here."

I laugh and scrunch up my nose.

"Okay. We can't just call up this..." I glance at the papers, "...*Frank* guy and explain my crazy theory to him. We need a plan."

Casey shifts so he's sitting on the floor across from me and unfolds his long legs. "Yes, we could. Just tell it to him straight."

I shake my head. "He'll think I'm crazy. And who wants to give information to a crazy person?"

An amused smile twitches on Casey's lips, the stubble catching in the early afternoon light. "All right then," he says, and he reaches for his guitar. He settles it comfortably on his lap, as if it always belonged there, and starts plucking the strings. "It helps me think," he explains. "Clears my head."

He plays contently, humming every now and then, his fingers moving along with his thoughts.

I lean against the wall, watching him, slightly entranced.

"I have a specific thinking spot," he adds, "but it'd be tough to go there right now."

"Where is it?"

His stops strumming. "Promise you won't laugh?"

"I promise."

"Chinese restaurants."

I pause for a moment. "You're serious?"

"I like to go there when I feel scunnered. It seems to help."

I laugh. "Scunnered?"

He smiles. "Oh, it umm…it means fed up, world weary, downtrodden. As if you're sliding into complete shitdom."

"You should write for Urban Dictionary," I reply.

"Anyway," he continues, "I like to work in the kitchens washing dishes. There's a place nearby that will let me wash dishes whenever I want, and nobody bugs me. Something about the repetitive motions, I don't know. It helps me clear my head."

I bite my lip and feel the laugh growing inside my chest.

"You promised you wouldn't laugh, now," he says, smirking.

"Well, if you're ever missing, I guess I'll check the local Chinese buffets first."

He picks out some complicated rhythm, and I marvel at how he's able to do different things with each hand and still carry on a conversation.

"You're very good," I say.

Excellent, actually. If I didn't think Casey was fantastic before, I certainly do now.

We sit there for a few minutes, he apparently lost in thought and me simply enjoying the music.

"So you're a firefighter, huh? How'd you get into that?" I ask.

"Can't talk," he says, strumming. "Thinking."

"Seriously, though," I say. "It must be stressful. How'd you get into it?"

He blows out a long puff of air. "I'm secretly a pyromaniac."

Before I can ask him any more questions, Casey's hand stills. His eyes are bright. Mischievously bright.

"I've got it. A wonderful, fantastic, brilliant idea."

CHAPTER 8

Jailhouse Rock

"Casey, this is a terrible idea," I hiss.

"Shh, they'll hear you," he whispers.

"It's illegal to impersonate an officer, you know."

"Only if we get caught."

I tug at my pants, which have a baggy butt and an uncomfortably tight waistband. Whoever designed these should be fired. "Where did you find these uniforms anyway?"

He knocks on the door. "The police station. Oakes got them for me."

"What?" I yelp. "Constable Oakes knows about this?" I lean against the side of the house, my heart pounding. "We're totally going to jail."

"We are not going to jail," Casey says quietly. He knocks a bit louder on the door.

"Didn't Oakes ask what you were using them for?"

Casey pauses. "Oakes and I have a, uh, understanding," he says.

Muffled footsteps sound from the other side of the locked door. Casey whips his aviator glasses down over his eyes.

"Okay, Thrift Shop Girl, game face."

He immediately adopts a stern, don't-fuck-with-me expression. I try to do the same.

I hope I don't giggle.

The gray, scraggly curtains are drawn on the door's window, and I see a distorted face behind the frosted glass. A moment later, the deadbolt turns over.

I'm holding my breath. For some reason, an enormous laugh builds in my chest. It feels like there's a beach ball stuck under my ribs, slowly inflating with air. If I don't let it out soon, I'm sure I'll explode.

Casey elbows me playfully. I nearly lose it.

The door opens, revealing a man with leathery skin and white tufts of hair just above his ears. He's smoking a cigarette and wearing a threadbare robe.

"What do you want?" he asks, looking supremely bored.

Shit. He doesn't look intimidated by us at all. I rub my sweaty palms over my pants. We are *so* busted. Casey expertly flashes a badge.

Where did he get that? It looks pretty real, all shiny and official looking. Surely Oakes wouldn't give him a real badge for our little project?

"Good evening, sir," Casey says. "I'm Constable McGuire. I have a few questions I'd like to ask. Is now a good time?"

Ugh! What's my cop name? We never discussed this!

Robe Man takes another bored drag on his cigarette. "Now's as good a time as any."

Casey smiles at him encouragingly. "Thank you, sir. We'll just need a few moments of your time."

I glance over at Casey. He's the picture of quiet authority, confident and unruffled.

He lifts up a black clipboard and starts flipping through some typed-up papers, complete with fancy-looking RCMP letterhead.

"Are you the owner of this house?" he asks.

Robe Man nods. "Yep."

Casey flips through the papers as if looking for something. "A mister...Frank Bailey?"

"The one and only."

Casey asks him if he used to live at such-and-such address.

Frank narrows his eyes. "Yes. Well, technically I never lived there. I rented it out. What's this all about?"

Casey nods. "We're looking for a missing person, a lady named Nancy Carlyle."

Casey and I look up at Frank in unison.

I hold my breath. This is it, the moment I've been waiting for. Maybe he'll know exactly who Nancy is and this stressful, highly illegal, OMG-I'm-so-scared-I-could-puke day will have been worth it.

I bet they were buddies. He probably knew her for years. Maybe they were even lovers! Oh my…could Frank be my dad? I scrutinize him a bit more.

Leathery skin. Long, wispy eyebrows. Bad fashion sense.

Shit. Is this my future? Am I going to have long, wispy eyebrows someday?

Frank shakes his head. "Never heard of her."

Phew. Dodged a bullet there.

But then the realization hits me. He doesn't know who Nancy is.

Casey takes his aviators off and tucks them into his front pocket. "We have reason to believe that Miss Carlyle lived at that address at one time."

Frank lifts his hand in an evaluative gesture. "It's possible. A lot of people lived there."

"How many do you estimate?" I hear myself ask.

Frank looks at me as if he's noticed me for the first time.

"It's hard to say. Too many to remember. I've been renting it out since the mid-eighties." *Since the eighties?* Damn. No wonder it looks a bit, umm, used.

"Did you keep any records?" Casey asks. "Renter's agreements? That sort of thing? Anything that might give us a list of names of who's lived there before?"

Frank rolls his eyes and turns down the hall, one hand waving over his shoulder. "Follow me," he says.

Casey and I hesitantly step into the entryway. A cold prickle of fear washes over my whole body.

"Is this even legal?" I whisper.

"Of course not," he replies.

"But don't we need a warrant or something?"

Casey briefly squeezes my shoulders in a side hug.

"Just roll with it."

I bite my thumbnail and follow Casey and Frank down the hall and into the basement, alarm bells ringing madly in my head.

Okay. There's no need to panic. Casey looks pretty capable. I think he could take Frank, or whatever creepy things might be in the basement.

We descend a flight of rickety, open stairs to a depressing unfinished basement. Frank ambles across the room and pulls a chain that leads to a single light bulb.

"Just a minute," Frank grunts while sifting through a lumpy pile in the corner.

The main room – or what I can see of it, anyway – is filled to the gills with junk. Normally I like old junk, but there isn't anything of merit here. Just stacks of outdated newspapers, piles of dirty laundry, and dusty couches piled with odds and ends that were set there once and never moved.

Casey stands straight as an arrow behind Frank, his arms crossed tightly over his chest. My own personal brick wall. I smile at him and mouth the words, *Thank you.*

He nods imperceptibly and turns his attention back to Frank. I'm glad Casey is here with me, even if the cops are going to haul our asses to jail.

Eventually Frank whirls around, still carrying his lit cigarette loosely between his lips, and plops an overflowing file organizer at Casey's feet.

"Here you go," he says. "Have fun."

An annoyed expression crosses Casey's face. "What do you expect me to do with that?" he asks, his accent showing more. I wonder briefly if his accent is stronger when he's caught off guard or stressed.

Frank starts to climb the stairs, wheezing as he hauls himself up each step.

"Do whatever you want with it," he rasps. "Everything in there is at least ten years old or more. Burn it, shred it, use it as ass wipe, I don't care. It's your problem now."

I pick up the organizer, and we follow Frank upstairs. Adrenaline races through my veins, the boom of blood in my ears yelling *Get out, get out, get out!* with every heartbeat. A swell of relief floods me as soon as I step through the front door and take a breath of fresh air.

Casey turns around, in pseudo-cop mode again.

"Thank you for your cooperation, sir. You've been most–"

The door slams in our faces.

"–helpful."

Casey and I stare at each other for a moment. I look up at him, not really believing what just happened. Or, more importantly, what we've just got away with.

"What do we do now?" I whisper.

He tugs my elbow and starts heading toward his truck that he parked down the street.

"Now, my darling, we haul ass.'"

"Well done, *Constable McGuire*," I say mockingly. I take a huge bite out of my Big Mac and melt into the passenger seat of his truck. "Thanks for the burger, by the way."

After we raced to the truck and were hurtling down the highway, we quickly realized that we were ravenous. Turns out that fearing for your life can really give you an appetite.

Casey stuffs several fries into his mouth. "Don't mention it," he mumbles through the fries.

I take another bite and reflect on what has most definitely been the most bizarre day of my life.

"McGuire. Is that your real last name?"

Casey shakes his head. "Giving him my real name wouldn't have been very smart, now would it?"

"Good point," I say. "So what is your real last name?"

"Nolan."

Hmm. Casey Nolan. Sounds good. Bet it rolls off the tongue nice.

Don't think about tongues around Casey.

He plugs a new tape into the cassette player, and the cab is filled with a sweet melody.

"Do you seriously like the Everly Brothers?" I ask, feeling amused. What man actually likes fifties pop?

"A better question is who *doesn't* like the Everly Brothers," he replies. "Just listen to that harmony."

The Everly Brothers lull us into a sense of quiet as they sing about their dream girl.

"Have you looked inside that thing yet?" he asks.

I lift the cover of the file organizer and run my fingers over the jumbled heap of paper. "A little. It's a complete mess. Nothing is alphabetized, or even organized by year."

"Surprising," Casey says, looking perplexed. "Frank gave the impression of being a great businessman."

I snort with laughter.

On the bright side, I don't think Frank ever threw anything away. There are decades of receipts, notes scribbled on ripped scraps, and renter's agreements stuffed into one tiny cramped space.

I rub my forehead. "It'll take me forever to go through all of this."

"Don't fret. I'll help you."

We hurtle back toward Casey's old, dirty house in his old, dirty truck, still wearing our "borrowed" police uniforms. He has me laughing every few minutes by singing along to songs in cartoony voices (he does a surprisingly good Mickey Mouse impression); making up lyrics, usually adding a dirty word or two; or making jokes about our "hot" outfits.

For the record, my pants are NOT hot. Why do they have all of these weird pleats? Do actual human beings have bums shaped like this?

I know I should be freaking out over how illegal and dangerous today was. Instead, I just laugh with Casey, eat my Big Mac, and enjoy the ride.

CHAPTER 9

If I Knew You Were Coming
(I'd Have Baked a Cake)

What a mess.

A sea of papers surrounds me. Yellowed papers, crumpled papers, wadded papers I have yet to flatten out.

There wasn't really a good way to go about it, so I decided to dump the whole thing on my living room floor and get to work. And now, several hours, two coffees, and one sore set of shoulders later, I have a list of names. People who might know something about Nancy. Casey still insists on helping me with my search, so we're meeting later this week to regroup. And talk about his sad, lamentable little office.

I rather like the idea of fixing his office up. It's kind of fun to have a project again, one where I can let my creativity run wild.

Well. That…and it gives me an excuse to be around him more. Men and women can be friends, right? Although I don't normally want to ravish my friends, so yeah. My intentions may not be entirely altruistic.

It makes me feel better, too, being able to do something for him. We'd started with ripping out the old carpet, blotched with decades of stains. Then, we dismantled the large desk attached to the wall. It had been built out of random pieces of scrap wood and was made more out of splinters than anything else. It might not seem like much, but it's my small way of repaying him for all of his help. I don't know how this journey would have gone without him. However, I sometimes worry that I'm taking over his house. More and more of my stuff is starting to accumulate on the side tables, I have my own mug in the kitchen, and I always seem to have an extra pair of shoes there. And I worry that I'm making it into "my" office, not his. But whenever I ask Casey for feedback on my ideas, he shrugs and tells me to do whatever I want.

"Go nuts," he says.

Ha. He may regret that when I start painting the walls pink.

The next day, I head over to Casey's house with a list of names.

"Lucy, I'm home," I announce, as I walk through the front door.

"Hiya Ricky," he calls out from the kitchen. Naturally, I'm impressed that he gets my Lucille Ball reference. He meets me in the hallway carrying a mixing bowl and wearing a shoddy old apron.

My mouth twitches. "Nice apron. What are you making?" I ask, trying to peer into the bowl.

"Muffins," he says.

I shake my head. "You're either the most adorable man on the planet, or you're completely and utterly gay."

He laughs. "Couldn't I be gay and adorable?"

"Good point."

He scoops batter into the muffin tins. "It's my mum's recipe, actually."

"Nice. Does your mom live close by?"

Casey opens the oven door, squinting at the heat.

"Nah," he says. "Mum remarried a few years after Dad died. They had a little boy together. They live in Vancouver now." He shuts the oven door. "I always wanted to be a big brother, and I never thought I'd get my chance. That is, until Liam came along."

"How old is Liam?" I ask while Casey hands me a glass of water. He really is a great host. I wonder if he entertains ladies here very often.

Not that I care.

"He's eleven now," Casey says. "In fact, you'll get to meet him this October. Mum's sending him up here when he's on fall break."

"I bet he's excited."

"I am too. I've got loads of fun things planned for him," he says, eyes sparkling.

I lean on one hand and look at him appraisingly.

He laughs. "What?"

"Just thinking," I say.

"About?"

I sit up straight and stretch my arms in front of me. "It's too bad you've written off the idea of having a wife and kids. I think you'd be a great dad."

Casey rubs his tattooed arm. "Yeah. Maybe." After a moment, he sits down at the table next to me. "So, let's see that list of names."

I dig the folded list out of my pocket. "Frank had hundreds of people pass through here," I say. "And who knows if the renters let friends live with them, off the record."

I glance around the kitchen, wondering how many people sat where we're sitting or used that stove.

How many house parties were thrown here?

How many people have fought here?

How many people have had sex here?

Eww. Maybe don't think about that.

Casey pulls his chair closer to mine. "How'd you narrow it down?"

I can smell his aftershave and see a splash of muffin batter on his chin.

I wonder what he'd do if I just licked it off...

"Umm, the letters addressed to Nancy are dated 1989. So, I figured that would be a good place to start."

I stare at the list for a moment. The clock ticks by.

"That's the year I was born," I say quietly.

Casey nods, his warm brown eyes meeting mine. "So we have ten names. Now what?"

"I still don't know why you're helping me with this," I say.

He angles his body toward me, his hand casually cradling his face. "You're my new best friend. Deal with it."

I laugh. "Whatever you say, weirdo."

The ancient timer on the stove buzzes. He jumps up, flashing a set of white teeth at me. "You're going to love these."

Casey pops the muffins out of the tin, burning a few fingers and reflexively sticking them in his mouth. My heart melts just a teeny, tiny bit.

He places a yellow china plate on the table, piled high with freshly baked muffins.

"Here you go, darl. My mum's famous Irish soda bread muffins."

"They look delicious," I say.

"We can't forget the butter," he says while slathering a generous helping onto the warm tops. I bite into mine, relishing the rich, fluffy goodness.

"Oh my god," I groan. *"Casey."*

"Now, there's a phrase I've heard before," he says, his tongue rolling over the Rs. I kick him under the table. "Do you like them?" he asks.

"Love them," I mumble, crumbs falling from my mouth. "The raisins are a nice touch."

He pops the rest of his muffin into his mouth and swipes the crumbs onto the floor.

"It's the middle of the afternoon on a weekday and you're at home, baking muffins. Don't you ever work?" I ask.

"I could say the same about you."

I lift a hand to my forehead. "The glories of charity work."

He leans back in his chair. "So, what do you do at the thrift store, exactly?"

"I'm the manager," I say. "I used to work at the hospital on the long-term care unit. It's mostly seniors. Now I just volunteer there on weekends, handing out breakfast trays and stuff."

I tell Casey about the ups and downs of being a manager for a non-profit. About Snake Guy and Sock Lady. About store theft and the amazing – and sometimes gross – things we find in donation bags. I explain that our store facilitates several community programs, too, so I'm in charge of making sure those run smoothly.

I tell him about our Bright Futures program, a social program designed for people with special needs. It's pretty great, actually. The program is kind of Cheryl's baby – she's the one who got us connected to Bright Futures as a way to support her special needs grandson. When I tell him about how it helps the people who join us, it makes me feel happy. It makes me wonder who designed the program in the first place. And it makes me wish I could do something like that.

Casey stares at me for a minute and then shakes his head.

I smile. "What?"

"You're officially too good for me," he says. "You work for a charity. You volunteer in your spare time. You don't drink. I don't think I've ever heard you swear." He leans closer to me and whispers, "In fact, I'm not sure that you *can* swear."

I pick up another muffin and nod at him. "These are fucking good muffins."

He grins cheekily and bites his lip. "I stand corrected."

I reflect on our conversation for a moment. "I really like the work," I say. "Although, lately, I sometimes feel like I'm just putting in time. I'd like to do something more meaningful, but I'm not sure what that is yet."

Casey just says, "Hmm," in reply, his warm brown eyes resting lazily on mine.

I shift my weight. I wish he'd stop looking at me like that. It makes me think naughty thoughts.

I look around the kitchen, trying desperately to avoid Casey. My eyes land on the microwave clock. It's already two thirty p.m. Where did the time go? I swear, Casey makes it speed up or something.

"Do you work today?" he asks.

"No, just some volunteering tomorrow," I say, turning to look at him. "I'm not really looking forward to it, though."

"How come?"

"There's a new guy in long-term care who cries every time he sees me."

Casey shrugs. "Maybe he's just sad about not being at home anymore."

"No, it's more than that. He'll be absolutely fine, talking or joking or whatever with other people, but as soon as he sees me, he bursts into tears and starts speaking in Polish. They sometimes have to reassign me to a different wing so I don't upset him."

"Maybe you remind him of someone," Casey suggests. "Try singing to him. It always worked with my nana."

He sang to his nana? Oh dear god. Why is this man still single?

"What'd you sing to her?" I ask.

"Just her favorite songs. It seemed to make her happy."

"Hmm. Might be worth a try."

"Try learning a few Polish words too," he suggests. "It might help him feel safe, if he thinks you can understand him."

"How did you get so smart?" I tease.

Casey clears the table and plops our dirty dishes in the sink. He sucks a breath between his teeth. "Dunno. I'm just a genius, I guess."

I tear off a small piece of my muffin and throw it at him. Unsurprisingly, he manages to catch it in his mouth, and he winks at me. I suspect he's good at everything.

He unties his apron and throws it onto the kitchen counter, and then motions for me to follow him down the hall toward his office. "All right. Time for phase two of our search."

I twist around, looking back. "But what about all the mess?"

He gently squeezes my shoulder. "Who cares? I'll get to it later."

My pulse speeds up at his touch, a fierce thud in my veins. I wish I didn't react to him like this; it's an intense, confusing, often consuming attraction. Though, perhaps I'm not so much attracted to Casey as I am to his "type." At least, that's what I try to tell myself.

I take a deep breath and feel a knot deep in my chest start to unravel.

"Okay," I say.

"Hmm. So much for that," I mutter.

Casey crosses out a couple of lines from the list and starts chewing the end of his pen. "On the bright side, we've eliminated two names."

We decided to start with a Canada411 search. Simple, easy, and free. Out of the ten names, we've found the phone numbers and addresses for seven. Three were unlisted. We've called six so far, some of which were long distance. I sure hope Casey has a good phone plan. I'd hate to see his phone bill next month.

We left messages for four of them and spoke to two, both of whom denied knowing anyone named Nancy Carlyle.

And even though it's a start, I can't help but feel overwhelmed by the task ahead.

Why did I ever think that this would be easy? These are only ten out of hundreds of names from Frank's files. Some could have moved or are dead. Some might lie. Depending on the lifestyle they lead, some may not remember.

And who knows? Maybe we're looking in completely the wrong year. Maybe Laura is right. Maybe this is all in my head.

Maybe, maybe, maybe.

"Maybe we should just call the whole thing off," I say.

Casey takes the pen out of his mouth. "What for?"

I rake my hands through my hair. "Listen, Casey, I appreciate all of the help, but…"

Casey swivels his office chair toward me. "You're not backing out again, are you?" he asks. "Need I remind you that I impersonated an officer for you?"

I smirk at him.

"I've still got the uniform in my closet," he says. "Shall I get it for you? Dance around in it? Refresh your memory?"

My pulse starts to pound again. Dammit! My mind is screaming to keep him at arm's length, but my heart wants to let him in. And right now my body really wants him to do a strip tease in that uniform.

Thankfully, I've learned how to trust logic, rather than impulse or emotion.

Seeing Casey in that uniform again would definitely be dangerous. I bet he can dance, too. I've seen him dance around the kitchen. The boy can move. I picture him throwing his hat at me first, and then ripping open his shirt, buttons flying everywhere. And then…

Ahem. Definitely dangerous territory.

I hold my hands up. "I'm good."

"Shame. Would my firefighter get-up be better?"

I grab his hand and pull him back down. "You are a shameless flirt."

He winks. "Lots of experience."

"I'm trying to be serious here."

He swallows and looks at me with intense eyes. "So what's the problem?"

Damn. He really is good with the whole eye contact thing. I struggle to not look away. Looking at him like this, I notice for the first time that he has flecks of gold in his eyes.

My face heats up, and my breath quickens. I deliberately rip my eyes away from his.

"Umm, so these papers," I say, my voice sounding squeaky.

I look at my stacks of papers, the notes I've hastily written from the few phone conversations I had tonight. "It's just so...overwhelming."

He wheels his chair closer to me, inch by inch, until our knees are touching.

"I told you I'd help you," he says quietly, his deep voice echoing around the sparse room. "And I'm here for you, whatever you decide. But you need to make a decision. Either you're in or you're out. No more waffling."

He reaches out to take my hand in his and traces circles over my palms.

Oh, sweet baby Jesus. "I don't know," I say shakily.

He gives me a stern look. "Here's what *I* know. I know that some crazy woman showed up on my doorstep one day on the chance that maybe, just maybe, she'd find a connection."

"I am not crazy."

"And that same crazy woman went along with my plan to impersonate police officers–"

"You kind of made me go along with your plan," I reply.

"–and she sorted through a mountain of paperwork and made several embarrassing phone calls to complete strangers."

I stifle a laugh. Some of those phone calls were really painful. There's no easy way to ask a complete stranger about someone they may or may not have known twenty-seven years ago.

"Do you think you'd go through all of that if you didn't really believe in it?"

I smile a tiny smile. "No."

He smiles back and continues tracing delicious, maddening circles on my hand. "So what's it going to be then? Are you in or are you out? Because if I have to hear one more time about you wanting to quit…"

"Okay, okay," I say. "You've convinced me. I'm in."

He nods. "Good."

I look down at my hands. He's still holding them. My stomach clenches.

"Are you always this touchy feely with your friends?" I ask, trying to keep my tone light.

He looks down at my hands in his and almost seems surprised. "Sorry. I guess I just wanted to make you feel comfortable." He backs the chair away from me and busies himself with the computer again. "One more call left," he says, his voice sounding a bit shaky. He quickly recovers, though, and flashes me a confident smile. "I'll do the honors."

Casey dials the phone, and I lean back against the wall – an area that's quickly becoming "my spot" – my mind buzzing with questions. Some about Nancy. Some about where this wild goose chase will lead.

But mostly, I wonder about Casey and just how many people he's touchy feely with.

CHAPTER 10

Mess Around

There are always dorks who don't feel the need to show up for work. So today, I fill in for another flaky volunteer at the store. I don't mind, though. It's not like I had anything else going on.

Millie and I assign ourselves to sorting duty. She seems unusually glum today. In fact, I've never really seen her like this before. It's as if the light inside of her has dimmed.

"You okay?" I ask.

She dumps another box of clothes onto the sorting table. "I've been better."

"Want to talk about it?"

"Just man trouble," she sighs. "Well, lack thereof."

"I'm surprised," I say. "I thought you'd be knee deep in wieners." Her eyes widen. "Natalie!"

"What? It's true! You're gorgeous."

Millie is truly beautiful. Translucent skin, perfectly painted red lips. Full hips and fuller skirts. Cool, short black hair with shaved sides. She's offbeat. And completely enchanting.

"Thanks," she says. "The truth is," she adds, quietly, "I haven't been with someone in over a year."

"A year!?" I hiss. "How could you go a year?"

She winks at me. "Oh, I have my ways."

I scrunch up my nose. "I don't need to know."

She grins. "You asked."

"Seriously though, I'm surprised you don't have someone," I say.

"I could. But I'm careful. I don't want just anyone around my kids."

I hold up a dress to the light, noticing a rather nasty grease stain on the chest. "You have kids?"

She smiles, as if remembering something sweet. "Two. Cara is four, and Elliot is six. I call him Ellie for short."

"Ha. I bet he loves that."

She shrugs. "He doesn't know any different. I've always called him that."

Millie pulls another box in front of her and covers her mouth as soon as she opens it.

"*Ohmigod…*" she says, the words lumping together, her face twisted in embarrassed horror. "I think someone donated their sex box."

I instantly rush over. Inside is a collection of phallic objects, an assortment of ropes, and some weird clampy things. "Look! It's an old edition of the *Joy of Sex*!" I exclaim.

Millie picks it up and starts flipping through the pages. "Just look at those big seventies bushes."

"Thank god they're just illustrated," I say.

"Eww! Some of the pages are stuck together!" she shrieks, and she tosses it at me.

"Ack!" I yelp. "Don't throw it at me, throw it in the garbage."

Millie is doubled over, giggling helplessly behind her fingers. I can't help but join in.

Gladys stomps toward us. "What are you two carrying on about?"

Millie and I try to quiet ourselves. I knot my fingers in front of me. "We, umm, we found…something."

Millie's nose erupts into a loud, unladylike snort.

And I'm done for. All I can do is point at the sticky-paged book and the box from whence it came.

Gladys looks back and forth between the two of us. "You're both nuts."

That sends us into fits of giggles again.

A while later, when I've recovered from giggling over sex like a kid in her first health class, I remember what Millie was talking about.

Her kids. She's never mentioned them before.

I glance over at Millie. "So…where's their dad?"

"Jackson? Oh, he's around. Though who knows for how long. He's thinking of moving to Vancouver," she replies. "The kids see him every other weekend." She's silent for a moment. "He's unemployed a lot, and money is tight, so…anyway. Volunteering here makes it easier to buy clothes and stuff."

"Oh Mill," I say, feeling instantly awkward. "I'm sorry."

She smiles sincerely. "It's okay. So that's why when I'm not at work or with my kids, I'm here."

I nod, taking everything in. Suddenly, it occurs to me that I've never asked her about her job.

"What do you do for work, anyway?"

Her forehead creases in thought. "I have a really long title. Suffice it to say, I work with computers."

Huh. Surprising. Millie doesn't really give off a "computer nerd" vibe. But, I suppose that's my own bias coming out. I suppose I don't give off a "former drug addict" vibe either.

She holds up a ratty old pajama set and wrinkles her nose. Most of the donations are good, but you do come across the odd thing that should've made it into the "toss" pile rather than the "donate" pile.

"However," she adds, while throwing the threadbare pajama bottoms into the trash, "having two kids does make it challenging to find someone."

I nod as if I know what she's going through, though I have no freaking clue.

"Ever wonder about who your ideal man is?" she muses.

"I dunno. I mostly want someone sweet and loyal, with a good job and a grasp of basic grammar."

Millie laughs. "Let me read between the lines: your last boyfriend was an obnoxious, unemployed cheating arsehole who only texted in emojis."

My mouth falls open. "How…how did you do that?"

Millie lifts and eyebrow. "Am I right?"

I nod. "Scarily so."

Millie taps the side of her head. "It's a blessing or a curse, depending on how you look at it. But I can usually tell what people really mean by how they say it."

"Okay," I say, "Let me try. Who would your ideal man be?"

"Oh, I've thought about this a lot. I think I'd like to be with a soldier. Well, I wouldn't like them being away for years and getting shot at. But my dream man is buff, has short hair, and would wear uniforms whenever I want." After a beat, she adds. "Ooh, and my dream guy is a *real* good dancer."

I snort. "Read between the lines: Millie's dream man is a stripper with a soldier routine."

Millie's laugh isn't a delicate tinkling sound. No, it's more like an infectious honk. After a few minutes of us discussing what a male stripper soldier routine would look like (and doing a few mock moves), we're both in tears and holding our sides.

"Having a good time, ladies?"

Millie and I turn around, still laughing weakly. "We sure are, Gladys," Millie says.

Our laughter slowly dies under Gladys's disapproving stare.

I pick up a new box of donations and start sorting through it. The moment I open the lid, a spray of foamy, emerald green fabric splashes out. It's the most beautiful color I've ever seen, with a slight sheen.

My fingers run covetously over it, and I pull the rest of it out of the box. There must be over twenty yards here. And it's good quality too. Whoever bought this paid a lot for it.

I hold it up, fascinated by how it catches the light. It would make a gorgeous dress.

I set the sea of fabric down and feel around the bottom of the box in case any other goodies are in there. My hands settle on what feels like a stack of thick letters.

My heart jumps slightly.

Calm down, Natalie. It's not like everything is going to be a clue about Nancy.

I pull the stack out. "Millie, look."

I'm holding a thick stack of vintage dress patterns tied together in a red ribbon.

Millie whistles and taps a finger on the top pattern. "They don't make dresses like that anymore."

I run my fingers along the ribbon. "They sure don't."

I can't wait to show these to my mother. Her little seamstress hands will be itching to open these babies up. I look at the stack of patterns and the gorgeous green fabric, and inspiration strikes hot.

I wonder if…

I haven't tackled a project like this in years. I know how to sew, of course. With a mother as a seamstress, it would be a sin if I didn't at least learn how to hem pants or sew on a button. But I can do way more than that. I could make something truly gorgeous, if I wanted to. I used to, all of the time.

Well, those things weren't exactly gorgeous. They were usually too tight. And too short. And made in fabrics that were a bit, umm, flashy (read: attention-grabbing). But the knowledge is there. Even if I have grown out of my spandex-and-sequins phase, I know I can do something with this.

I scoop up the fabric and dress patterns and try to stuff them back into the box they arrived in. I pay for them as soon as my shift is over (thank you, employee discount) and happily squirrel them away in my car.

CHAPTER 11

Mystery Train

My ringing phone is a welcome distraction as I'm trying to mentally erase what I just saw at the grocery store – a pregnant lady throwing up into her purse in the checkout line.

"Hey, Casey," I say.

"Hey, Nat. I've got some news."

I cradle my slippery cell phone between my ear and shoulder and continue putting away groceries.

"Oh yeah?" I say.

"One of the guys we left a message for called back. Said to come over and he'd tell you everything you ever wanted to know about Nancy Carlyle."

My phone slips and hits the floor.

"Nat? Natalie? Are you still there?" says Casey, his voice sounding tinny and hollow from the floor.

I pick it up, cursing.

"Yeah, I'm here." I run a hand through my bangs. "So…what now? Did he tell you anything about her?"

"Nothing. He wants to speak to you in person."

"Oh. Why?"

"Dunno. The guy sounded a bit, umm, eccentric."

I pause. "And by eccentric you mean…?"

"High as a kite."

Hmm. An eccentric, high-as-a-kite man who may or may not know anything about Nancy Carlyle wants me to come to his house.

Alarm bells start ringing in my head.

"How do we even know that he's talking about the same person? Or if he's making it all up? I mean, what if this is a total scam?" I say.

"I considered that too, but I don't think it's likely," Casey says. "When I asked if he'd ever known anyone named Nancy Carlyle, he started laughing, and it was a really creepy fucking laugh too."

I snort into the phone.

"Anyway, he said that he hadn't heard that 'crazy bitch's name' in years. Said she was the best lay he'd ever had."

"Whoa. Way too much info."

"I know, right? Anyway, in his rambling, he said that he used to party with her at this old house that he rented in the late eighties."

My hands are sweaty and shaky, and my phone nearly slips again.

"What else did he say?"

"Not much. When I asked him for more information, he said that he didn't want to talk about it over the phone, whatever that means."

I sit down at the kitchen table, blood hammering away in my ears.

"Well, let's go see him. Where does he live?"

Casey sighs heavily into the phone. "That's where it gets weird. He said he that lives about an hour or so northwest of the city limits. He gave me a complicated set of directions, all back roads and stuff."

"Okay..."

"I looked up the area he said he lived in, and according to Google, it's all parkland. No one should be living around there. Legally, anyway."

I twirl some hair around my fingers. "And he absolutely refuses to just talk over the phone?"

"Yep."

"Hmm. Okay, let me think."

I consider what's being laid out before me. A weirdo stranger who lives in the middle of nowhere wants me to come to his house. This has "scary" written all over it.

"I don't suppose you'd want to come with me?" I ask.

"Pfft," he says. "Way ahead of you. I've already planned out a route and everything."

"You have?"

"Of course."

I smile like an idiot, until I glance over at my groceries still sitting in their carrier bags on the counter. A carton of frozen yogurt is melting into the bag and leaking through a hole into a sticky puddle.

Would licking it straight out of the bag be considered cleaning up? Ugh. I'm so stupid. I should've put the groceries away as soon as I got home. I hate making mistakes. I've already made enough for a lifetime.

"Natalie? You still there?"

I shake my head, feeling distracted and mad at myself. "Yeah, sorry. You were saying?"

"What day do you want to go? The guy said we could drop in anytime."

My forehead crinkles. "Anytime? What, is he some kind of hermit who doesn't leave his place?"

"It wouldn't surprise me. How about Friday? We can go that afternoon when I'm done work."

I walk over to the calendar hanging on the wall. No shifts at the hospital or thrift store.

"Yep. Friday works for me," I say.

"Super. Okay, meet me at the fire station at about three p.m. and we can leave together from there."

"See you then."

Friday afternoon rolls around and I pull into the fire station parking lot. It isn't too far from Casey's house, a fifteen-minute drive at most.

I walk into the air-conditioned foyer of the fire hall, my mind whirring.

I still can't believe it. We might find some answers about Nancy today. I'd be a little worried if I were going on my own, so I'm glad that Casey is going with me.

No, I'm more worried about what this guy *did* say about Nancy.

Crazy bitch. Best lay he'd ever had.

Who was this woman?

A man clears his throat behind me. "Can I help you?"

I shriek and jump as much as my wedge heels will let me.

"Sorry," the man chuckles. "It's just that you've been staring at that fire hazards poster for a full five minutes. I thought maybe you were lost."

I pat down my hair and smooth over my dove-gray skirt.

"Yes, I umm, I'm looking for Casey. Casey Nolan."

He nods. "I'll fetch him for you. Your name?"

I extend my hand. "Natalie."

The man's eyes light with recognition and he crosses his arms. "Ah, so you're the girl he keeps talking about."

"He's been talking about me?" I ask, trying to resist the giddy smile that slowly builds on my face.

"Won't shut up."

I have no idea how to respond to that. So I don't.

"I'm Marty, by the way," he says, finally shaking my hand. "Come on in."

I follow Marty down a dimly lit hallway and into a large bay area where several fire trucks are parked. Hooks and shelves line the far wall. Helmets, coats, boots, and other gear hang in neat rows, waiting in anticipation.

"Casey's a good guy," he says. "He's the sort of guy you want on your side." Marty looks ahead, craning his neck, and slows his pace. "Especially when you're trying to pull an epic prank. You picked a good day to drop by," he says. "We're going to antique the rookie."

"Antique?" God. I hope that's not code for some weird sex thing. (Note to self: Why is that my first thought?)

"Yeah," he says quietly. "First we...well, you'll get the idea in a minute." We're about to pass the last fire truck when Marty holds his hand up. "Just wait," he whispers. "We can watch from here."

I glance to where Marty is pointing and see several guys sitting around an ancient-looking plastic picnic table. Even though all of the men are facing away from us, I instantly recognize one. I'd recognize those broad shoulders anywhere.

"Watch the door," Marty whispers.

A door a few feet away from the table is standing slightly ajar. A bucket of water is set strategically above.

"No!" I say. "They're not going to–"

"Here he comes," Marty says.

Tension fills the air. Everyone's eyes are trained on the door. Even I'm holding my breath. A moment later, I can hear deep voices echoing in the hall beyond the door, and my body stills in anticipation.

The door swings open, the bucket slips, and the young man standing in the doorway is drenched from head to foot.

He gasps in a shocked, wide-eyed way, much to the amusement of his onlookers. After a moment, he puts his hands on his hips and smiles. "You assholes."

Casey claps him on the back. "Ah, it's a rite of passage." He hands him a towel. "Here, go get yourself cleaned up."

Rookie Man takes the towel and walks toward another door across the room. I start to walk away, when Marty holds up an arm.

"Just wait," he says.

As I watch Rookie walk away, dripping with water, I wonder what Gladys would do if I threw a bucket of water on her. Probably scream, "I'm melting, I'm melting!"

Rookie swings open the door, which turns out to open to a bathroom. There's a muffled "poof" sound and a strangled, "Ack! What the fuck!?" A delicate white cloud curls out into the room.

Rookie emerges covered head to toe in a sticky white paste. The only thing visible on his face are his eyes. He places his hands on his hips and looks around the room where his "buddies" are bent double, holding their sides with laughter.

"And that is what we call antiquing," Marty says, chuckling to himself.

"What is that stuff?" I ask.

"Flour."

"I can really feel the love, guys," Rookie says, licking his lips. "In fact, I think I might have to share it," he shouts, stumbling toward Casey with open arms.

"Don't you dare," Casey laughs. "I've got a hot date with a cute girl in a few minutes."

My heart feels like it's trying to scramble up my throat.

Marty flicks a glance at me. "See what I mean?"

Some of the other fire men say "Oooh" and give a few cat calls, teasing Casey.

"Nah, it's not like that. We're just friends," he says, smiling good-naturedly.

"Yeah, but none of them ever stay just friends for long, do they mate?" one of them calls out.

"Remember that one chick he used to bring to the station?" another man says. "The blonde?"

Everyone around the room groans with appreciation.

An uneasy feeling swirls through my stomach. I don't really want to think about Casey bringing other girls here, friends or not.

Marty shrugs. "Boys will be boys."

We emerge from our hiding place, and Casey lights up as soon as he sees me.

"Hey Natalie," he says.

"Hey look guys, it's Thrift Shop Girl!" one of the men calls out.

Casey rolls his eyes. "Ignore them. Wow, you look nice."

I smooth my hands over my skirt and feel my face flush. "Thanks."

"You ready to go?"

I reposition my purse on my shoulder. "Sure," I say, glancing around. "I've been here for a little bit. Marty wanted to show me what antiquing was."

Casey lets out a short, throaty laugh. One that I quite like. I'll have to try to make him laugh more often.

"You saw that, did you?" he says. "He had it coming too," he says quietly. "The little bastard is a bit of a cowboy, thinks he knows everything."

I smile up at him. "Remind me to never act up around you."

"Nah. A real man likes a woman with a bit of sass."

We wander through the aisles of trucks, and I notice that they all look a bit different. "I had no idea that there were different kinds of trucks. I figured there was just one type."

"Oh no, there are ladder trucks, rescues, tankers, pumps..." He glances at his watch. "We have a bit of time. Would you like a tour?"

I stand on tip toe, trying to look inside one of the truck windows. "Can I go inside one?"

"Sure. If you want." He climbs up first and reaches his hand to help me up. "If you're a good girl, I'll even let you turn the siren on."

Casey, it turns out, is an excellent tour guide. He shows me the trucks, the kitchen (those boys sure can eat), and their gear. Casey even gears up, showing me how fast they need to put everything on when they get a call.

At one point, he slips this hood piece on that covers most of his chest.

"That looks like a dickie," I say.

He stops and whips his head up to look at me. "A *what*?"

"You know, a dickie. They're sort of a mix between a scarf and a turtleneck? My grandma wears them."

He shakes his head. "You've got one kinky grandma." He pauses. "Can I meet her?"

I playfully smack his shoulder. "Gear up, firefighter."

He smirks at me. "Yes, ma'am."

It all looks quite heavy. I'd be exhausted just wearing it, let alone having to work in it.

I circle Casey, taking in everything from his heavy boots and coveralls to the coat and oxygen tank. "How much does all of that weigh?"

"Sixty pounds, give or take, when you've got your bunker pants, jacket, boots, helmet, mask, and tank. But you'll usually take some sort of equipment with you, depending on the call, so you can add another ten to thirty pounds on top of that."

I whistle. "No wonder you're so ripped." I resist slapping a hand over my mouth. "Of course, you have a physical job," I babble. "It's important to be in shape. I mean, you know, I uh..." I shift my weight from side to side and start playing with my necklace.

He grins. "Anyway, we have bunker gear races all the time," he says. He leans toward me and adds, "I always win."

"Oh yeah? What's your best time?"

"Forty-seven seconds."

I secretly wish I could dress that fast every morning. It would definitely save time.

When my private tour of the fire hall ends, Casey hands me a red helmet.

"Put this on," he says. He pats the front bumper of one of the trucks. "We'll get a picture of you sitting on the truck." He extends his hand for my phone. "We end all of our tours this way."

I smile at him. "Cool." I hand him my phone and pose for a few shots. Eventually, I pat the spot beside me. "Come sit, I want one with you."

"Why?" he asks.

"Well, I feel a bit silly sitting here on my own, like I took a tour by myself or something."

"You did."

I roll my eyes. "That's beside the point."

Casey rubs his chin a bit but doesn't say anything.

I throw my head back in mock exasperation. "Just come sit by me already and get your picture taken."

He does. Another firefighter offers to take our picture, while several others stand to the side, making cooing and kissy noises at us.

"Fuck off," Casey says, while smiling.

They simply laugh and smile back.

I swear, the relationship dynamics between men are weird. I could never say, "Fuck off," to a woman and still be besties. They'd smile back and start plotting my slow, painful demise.

"Ready to go?" Casey says.

"Sure," I say, scrolling through the pics we had just taken of us.

Damn. I'm looking pretty cute today. Even my nose doesn't look as huge as usual. And Casey...well, Casey always looks gorgeous. All dimples and tight T-shirt and glittering brown eyes and...

Anyway.

"Just give me a second," I say. I open up Instagram and post a few photos. "It's not every day that I get a private tour of my local fire hall."

I say goodbye to the rest of the crew, and Casey and I walk together to the parking lot. Already the comments on my newly posted photos are rolling in.

And they're all on the one of me and Casey.

LawdyMissClawdy: omg! He is gorgeous!!!

whatdreamsmaycome: Hot daaaaaayum. Who is THAT!?!

chalupabatman12: I think my house is on fire.

I stuff my phone into my purse and resolve not to look at it again today. Nerves swirl in my stomach as I think once more about who we're going to see.

"Thanks for the tour," I say. "And for offering to come with me today."

"You bet," he says. After a beat, he looks over at me. "And just so you know, I'm driving."

"Oh, that's all right," I say, trying to sound casual. "You've drove me around the last few times. I'd like to return the favor." I kick at a few rocks, feeling like this has all become too real. I wonder if he really wants to be here. "Honestly, you don't have to come along, if you don't want."

"I want to." He throws keys up into the air and catches them. "And I want to drive."

We walk to the end of the parking lot, and I stop.

"What?" he says.

"What happened to your truck?" I ask. God, I didn't think the truck could be any uglier. But I was wrong.

"I buffed it out. I'm taking it to an auto body shop to have the paint redone. They've already been working on the body."

He opens the passenger door, his hands doing a grand, sweeping gesture. "Look, see? No holes in the floorboard."

I slide into the passenger seat and glance down at my feet. "Charming." Casey closes my door, and I roll down the window. "It's like a sauna in here," I say. Spring has slid into summer, the days alternating between scorching heat and heavy rain.

Casey leans into my open window and rests his chin on crossed forearms, looking boyishly handsome. "Oh, it's not so bad," he says. His accent sounds thicker, I've noticed, when he's really happy or stressed or nervous. I wonder what he's feeling right now.

"We'll get some fresh air coming in once we get on the highway," he says.

With his forearms on display so close to my face, I can't help but admire his colorful sleeve tattoo. Blue and green waves.

"Your sleeve is beautiful," I say. "What's the story there?"

He tenses ever so slightly. "Why does there have to be a story?"

"Dunno. I figured you'd have flames or something. Being a firefighter and all."

He glances at his watch and whistles through his teeth. "Damn. That tour took a bit longer than I wanted it to." He slaps the window frame playfully and runs around to the driver's side. Before I can ask any more about his tattoos, he pushes another ancient-looking cassette into the player. "Ever heard of Johnny Burnette?"

"No, I haven't," I say, not sure how to read his mood.

He smiles. "You'll love this."

He cranks the volume and sings along, acting as if the cab of his truck is his own personal stage. He sings loudly, yelling out the chorus for comic effect and bobbing his head along to the rhythm. After a while my questions fade and are eventually forgotten.

CHAPTER 12

Running Scared

Casey turns down the volume and slips into a more relaxed mood.

"What's it like to work there every day?" I ask, scrolling through the pictures of the fire station on my phone.

He sucks in a breath, trying to look serious. "Oh, you know, it's all flinging damsels over my shoulder and standing around shirtless."

"That sounds fantastic."

He smiles and then says. "It isn't all fun and games. It can be a pretty stressful job."

"I believe it."

"But we have some fun days too."

I angle my body to face him. "Like what?"

"Well, getting to teach school kids about fire safety is pretty cool. Oh, and lately, we've had this one old lady who keeps dialing 911."

"Is she just really accident prone or something?" I ask. "Starting fires in her kitchen and what not?"

"No. I think she's lonely. She presses her life alert button about twice a week. And when we get there, she meets us on the step with a plate of fresh-baked cookies. We've had to give her a few warnings not to call us unless it's a real emergency."

"Now *that's* brilliant," I say. "I'm totally going to be that old lady who dials 911 just to have the fire department show up on her doorstep. I'll be all like, 'Oops, false alarm. But now that you're here, why don't you make yourself comfortable. Take off a few layers. Or, you know, all of them…'"

Casey snorts with surprised laughter. "You don't have to wait until you're an old lady," he chuckles. "Call me anytime, babe."

After a moment, his laughter turns into deep, throaty hacking.

"If I didn't know any better, I'd say that sounded like a smoker's cough," I say.

"Hazard of the job," he says, jokingly. "That, or I really need to clean out this truck."

I glance at the McDonald's hamburger wrappers layered around my feet. How can he eat this much fast food and still look fit?

"Did you ever smoke?" I ask.

A dark cloud seems to pass over his face. "Yeah. A long time ago." He shakes his head. "Filthy habit." He glances over at me. "You don't smoke, do you?"

"Not anymore," I say. "I used to, but just when I was at parties and stuff."

There. Nice and vague. He doesn't need to know exactly *what* I was smoking.

"Good," he says. For some reason, I feel like I've passed some sort of test.

"How long have you been a firefighter?" I ask.

"Six years," he says. "I started off volunteering, and then decided that's what I wanted to do. The rest is history."

His words bring back warm, distant memories of watching old TV shows with my grandma. "Have you ever seen that episode of *The Lucy Show* where Lucy and Viv are volunteer firefighters?"

"No. Is it good?"

"Lucy is always good," I say emphatically.

"Well then, we'll have to watch it together."

I smile, thinking that no one else my age probably knows what *The Lucy Show* is, let alone wants to watch it with me.

"Deal," I say.

My mind drifts back to the "antiquing" ritual I saw at the fire house.

"Speaking of firemen, are you bad to all of them?" I tease.

"If you thought that was bad, you should see what we do to them in the bathroom."

I pause. "In the bathroom?"

Casey grins. "When they go into the stall, we'll either throw a bucket of ice water over the top–"

"No!"

"–or," he continues, clearly enjoying himself, "we light wee bits of paper and toss them at their feet while they're sitting on the throne." Casey chuckles. "It's really funny, watching them stamp out the fire while their pants are down around their ankles."

"That's horrible," I say, shaking my head, though secretly wondering if I could get away with this at work.

"It's all in good fun," he says. "Sometimes we go hours without a call. It keeps us occupied." Casey squints into the afternoon sun. "I think that's our turn," he says.

I look ahead. We've been driving for nearly an hour and a half into the backwoods that lie northwest of the city limits. It's all winding gravel roads, the treeline thick on either side of us.

I look ahead too, trying to see an intersection or a traffic sign, maybe a gate along the side of the road.

"Casey, there isn't anything here," I say. "Well, that dirt path, maybe, but that doesn't look like it goes anywhere."

"According to our buddy on the phone, that's where we've got to go."

Casey turns left, into a barely visible break in the treeline, and we slowly creep down a dirt road. It's overgrown with grass, and dark trees hang above, forming a shadowy canopy.

"This looks like some abandoned service road," I mutter.

I peer out into the dark forest. Despite the early summer heat and lack of modern air conditioning, I roll up my window. "You said this was parkland, right? Government land?"

Casey shrugs. "Maybe he's a park ranger or something."

He cranes his neck and narrows his eyes, trying to look around the bend in the road.

"What is it?" I ask.

His mouth is pulled into a thin line. "There's a log across the road, just up ahead."

Sure enough, an enormous log stretches across the road. An effective barricade. The treeline is so thick on either side that driving around it won't be possible. If we're going any farther, it'll be on foot.

We stop in the middle of the road, engine idling. A growing sense of unease blooms in my stomach. "I don't know about this, Casey."

A loud tapping noise on my passenger window startles me so much that I yelp.

Outside of the passenger-side window stands a tall, thin man wearing dirty jeans and a greasy button-down plaid shirt that's rolled up to the elbows. The bones of his face stick out so far that his eyes look like they're sinking into his head.

"Who the hell are you?" he asks.

Casey angles himself more toward the passenger-side window. "We spoke on the phone earlier this week. You said we could come over today?"

The man runs a grubby hand over his face and peers at me a bit more intently. A smile spreads over his gaunt face, revealing mainly toothless gums.

"I'll be damned. You sure do look like your mama."

My madly beating heart scrambles up into my throat. Casey and I stare at the stranger, not moving. Not saying a word.

He frowns at us and spits on the ground. "Well, are you coming out or not?"

We unbuckle our seatbelts and start to open the doors.

"Russell, is it?" Casey asks.

The stranger clicks his tongue. "Everyone calls me Rusty. Come on up to the house. I'll make us some coffee, and we can have a good talk about Nancy Carlyle."

Rusty motions with his chin for us to follow, stuffs his hands into grubby jean pockets, and awkwardly leaps over the log with his long, stork-like legs.

As Casey starts to get out, I grab his forearm. Casey's body, half hanging out of the truck, half hanging in, freezes at my touch.

"Do you want to go?" he asks, looking at me seriously. "Because we can leave right now, if that's what you really want."

Rusty yells at us from outside. "Are you coming or not?"

Casey leans back into the cab, his face a few inches from mine. "Your call," he says.

I glance at Rusty, who is pacing like a caged cat, his eyes darting around wildly. Butterflies beat my stomach from the inside out.

"I'm not sure," I whisper. "Can we trust this guy?"

Casey pauses. "Not one bit."

"Well, at least we agree on that point," I say, feeling slightly nauseous. "What if we follow Rusty and he legitimately knows things about Nancy Carlyle, and what if I find out more about her, and…"

"And?" Casey asks.

My chest feels tight, like a wire wrapping and squeezing around my lungs. "What if I don't like what I find?"

Casey scratches his stubbly chin. "Then I guess you have to decide whether that's a risk you're willing to take."

My eyes dart back to Rusty's emaciated form. His clothes must've had colors once. Now they're almost black with grease and dirt.

His words come back to me, making my chest feel both elated and hollow.

You sure do look like your mama.

I think about all of the years I've spent wondering where I come from. Who is this mysterious person that I would have called "mother"? What was she like? Why did she give me up? Where is she now?

Questions I want answers to.

I blow out a shaky breath. "Well, we've come this far."

Casey gets out of the cab and offers me one of his large, callused hands. I step down from the truck, and Casey slams the driver-side door behind me. Despite the early summer heat, my body feels cold. I start shivering, and I squeeze his hand tighter.

"Remember, you're calling the shots here," he says, quietly. "The second you say go, we'll go."

I nod and walk with Casey down the dirt path toward Rusty, all the while repeating Casey's words in my head.

We quickly catch up with Rusty and follow him down a meandering trail. It eventually opens up into a small clearing. A shed with a saggy roof stands to the right. A small porch has been built onto the front of it, and an ancient plaid brown couch sits in the garbage-strewn yard. A skinny young woman wearing a baggy gray hoodie is asleep on it. A man sits at one end of the couch, her feet propped up on his lap. His head keeps bobbing up and down, as if he's dancing on the brink of sleep. Their clothes and the couch are covered with small, circular burn marks.

I slow my pace.

Rusty lets out a dark snicker. "So, you decided to follow me, eh?" he says.

I force down the lump in my throat and smile pleasantly. "You bet."

He stares at me for a brief moment. "I wish I had a picture to show you."

"Of Nancy?" I ask.

"Well, of course, dummy," he laughs.

Casey is still holding my hand. I feel the muscles in his forearm tighten, and he stands just a little bit taller.

Rusty beckons for us to follow him into the dark shed. This scene screams all kinds of creepy, and I squeeze Casey's hand. He squeezes back.

"You know what, mate, why don't we stay out here," he says, gesturing to the grand clearing around us. Were it not for the garbage lying around everywhere, you might call this place beautiful. "It's a sunny day and all, might as well enjoy it."

Rusty shrugs. "Suit yourself." He flicks on a light inside the shed. "Gonna make some coffee. You want some?"

"Sure," Casey and I say in unison.

From my vantage point on the porch, I peek through the open door, curious about who these people are, what they're doing out here, and how they live.

And I'm instantly glad we aren't inside that shed.

The moment the lights turn on, about a dozen cockroaches start jumping off the walls and scurrying into dark corners. I shudder and resist the urge to gag.

Moments later, Rusty comes out with three steaming cups of coffee. His toothless smile has been replaced by a very dark, very irritated look. "Here's your fucking coffee," he barks. He walks away, muttering to himself. I only catch the odd phrase, something about, "Idiots…show up and demand coffee…I live on a budget…"

Casey and I exchange a look. "But, didn't he…?" I start.

Casey subtly shakes his head, and I shut up.

I stare down at the brown sludge and notice bits of God knows what floating on top. "Thanks, this is great."

Maybe I can discreetly fling the contents into the bush when he isn't looking.

A small plastic patio table and a set of mismatched chairs are set outside, not far from the couch where the young man and woman are slumped. Somehow, despite the cigarette burns and the fact that they're not even aware that we're here, I find their presence comforting.

The word "witnesses" runs through my head.

Rusty leans back in his chair, his tongue licking over his mostly toothless gums and chapped lips. Despite the dirt and lack of oral hygiene, I can see how he would have been nice looking when he was young.

"So, are you two bounty hunters or something?" he asks.

Casey and I freeze. Has Rusty already forgotten why we're here? His mood seems to have changed with the wind, but still.

"No…" I finally say, feeling off balance. "I'm looking for Nancy Carlyle because I have something that I think belongs to her."

"A photo album," Casey says. "And a few letters, all addressed to her."

"They were written the year I was born," I say.

Rusty runs restless hands over his face. He's got a knowing smile. It seems like happy Rusty is back.

"And so you think she might be your mother," he says.

I shrug, noting that he seems to have returned to his earlier self. "It's only a theory."

Rusty nods. "I knew she'd had a kid, a few months before she moved in with me." He shakes his head in wonder. "Honest to God, you are the spitting image of her."

My stomach clenches. "What can you tell me about her? What was she like? How long did she live with you? Do you know where she is now?"

Rusty's leathery face pinches together. "What is this, fucking 'How to Be a Millionaire'?" He runs a hand through his greasy hair, muttering a string of curses. "She lived there with us for about a year, I think. It's hard to remember, it was a long time ago," he says. Then suddenly his eyes glint. "But I'll never forget her. You never forget the best sex of your life."

He makes an obscene, waggling gesture with his tongue. I try very hard to keep my expression neutral and my stomach from roiling.

"Do you know where she is now?" I ask quietly, wary of setting him off again.

He spits into the tall grass. "No idea. Last I heard, she moved to Calgary and got married."

Married. So her name might not be Nancy Carlyle anymore.

My sinking heart is momentarily distracted by the girl on the couch. She's sitting up now and rubbing her eyes, her baggy hoody swelling up around her bony frame. She wanders over to our table but doesn't make eye contact.

"Is there any left?" she asks.

Any what? I wonder.

Rusty's eyes light with fury, but he maintains composure.

"Sadie, these are our guests," he says, a fake smile plastered on his face. "Be a dear and get us some cookies or something, eh?"

Sadie sleepily scrubs at her ashen face with her sleeve and ambles toward the shed.

"She makes the best cookies," Rusty says proudly after she leaves. "I have such a sweet tooth too, can't get enough of them."

His eyes glint and his mouth pulls into a sideways grin. "I can't get enough of her sweetness either. Know what I'm saying?"

Casey and I laugh uncomfortably, the strangeness of the situation hanging thick in the hot summer air. How long have we been out here? I take my phone out of my bag and glance at the time. When I look back up, I see Rusty's sharp eyes watching me.

Sadie returns a few minutes later, a plate full of cookies in hand, her eyes looking more glazed over than before. She sets the plate on the table.

Rusty stares at it for a minute and then bangs a fist on the table. "What the hell is this? You know I'm diabetic." He picks a cookie up and takes a huge bite. "Bunch of assholes," he says.

The young guy on the couch is up now too and wanders over to us. He sits down, legs spread wide, a casual smile on his face.

"What are you guys doing out here?" he asks.

"They're looking for an old friend of mine," Rusty says.

"Oh yeah? Cool."

The young man leans toward Casey and slips an arm around the back of his chair. A bit of his long-sleeved shirt rides up. Blisters and purple bruises track up and down his forearm.

"Hey man, do you think you could lend me twenty bucks?"

"No. I don't think so," Casey says, his tone friendly but authoritative.

"Aw, come on bro," he says, "It looks like you have some to spare, all clean shaven and preppy and shit."

I flick my eyes to my phone again. Time to get a few more questions answered and go.

Rusty slams his coffee cup on the table. It makes me blink. "Who are you texting? Are you telling people to come here?"

"What? No!" I say. "I'm just checking the time."

"Are you cops?" he says.

"No," I say.

"You're cops! I knew it, goddammit!" he shouts.

"Time to go," Casey says quietly to me, and we get up.

"Nice to meet you," I say, mostly because I'm not sure of what else to say. Casey and I head toward the trail, our walk quickly transitioning into a jog.

"Now look at what you did," Rusty says, followed by what sounds like a loud slap across the face. I'm not sure who was hit. We start running.

"You tell that fucking Nancy Cox that she still owes me money!" he bellows.

Casey and I race down the trail, me desperately afraid that his long legs will outrun me and I'll lag too far behind. Somehow, though, we manage to stay in step (I wonder if he slowed his pace for me), and we pile into the truck.

Casey wordlessly locks both of our doors and throws the truck into reverse. He expertly maneuvers through the dark, winding path until we hit the main highway. I feel like we can't go fast enough.

After a few minutes of racing down the highway, I lean my head against the window, my mind reeling. "Well, that was the weirdest shit I've ever seen."

The cab is quiet.

"Casey?" I say, glancing over at him.

His brow is furrowed, resolute. "I'm so sorry."

"For what?"

He shakes his head. "I should've never brought you there."

"You couldn't have known," I say gently.

"I should have just gone by myself."

"Oh yeah? And who would've taken care of you?" I ask.

A small grin plays over his features. "I can take care of myself."

He flexes one of his biceps for me, and I laugh. "I bet you can," I say.

We travel some more in silence, but the mood has lightened a bit.

"I'm sorry you didn't learn more about Nancy," he says. "I think we're on the right track, though. Rusty seemed to think you look like her."

I nod. "Yeah. Although, who knows if he's a reliable historian. He seemed to be all over the place."

"Totally. I think I have whiplash from all of the mood swings," Casey says. "Do you think it was some kind of drug op?"

"Probably," I say, knowing the real answer is "definitely."

"I'll mention it to Oakes when we get back to town."

"And what if he asks why we were out there? Doesn't that implicate us or something?"

Casey taps the side of his nose. "Not to worry. I've said before, Oakes and I have an understanding."

I smile. "Do you have dirt on him?"

He throws another one of his old cassette tapes in the player. "Something like that."

I feel myself relax into the happy melodies of the 1950s, tapping my foot along with the beat. It seemed like a simpler time. Songs titles like "Gingerbread" and "Lollipop" were taken seriously.

"We got one good thing out of today," I say.

"And what's that?" Casey asks.

"We know Nancy's married name."

"We do?"

I nod. "Yup. He called her Nancy Cox while we were running away. And said she was moving to Calgary."

I try to celebrate this small victory. But inside, I keep turning over the day's events as if they were objects, inspecting them for clues, wondering how I really feel about it.

I want to feel excitement. But a big part of me feels dread.

If that was the sort of people Nancy hung out with, do I even want to find her?

CHAPTER 13

Tell Laura I Love Her

I flop back onto my bed, my cell phone pressed to my ear. "And then, we basically ran to the truck and sped off."

"God," Laura says over the line. "What a nightmare."

"Well, it wasn't all bad," I say.

For example, I got to watch Casey run. He was sweaty from the heat, and his muscles were pumped up from the adrenaline. Mmm. That part was kind of fun. Even if we had just narrowly escaped an encounter with a guy who could easily be cast on *Breaking Bad* as "Evil Drug Dealer #3."

"At least we got some new information to go on," I say.

"How's your mom handling all of this?" Laura asks.

"Okay, I think," I say. "She asks a lot of questions, but seems supportive."

Although, sometimes, I feel flooded with guilt. Like somehow looking for my birth mom means that I'm not thankful for my parents. That they weren't enough, or were deficient in some way. I sometimes wonder if I'm being terribly cruel.

"We're starting a new project together, actually," I say.

"What kind of project?"

"A dress. I found this gorgeous emerald green fabric at the thrift store. Yards and yards of it. So I bought it, and—"

"Wait. You bought pre-owned fabric?"

"What? It's probably vintage."

"You know it came out of some old lady's basement, right? She probably kept it beside her litter box for years."

I giggle. "Shut up, please. I'm telling a story."

"Okay. But if you find any shriveled-up cat turds in there, don't say I didn't warn you."

Laura thinks my thrift store obsession is strange. While she'd much rather buy new from the local box store, I'd rather forage for that perfect little something that I can make entirely my own. I've resolved to never buy anything from Old Navy again. It all ends up at the store anyway. Same thing with Ikea. It all ends up on Kijiji.

I like to gross her out with some of my personal "strange stories from the thrift store." Like the Hutterite and Mennonite women, for example. They come in wearing long, plain dresses and covered hair, talking in soft German accents…and buy the raciest lingerie they can find.

Second-hand racy lingerie.

That story makes Laura gag every time. Naturally, I mention it often.

"Anyway," I say, with mock exasperation. "I also found these vintage dress patterns from the fifties, and they're absolutely to die for."

"To die for," she coos.

"So I brought the patterns and fabric over to Mom's house, and she was totally thrilled. We're going to combine elements from different patterns to make a truly unique dress. I have no idea where I'm going to wear such a fancy thing, but it'll be fun making it."

And with the way her hands are going downhill, I imagine it will be the last big project we'll ever do together.

"Sounds fun," she says. "Hey, since when do you sew?"

"Oh, umm, I used to sew all of the time. All kinds of things. Dresses, bags, curtains, you name it."

"Go figure. You think you know a person."

"I've got to keep a little mystery," I laugh.

"Has Snake Guy come back into the store?" she asks.

"No." I draw my curtains to look outside. Thunder softly booms in the distance and water hammers on the window. It makes me wonder where that young man stays on nights like this. Whether his shoes are holding up. Whether he's warm. Whether he feels any hope for the future.

"I think about him, sometimes," I say. "I wish I could've done more for him. Or for anyone in that situation, really."

Laura hums in agreement. "Who knows? Maybe someday you will."

I flop back onto my bed, wondering if I should tell Laura my story.

I was a quiet little girl. Got good grades; never drew attention to myself. I hung out with girls with cute names like Brooke or Ashley. They dressed in pink and had big, splashy birthday parties. I'd spend time with them, hoping that their self-assurance might rub off on me. Coolness by proxy. But it never did. I played the part of the nice, perfect little girl, all the while feeling like a fraud.

I didn't think anyone truly liked me. I figured they hung out with me out of boredom or pity, or because my mom sewed princess dresses for everyone or Dad had installed a pool in the backyard. Fear stewed in the back of my mind, reminding me that my friends would most likely drop me as soon as they discovered that I wasn't really like them.

By high school, fear of abandonment had mixed with teenage hormones and whipped my insecurities into a frothy mess. I figured that it'd be in my best interest to put people off before they had a chance to like me.

I found groups of misfits. The artsy kids, the kids from rough homes, the kids who dressed in black and listened to loud, angry music, the ones who sold drugs in playgrounds after dark. There was a turbulent loneliness about them, an anguished urgency that they were so desperately trying to fill or cover up.

I felt like I'd found my people.

It starts out slow. You might steal a few things to be accepted by the group, to feel something. Anything.

Your boyfriend is growing pot outside of town and pressures you into taking it, then selling it. You start staying out late at parties. You start going to raves, dancing the night away in a neon blur. You start fighting with your parents and storming out of the house, a cloud of profanity and hurt feelings carrying you to whoever's couch you can find. Sometimes, it's not a very safe couch. Sometimes, your friend's creepy uncle takes advantage of you during the night.

You start thinking that nowhere is safe, and you sleep outside a few nights.

I don't remember most of high school. There are huge gaps from the year I turned seventeen. I'm almost afraid to start digging for information. The memories I do have from that time are scary enough.

I got used to people, loved ones and strangers alike, calling me trash, calling me worthless. After a while, it didn't hurt anymore. Because deep down, I agreed with them.

My parents, desperate to do something for me, got me into counseling, and I begrudgingly went. It didn't go well at first. I figured my therapist would reject me, just like everyone else, but after a while I warmed up and was willing to let her in. I was okay for a few years after that. Stuck to myself, buried my head in my textbooks. Got an okay job as a nurse's aid. Got my first place. I felt like I was finally turning into a person I could like and maybe even respect.

Then, I met Kelly…and down the rabbit hole I went. Again. It amazed me how quickly I relapsed when I was around him. This perfect little life that I'd worked so hard to create went to shit in a matter of months.

My therapist might say that it was just my usual pendulum swing. Me trying on my familiar roles: the good, perfect girl and the bad party girl. Both masks are meant to keep people at arm's length.

I've decided that I've had enough of this stupid pendulum, this sick carousel. I'm done. No more men who use me; men who don't care about me. No alcohol. No drugs. Nothing that could send me down that dark path again. And if it means that I have to keep striving toward perfection, then so be it. It might be boring, but at least it's safe.

Casey's smiling face comes to mind. I note, with a sinking heart, that he's sooo my type.

Anyway. I've mentioned bits and pieces, but Laura doesn't know everything. When you're deeply ashamed of something, you tend to never mention it.

Or, if you're like me, you try to do everything you possibly can to distance yourself from it.

"Anything new with you?" I ask.

She yawns. "Not much. Just an early morning meeting. I should probably get going."

I glance at the clock. It's only nine p.m. I still have three hours to kill until I'm tired.

"Yeah, me too," I say.

We make plans to meet for coffee next week and hang up. I wrap a cuddly sweater around my shoulders and walk leisurely around my bedroom. I stop to look at photos I have framed on the wall. Family and friends. I look closer at my favorite photo of Laura and me, taken last year at a summer barbecue. We'd just been in a very lame food fight (how very *Fried Green Tomatoes* of us) and have barbecue sauce on our chins. I'm laughing like an idiot, and Laura is blowing a leisurely kiss at the camera. Everything about her is shiny and flawless, yet understated. When people look at her, they think classy. Worthwhile. Important.

And with startling clarity, even though I'm technically an adult, I realize that she's who I want to be when I grow up.

CHAPTER 14

Lucille

Cheryl picks up a ripped pair of jeans. "Now, who would want to buy these? They have holes in them," she clucks.

"Throw them in the scrap pile," Gladys mumbles.

The scrap pile is for items that aren't good enough for wear but could be used for crafts. It's made up of bolts of upholstery fabric, stained T-shirts, and worn-out overalls. And today, a pair of expensive Diesel jeans with purposely ripped thighs and knees is part of that pile. I wonder what other designer goodies have been sold for outrageously cheap prices. We're trained to look out for designer pieces and sell them for a bit more money. It all goes to charity, so why not? But I'm guessing that a *lot* flies under the radar.

I pick up another box and rummage around. I sometimes like to play a game, using the contents of a box as clues as to who the previous owner was. Like a detective.

Rubber ducks, cloudy bottles, and faded swaddling blankets? My guess is that someone out there is cleaning out a nursery.

A Slap Chop, an unused Miracle Bra, and a spidery-looking head massager? Someone was addicted to shopping channels.

Playing little games like this makes the day more interesting.

"What do we have here?" I mumble to myself.

An elaborate doily collection, one of those hideous dolls with crochet dresses used to cover toilet paper rolls, and various books on rose gardening. My guess is that someone is helping Grandma clean out her house.

As I continue sorting, something else catches my eye.

It's a VHS boxed set of *The Lucy Show*, seasons one through three. Lucy and Viv are smiling widely on the glossy pink cover. Lucy's iconic bright-red hair stands out in stunning contrast. I've secretly always wanted to have hair like hers, ever since I was a little girl and I watched this show with my grandma.

I bring out season one and read through the episode titles. I'm pretty sure that the volunteer fireman episode is on here.

Aha! There it is. Season one, episode sixteen. I wonder if Casey would want to watch it.

Just then, my phone rings.

"Hey missy, what you are up to?" he says.

"I was just thinking about you."

"Hmm. Do tell," he says, his voice sounding rich and deep, as if he's smiling.

My cheeks flame, my body betraying my emotions once again. Damn hormones.

I clear my throat. "Nothing like that," I say lightly.

"Shame."

"I'm just at the thrift store, sorting through a box of stuff."

"Fun. Who do you think owned it before?" he asks.

"Hey, that's my game," I tease. I survey the mountain of yellowed doilies. "A grandma."

"And you thought of me? Seems weird."

I laugh. "No, I found old seasons of *The Lucy Show* and thought of you," I say, feeling vaguely silly for even talking about it.

As if a hot young guy like Casey would care about watching fifties sitcoms.

"You wanted me to see the volunteer firefighter episode, right?"

"You remember?" I ask.

His smile colors the tone of his voice. "Oh, I have many talents, a good memory being one of them."

"What are you up to?" I ask, choosing to ignore his flirting.

"Someone else returned a phone call about Nancy today. I thought you might want to know what they said."

"After the Rusty fiasco, I'm not sure I want to take any more phone calls."

He clears his throat. "This one at least sounded sane. She said she'd lived with Nancy and Rusty for a while. Apparently those two had a nasty break-up or something, and so Nancy and this lady moved out and got an apartment together."

"So, they were friends?" I ask, feeling hopeful.

"Sounds like it," he says. "Do you want to meet up for coffee? I'll tell you all about it."

I glance at the clock on the wall. Almost quitting time. "Sure. Why don't you pick up coffee and come over to my place? We can catch up, maybe watch some *Lucy*."

"Okay."

"Okay," I reply. "I'll text you my address."

The last half hour of my shift, which had been clipping along just fine, seems to drag on now that I'm waiting to get out of here. I barely make it home in time to throw on a clean shirt before Casey walks through the front door.

He kicks off his shoes and whistles at the living room. "Nice place."

"Thanks," I say, admiring how he makes himself comfortable everywhere.

"Is my place going to look this nice when you're done?" he asks, eyes roving around the room.

"The office will, at least." I settle onto the couch. "Thanks for the coffee."

He flops onto the seat beside me. "Took them forever to get the order right," he says. "The barista couldn't understand me."

"What? Your accent isn't that thick," I say.

"Who knows? Some people don't seem to notice. Just depends, I guess."

"Has it ever got you in trouble?"

"Sometimes. My GPS doesn't understand me, for one thing. Or, if I go to a restaurant and order neeps and tatties, they always look at me weird."

"Well, no wonder," I say. "It sounds like you're saying nips and titties."

Casey makes a half choking noise and struggles to keep his mouthful of coffee down. "You've got a dirty mind, Thrift Shop Girl," he says after he's composed himself. "I kind of like it."

"Just for the record, what are neeps and tatties?"

"Turnips and potatoes," he says. He sits one leg up on the opposite knee, nestling into my couch as if he belongs there. "Even general names for things can be a problem."

"Such as?" I ask.

"My mom always said that sports shoes were called runners, while Dad insisted they were called trainers or joggers. And when we moved to Texas for his job, everyone there called them sneakers. When I was a kid and the shoe salesman would ask me what kind of shoes I was looking for, I'd panic."

I smile into my coffee. "That's kind of sweet, actually."

We relax into a comfortable silence.

Casey's eyes flick up to the ceiling. "When did you last check your smoke detector battery?"

I pause for a moment, reflecting. "I don't think I ever have."

His eyes widen. "You should check it every month. What about your carbon monoxide detector?"

I shrug. "Don't have one."

Casey looks so bewildered for a moment that I can't help but laugh. A moment later, he gulps down that last of his coffee and puts on his coat.

"Come on then," he says.

"Come on where? You just got here."

"We're going to the hardware store."

Within seconds of entering the store, Casey directs me to the aisle where they keep smoke detectors. Good Lord, who knew they made so many kinds?

"Here's a good one," he says, turning the package over in his hands. "Guaranteed to last ten years, without changing a battery. And it's a smoke and carbon monoxide detector all in one." He tosses it into my shopping basket.

I lay a hand on my forehead and flutter my eyelashes. "My hero."

He bows gallantly. "At your service."

When he stands, he offers me his elbow. It just seems natural to take it.

"So, tell me more about Nancy's friend," I say.

Casey clears his throat. "Well, like I said, they lived together for a while after Nancy broke up with Rusty."

"Did she give you any leads?" I ask.

"Kind of. She said that Nancy had given up a baby but didn't like to talk about it."

"That might not mean anything. It might be a coincidence."

One hell of a coincidence.

I chew my lower lip. "At least it confirms Rusty's story."

Casey nods. "Nancy and this lady lived together for a while and kept in touch by phone for a few years after that. The last thing she'd heard was that Nancy moved to Calgary and was getting married."

"Cox is an even more generic name than Carlyle," I say. "And, hypothetically, she could have married or changed her name after that."

"Hypothetically, she could use aliases too," Casey points out.

"You're good with brilliant ideas. What should we do next?"

"Knowing which city to look in helps," he says.

"That is, if she's still in Calgary," I say.

"And if she still has the same last name," Casey adds.

We look at each other for a moment, perfectly mirroring *What the fuck do we do now?* expressions.

We've almost reached the cashiers when I spy the decorating section of the store.

"Ooh, I just want to look at paint colors for a minute."

We walk into the paint aisle, standing side by side, surveying a rainbow of square paint chips. "What's your vision, Casey? What does your dream office look like?"

He shrugs.

I dig out my phone. "I thought it might come to this. Here, I have some ideas."

He scrolls through the photos. "What is this?"

"It's my office inspiration board on Pinterest."

"What the hell is Pinterest?" he asks, squinting at the screen.

"It's my preferred way to waste time," I say breezily. "It's basically a place to keep online inspiration boards."

He turns the phone back to me. "I kind of like this one."

It's a very masculine space, with clean lines and dark furniture. The walls are really boring, though. Eggshell.

"I can work with that," I say. "Would you be open to more color, though?"

"Sure."

I suddenly feel like teasing him. "What would you say to hot pink? The light is perfect in there. Just a feature wall, mind you. Not the whole thing." I pick up a paint chip board with names like "Electric Flamingo" and hand it to him.

Casey nods. "Whatever. I trust your instincts."

I snort. "I didn't really mean it. Trust me, you don't want a hot pink feature wall in your office."

He holds the paint chip up to the light. "I think it'd look cool." He turns his head to face me and smiles. "Do what you want, darl."

Well, shit. I can't believe he actually went for it.

"Deal. Oh, while we're here," I continue, "I just need to look at the mis-tint section."

"And you're looking for mis-tints because…?"

I crouch down and shuffle my feet closer to the cans of discounted paint. Each can has a spot of the color on the lid along with the marked-down price. "For the thrift store," I say, distractedly. "I want to paint a feature wall in the book section. Make a funky little reading area."

I drag out a can with a bright purple splotch on top and a label that says, "Sizzling Orchid." Perfect.

"Why not just pick a color you really want?" he asks.

I shuffle the can off the shelf, admiring the glossy purple splotch on top. "Because this is affordable. And besides, this is more fun."

"Excuse me," a small voice says from behind us. Casey and I turn to see a short lady with curly gray hair waiting for us to move out of the narrow aisle. "Thank you," she says, smiling as she passes. "You and the missus are picking out paint colors, huh? Oh, it's such a fun time in life. Enjoy it."

"Oh, we're not married," Casey replies.

"Sorry, your girlfriend then."

"We're just friends," I explain.

"Really? Well, you do make a really cute couple." She smiles at us once more and bustles toward the cashiers.

Casey might be a great friend, but he'd never be a great boyfriend.

Despite the fact that he isn't conventionally handsome, he has a certain *je ne c'est quoi* about him. An *x* factor that I can't put my finger on.

Confidence, in other words.

I'm clearly not the only one who thinks so. I see the way his phone blows up with texts from women. But I don't want to be one of many; I don't want to be just another woman passing through his revolving door of casual sex. And besides, even if I did think it was a good idea, I doubt I'd be his type.

Well. Not that it would stop him from hitting on me. I've noticed him flirting with me and slipping innuendo into our conversations. But I think it's just part of who Casey is. He seems to flirt with everybody. I doubt that he means half of what he says.

I picture him being with polished, career-driven women with glossy hair, firm handshakes, and stories about the year they spent in Brazil. That so isn't me. I'm more like the weird friend with the funny nose who routinely embarrasses herself in public.

"Isn't that ridiculous? Her thinking we were a couple," I say with a laugh.

Casey pauses and scratches his forehead. "Yeah. Ridiculous."

It doesn't take Casey long to install my new smoke detector.

"Thanks for doing that," I say. "Do you have some time? Maybe we could watch that *Lucy* episode I was telling you about?"

"On one condition." He flops onto what I'm now considering "his" side of the couch. "We don't start at episode sixteen. We watch the whole season, right from the beginning."

"We probably won't get to episode sixteen tonight, then."

"Fine by me," he says with a smile.

We end up watching several hours' worth of *The Lucy Show*. I was worried at first that he might just be humoring me and isn't really interested in the adventures of eccentric fifties housewives. But he seems to be having a good time.

Every so often, his phone buzzes and he glances at it. I notice that he rarely texts back.

"You seem popular today," I say, trying to gauge his reaction.

He frowns at his phone, eyes flicking back and forth over the screen. "I kind of let things get a little too serious with this one."

"Meaning?"

"Meaning that it's time to move on," he says, sounding resigned.

Casey turns his phone off and scrubs his face. "I love that you have these on VHS, by the way."

"You're a closet nerd, aren't you?"

He picks up the season one boxed set. "Nah, I came out a long time ago. Mark my words," he continues, "VHS will be cool again someday."

I laugh. "Highly unlikely."

"Just you watch. It'll have a comeback, like vinyl records."

"If you say so."

He scratches his cheek thoughtfully for a moment. "That, and I'm too cheap to replace my old VHS collection with DVD and Blu-Ray. And I can find pretty much any title I want for a dollar."

"You're so weird."

"I find the best ones at Goodwill. You should come with me sometime."

"Oh, I don't know if I could do that. I'd feel like I was cheating on my own thrift store," I say, and he laughs.

"You wanna watch more *Lucy*?" I ask hopefully

He taps his watch. "Don't you have to work tomorrow?" he asks. "You're gonna have a lot of 'splainin to do," he says in his best Ricky Ricardo impression.

I shake my head. "Not until the afternoon."

He tilts his head back and empties his glass of water. "Thanks, but I should probably go. I need to be up at five."

I look at the time. It's ten p.m.? How did it get so late? I throw on a thin sweater and walk Casey out to his car.

"Thanks for having me over," he says. "I had a really good time."

"Anytime. And thanks for taking that call about Nancy. I'm not quite sure if it's enough of a lead, but it's a start anyway."

He nods and shuffles his feet. "So, I'm playing at Nifties next month. You should come by, check it out."

"You play there?"

"Sometimes."

"Sure," I say, thinking about how Casey must look performing for a live audience. I've had a few private performances already, but seeing him playing on a stage with a band and lights and sound equipment would be amazing.

"Great. See you later."

He jogs back to his horrible, ugly truck and waves as he gets in. He doesn't drive away, however, until he sees that I'm safely inside the house, and I can't help but think to myself that, despite being a cocky flirt, he really is very sweet.

That night, I crawl into bed, ready for sleep. Only I can't get my thoughts to turn off.

I think about Nancy, and make a plan to Facebook search for anyone named Nancy Cox, Carlyle, or Carlyle-Cox in the Calgary area.

My thoughts wander over to Casey and *Lucy*, too. It's easy to have fun with him. I don't think I even have this much fun with Laura. I can just let go and be me, and I don't have to worry every second if I'm doing or saying the right things.

I tuck the sheet up under my chin, curl up in my big, empty bed, and wonder, just for a minute, what it would be like to have Casey lying here with me.

CHAPTER 15

Tear It Up

Okay, Facebook. Let's get down to business.

I sit down at my computer and type "Nancy Cox" into the search area and narrow the results to "Calgary, AB" and "female." (Side note: who would ever name their boy "Nancy"?)

Sorry, we couldn't find any results for this search. Showing partial matches instead.

What? Surely there must be *someone* named Nancy Cox living near Calgary. Okay. No biggie. Let's try "Carlyle" instead.

The same message pops up.

"Stupid Facebook," I mutter. I type in "Nancy Carlyle-Cox" and take off the search filters.

Sorry, we couldn't find any results for this search.

I take a deep breath and stare at my laptop screen for a few seconds.

"This is not a big deal," I say aloud. "Facebook is only one option. I can always try Google, or the White Pages, or Canada411, or Twitter, or Instagram…"   1`

I feel buoyed by the many options I have. I will find Nancy Cox, Carlyle, whoever she is. Today.

Three hours later…

That was a waste of a time. All that work for nothing. Well, nothing definitive, anyway.

I even looked at online newspaper archives. Wedding announcements, obituaries, public notices of name changes …anything, really.

I gently press the heels of my hands into my eyes, which are sore from staring at a computer for so long. Where do I go from here?

Feeling bored and more than a little defeated, I start scrolling through my Facebook home feed. Several of my friends have shared the same post. It's a picture of a woman from Florida holding a poster board that says, *Help me find my birth parents! My name is Sarah Beth Rindle. I was born on March 2, 1982, at the Memorial Hospital in Jacksonville, FL. If you have any information, call the number below. Please like and share!*

I look back at the original post. Sarah Beth posted it at eight a.m. It's now ten a.m. That post from Florida made it all the way to my laptop in my cramped little office in Edmonton. All within a matter of hours.

I wonder…could I?

I pick up my phone and call Laura.

"Hey. Do you think you could come over and take my picture? I've got an idea."

Well, that's that. The picture that Laura took of me holding up my very own *Help me find my parents* poster board is online. It's already been shared ten times. And, for good measure, I held up my doppelganger portrait too.

I didn't, however, mention Nancy's name. I can imagine whackadoo imposters messaging me, claiming to be the "right" Nancy Carlyle (or whomever). That, and despite my gut instinct and circumstantial evidence, I still don't know for sure what my birth mother's name is.

Laura also had a really great idea of posting the same information on adoption websites, just in case. Now, that's all said and done, and all I have to do is wait.

And wait.

After checking my Facebook page and phone and email for the bazillionth time, I decide it's time to distract myself with something else. Like working on my green dress.

I take out the bodice pieces that my mother and I painstakingly cut out last week. It took us a little while to figure out our own design, but what we've come up with is going to be a one-of-a-kind stunner.

I pin the pieces together, being careful to make sure the edges line up. Taking a deep breath, I place the fabric under the needle. It's been so long since I've sewn anything on my own.

"Here goes nothing," I say quietly.

About five seconds in, my thread breaks. I fiddle with the tension and rethread my needle. After about five stitches, it breaks again.

Fuck.

I start all over again, making sure the tension is at the right setting, and wondering why my new, high-quality thread keeps breaking.

"I've sewn hundreds of things before," I say out loud. "I know what I'm doing. This is going to go perfectly."

About thirty seconds later, my bobbin thread snarls under the fabric, creating a knotted forest of string on the underside.

"Argh! Piece of shit sewing machine!" I yell.

I stare dejectedly at it for a few minutes and briefly contemplate throwing it out the window, before I pick up the phone.

"Mom? Do you think you could come over and help me?"

She arrives a little while later carrying her sewing kit and a box of cookies under her arms.

"I don't understand it," I say, showing her the machine and what it's done.

She takes everything apart, rethreads the machine and bobbin, and readjusts the tension. It looks exactly the way I had it. Of course, it works fantastic for her.

I sneer at the fickle contraption. "Traitor," I say, and she laughs.

Every few minutes, I notice her massaging her hands, as if they hurt. I wonder how many years I have left to do this with her before her hands are too stiff and she can't do it anymore.

My throat tightens, and I feel the urge to hug her. This green dress project seems a thousand times more precious to me now.

"How've you been?" I ask.

She sticks a few pins between her teeth and mumbles around them. "I'm good," she mumbles, and takes the pins out of her mouth.

"Keeping busy with summer weddings and dress fittings. Keeping your dad out of trouble."

"Oh?"

She sighs, a perplexed smile on her face. "He just learned how to use Facebook."

I snigger. "Did he start playing zombie Facebook games?"

"Yes!" she exclaims. "It's consuming him." She clucks her tongue. "I swear, he never used to be this weird. Anyway, that's not the worst of it. He friended cousin Clara."

I snigger. Clara is a doctor, and Dad seems to think that, just because she's related, he can tell her all about his body.

"He didn't," I protest.

"He so did," my mom says. "He's been messaging her all day, telling her about his bowel movements–"

"Ack!"

"–his weird thick toenail, the one he calls his 'horse hoof'…"

"I bet she loved that," I mutter.

Mom shrugs, finding it more amusing than disturbing. "I imagine she'll just block him. So what've you been up to?" she asks while peering at the needle bobbing up and down.

I lean against the desk. "Work, mostly." She nods, the hum of the sewing machine conjuring up memories of my childhood. "I've started going to this fun place called Nifties," I continue. "My friend Casey is this amazing guitarist who plays there."

"Sounds fun," she says. I notice her licking her lips. She always does that when she sews or is concentrating really hard. "Is Casey a guy or a girl?"

"A guy."

"Are you dating him?"

"No, he's just a friend," I say.

She says, "Hmm," and her eyebrows rise the smallest amount. "You know, Martin is still single." I raise an eyebrow, mirroring her. "He's so nice. And tall, and handsome. And he's really done wonders with our accounts," she says.

I smile. She isn't going to give this up, is she?

I suppose I haven't dated anyone in a while. And maybe dating someone else will help me, you know, not think about being with

Casey, the shameless flirt who's afraid of commitment. The friend I'm slowly starting to adore, even though I know better.

"Okay. I'll think about it."

She swipes a wispy hair behind her ear, grinning. Victorious. "Good," she says.

Our talk rambles leisurely from here, circling around the usual topics. My brothers, weirdo Dad, our plans for the rest of the year. But then we talk about something new.

"How's your, umm, search going?" she asks, the sewing machine humming away.

I bite my lip. "It's okay. Casey's helping me find Nancy."

The humming stops, and then quickly starts again.

"Have you found anything new?"

I tell her about my adventures with Casey, leaving out some of the shadier details. Somehow, I don't think, "And then we stumbled upon a meth lab in the woods," would go over well.

I also tell her about my futile afternoon of searching online. "So that's why I've decided to try Facebook. Hopefully something comes up."

I stop talking, unsure of what else to say.

It feels awkward, telling my mom that I'm looking for another mom. I wonder what this feels like for her. I imagine it might feel like she's being laid off.

I have a vision of Laura sitting in her office at human resources, talking to my mom about upcoming replacements.

"Thank you for your twenty-seven years of active service as 'mom,' but unfortunately the position has been filled by someone else. We're going to have to let you go."

The silence stretches between us, becoming thick and suffocating. My heart beats an anxious rhythm as I knot my fingers.

"Do you think...?" I begin "Do you think this is wrong of me?"

"Wrong?"

"Well, maybe *wrong* isn't the best word," I say. "But, is this... selfish? For me to be looking?"

She stops sewing and looks me in the eye, her expression soft. "A part of me is worried about what or who you'll find. But no. I don't think it's wrong or selfish to want to find your roots." The sewing machine starts whirring away once more. "I just don't want you to get hurt."

"I know." I pick up the letters stacked on my desk. "I just want answers."

My mother stares at me for a moment. "This really means a lot to you, doesn't it?"

"Yes," I admit.

"So…what if nothing comes of it? What if you never get the answers you're looking for?"

I smile. "Then I guess I'm still stuck with you."

She smiles back. "You always will be." She winks at me, takes a bite of cookie, and pushes the plate toward my side of the desk. "Now eat up. We've got a lot of sewing ahead of us. We'll need the sugar high to get us through."

Later that night, Casey calls me.

"Miss me already?" I tease.

"You up for a little Lucille Ball?" he asks.

"I hope that's not some dirty euphemism."

"I wonder what the Lucille Ball would be," he snorts. "A red pubes fetish, maybe?"

My imagination is going now too. "No, it's having sex while wearing an apron and crying."

"You're so twisted," he says.

"You know it," I say. "My place?"

"See you in twenty."

We've nearly made it to season two of *The Lucy Show* when we decide to take a break.

"I love her," he says through a mouthful of takeout pizza. "I would marry Lucille Ball if I could."

"Why do you say that?" I ask, sloppily trying to lap up the cheese string dangling from my lips.

"Because she's fun. I'd love to come home to that little redheaded weirdo every night." Casey picks up our coffee cups. "Want some more?"

"Please," I say. I cross my arms behind my head and prop my feet onto the coffee table. "It's kind of nice having a butler."

"I prefer manservant, thank you," he says, his accent thickening. A minute later, he walks back in with two mugs. We visit for a while, and I fill him in on the events of the day.

He whistles. "A shared Facebook post. You're going to go viral. I'm so honored to know a famous person."

"I hope it goes viral," I say. "I thought I would've found more by now." I lean my head against the back of the couch and stare up at the ceiling. "I think I need a break from the search," I say. "Clear my head a bit."

"What you need to do is have some fun," he comments. "Wanna come with me to the Rockabilly Riot next weekend?"

I blink. "The what?"

Casey digs his phone out of his pocket. "You know, big music festivals? Like Boonstock? Big Valley Jamboree? Coachella?" he asks.

"Yeah?"

"Well, it's like that, but with a rockabilly twist. It's basically a three-day concert held in the middle of nowhere."

He hands me his phone. He's brought up a beautiful poster for the event, with vintage typeface and drawings. It advertises bands, tattoo booths, burlesque shows, a vintage car show, and a drive-in movie.

"Millie's going too," he says.

"Oh yeah?" I ask, surprised. It had never occurred to me that Casey and Millie might hang out socially.

"Yeah, I saw her at Nifties last weekend," he explains. "She asked if I was going."

I hand his phone back. "Sounds fun," I say. "But I don't know where I'd stay. I don't have a trailer or anything."

"Some people only come out for the main events on Saturday, but most bring their campers," he says. "I'm just going to sleep in my truck, but you could probably bunk with Millie. She has a tent trailer, I think."

"You're sleeping in that rusty old thing?" I say.

"Shush, she'll hear you!" he says in a stage whisper. "Don't worry about me, I'm bringing a blow-up mattress and lots of blankets."

"What if it rains?"

"Then I guess I'll sleep in the cab."

I shake my head. "You're crazy."

He shifts his body a bit closer to mine. "You could get a tattoo."

Unbidden memories of needles piercing my skin come to mind.

"Not likely. Needles freak me out."

"You could dress up," he offers, not one to be deterred. "Look like Lucy for the weekend."

I think of the lovely midnight blue halter dress I found along with the photo album and letters. It's hanging sadly in my closet. It really deserves a weekend out.

"They have a drive-in movie on Saturday night," he says.

"So I read."

"We could watch a burlesque show together," he says.

A small smile breaks across my face. "Maybe."

"A drive-in movie didn't sell the idea, but burlesque does?" He grins.

"What can I say? I'm a sucker for scantily clad women dancing around," I say.

He clinks his coffee cup with mine. "Another thing we have in common."

Hmm. A whole weekend away with Casey. My heart starts beating a little bit faster.

"Okay," I say. "I'll go."

CHAPTER 16

Heeby Jeebies

I turn onto the street where Millie lives and see her standing in her driveway. She's wearing a full bright-yellow skirt and her hair is tied up in a sheer yellow scarf. She waves when she sees me, and I'm momentarily stunned by her fifties-style glamor.

I glance down at my plain white t-shirt, skinny jeans, and ballet flats, feeling like I'm in way over my head.

"Hey! Glad you could make it! Find the house okay?" she asks, shading the afternoon sun with her hand.

"No problem at all," I say, lying. Turns out that Millie gives horrible directions. I doubt that "turn left by the pizza and donair shop with the hairy waiters" would help anyone.

Thank god for Google Maps.

"So, this is it, eh?" I ask, pointing at the tent trailer. The finish is crackled by the sun, and the orange and brown decals are peeling off in places.

She pats the top. "It's not pretty, but it'll keep us dry."

"Thanks for letting me tag along," I grunt as I haul my weekend bag out of my car.

"You're going to love it."

"Where are your kids?"

"In the house," Millie says. "My mom's taking them for the weekend."

"And they'll be okay, being away from you all weekend?"

I remember having such separation anxiety as a kid. I hated being away from my parents for too long. I always wondered if they were ever going to come back.

Millie rolls her eyes. "Please. They'll spend all weekend watching cartoons and eating candy. They'll be like, 'Mom who?'"

The sound of a screen door slamming open startles me. I turn to see two small children bounding across the front yard. A woman with short brown hair and wearing yoga pants trails behind, her arms loaded with pillows and colorful backpacks.

"Natalie, this is my mom, Lisa. Mama, this is Natalie. I work with her at the thrift store."

Lisa drops the bags on the ground and wedges the pillows tightly under her arm. She has a round face with deep laugh lines. Her short hair spikes up a little in the front, and her bright blue eyes twinkle with mischief. I like her immediately.

I shake her hand and say, "Nice to meet you." I notice that she and Millie have the same smile. I wonder, briefly, if I have the same smile as my birth mother.

She pats my hand. "You two have fun this weekend, eh?" She turns away, and I suddenly miss the warmth of her hands on mine. "Mildred, did you remember to pack your kids some extra pajamas and underwear this time? Because last time…"

Millie sighs, looking weary. "Yes, I packed extras." She turns and stage-whispers to me, "Trust me, you don't want to know."

Loading children into a car is a rather grand production, filled with kisses and hugs and making sure that special teddy bears aren't forgotten. When that's done, Millie and I load up the last of her stuff into her SUV and climb into the front seat.

"Thanks for the ride, *Mildred*," I say, straight-faced.

She laughs. "Watch it, lady. I know where you sleep tonight."

When we finally get on the road, Millie turns her CD player on. "Ever heard of July Talk?" she asks.

"Nope."

"They're incredible."

I listen to a few bars. "I like his raspy voice," I say. "It sounds a lot like the stuff they play at Nifties."

But what I mean is, It sounds a lot like Casey.

Millie turns onto a bumpy dirt road that wanders through a field. I'd think we were taking a very weird turn were it not for the dozens of trailers and vehicles already parked up ahead.

It doesn't take long to set up the tent trailer, and we haul our bags and coolers inside. As we squirrel things away for the weekend, I glance out the window every so often. Trailers are packed tight together, laughter and beer-fueled stories ringing in the air.

"What are you wearing to tonight's show?" Millie asks.

I look over at her sitting on her bed, one foot held high in the air as she rolls a seamed stocking down her calf.

I dig around my bag and fish out the blue halter dress. "Will this do?"

She whistles. "Wow, is that the dress you found with the photo album?"

"Yes," I say, dangling the garment in the sunlight.

She runs her fingers slowly over the fabric. "This will totally do."

After messing around with my hair and makeup and wriggling myself into the dress, I stand tall in the middle of the tent trailer.

Millie takes one look at me and crosses her arms. "Oh, this won't do." She circles around me, lost in thought. "The dress is fine. But this…" She picks up my straight, flat-ironed hair. "We can do better than this." She touches my chin and turns my head from side to side. "I'll help you fix your makeup, too."

"What's wrong with my makeup?"

"Nothing," she says sympathetically. "If you were becoming a nun."

Millie cleans off my barely there makeup and applies primer on my nose, then spreads it over my cheekbones. I shift uncomfortably.

"I've never really liked my nose," I say quietly.

Millie applies bronzer to my cheeks. "You know who you look like?"

"Who?"

"A young Sophia Loren."

I sputter with laughter. "You're such a liar."

"Seriously, you do. Do you know what Sophia Loren said about beauty?"

"What?"

"Nothing makes a woman more beautiful than the belief that she *is* beautiful."

"Interesting theory," I say while trying not to move my face too much.

I bet there's some truth to that. Casey is a good example. He thinks he's the shit, and consequently, so does everyone else.

Millie spends extra time applying my eyeliner and lipstick. "And...voila!" she says, as she hands me a compact mirror.

For the first time in years, I recognize the girl looking back at me. It's like slipping on a cozy pair of slippers that you love but lost and forgot about.

"You like?" she asks.

I smile. "I like."

Millie snaps her compact shut. "Good. Now, let's do something about your hair."

About thirty minutes and half a can of hairspray later, I walk out of Millie's trailer a new woman. Gone are the beige flats and skinny jeans that I arrived in. Millie loaned me a pair of cherry-red high heels and a skinny red belt to wear over my dress. My hair has been teased and curled within an inch of its life, and it has been reimagined in a complicated set of victory rolls, topped off with several large roses and a rhinestone clip.

Millie slips herself into a gorgeous white dress with a red rose print.

"Where do you find your clothes, Millie?" I ask. "It's not exactly something you can find at Wal-Mart."

"I find a lot of stuff online," she says. "Though, I usually find the best stuff at Rowena's on Whyte Ave."

I'm feeling so glamorous in my new get up that I make a mental note to shop there when I get home. Why did dressing up ever go out of fashion? Nowadays, if you wear a dress or tuck your shirt in, people ask, "Why are y'all dressed up?"

Just as Millie is putting the finishing touches on her own hair, I get a text.

Casey: Hey Miss! Are you here yet?

I text him back, telling him where he can find us.

"I'm just going to go outside for a bit," I say.

Millie nods and picks up a rat tail comb. "Catch up with you later."

I stand outside the tent trailer and feel my stomach clench. What felt like old Hollywood glamor just moments ago now feels like a cheap costume.

Stupid insecurity. I thought I was supposed to outgrow that shit in my teen years. Here I am, closer to thirty, and I'm still worried about what other people will think of me. Does it ever end, I wonder?

I shift from side to side and rub my arms, which feel cold despite the dry August heat. I'm just about to go back inside the trailer when I spot Casey.

He's walking toward me, hands in his pockets, talking to someone over his shoulder. He stops and his mouth forms a small O shape when he sees me. He whistles. "What a stunner."

My hands run over my skirt. "Thanks. I feel a little silly, though."

"You look cute. Especially with those little bobbles in your hair."

"Bobbles?"

"Ah, it's what my mum called them. Umm, you know. The hair thingies."

I feel some of the tension release from my shoulders. "Thanks. You look pretty cute too."

His hair is slicked back, and the sides look freshly shaved. He's wearing black dress pants, a light blue dress shirt with the sleeves rolled up, a bow tie, and suspenders.

"Suspenders?"

He stretches them out and releases them with a snap. "I make 'em look good at work. Why not here?"

We've got about two hours before the Friday evening concert starts. Millie has made plans to meet up with some friends of hers – she seems to know everyone here – so it's just Casey and I. We take our time wandering around the grounds. It looks like we've wandered onto the set of *The Outsiders*. It's all slicked-back hair, victory rolls, and Bernie Dexter dresses as far as the eye can see.

Whoever organized this event really went to a lot of trouble. There's an enormous, professional-looking stage toward one end of the field, complete with huge speakers and fenced-off areas. Dozens of vendors are lined up around the perimeter. There's the usual concert fare: food, drinks, and band T-shirts. Some booths sell rockabilly dresses and complicated-looking lingerie, while others focus on collectibles and old cars.

We're ambling between the rows of vendors when Casey bumps my shoulder.

"We've passed the same tattoo booth a dozen times now," he says.

"No, we haven't."

"Yes, we have. What do you keep looking at?"

I relent and point out a poster toward the back, where the artist has displayed pictures of their previous work. "That one," I say.

The woman in the picture has an extremely realistic rose tattoo on her shoulder. Clusters of small roses and leaves trail down her arm into a half sleeve.

"Do you have any tattoos?" Casey asks.

"No," I say, tilting my head to look at the photo from another angle. "I thought about it once, a long time ago."

"Do you want to get one now?" Casey asks.

I laugh. "Getting a rose tattoo is so cliché. It's like a belly button. Everyone has one."

"I don't have one, so there goes your argument," Casey says.

"You don't have a belly button?" I ask innocently, hoping that I can conceal my smirk.

He rolls his eyes. "Smart arse," he says, drawing out his accent.

Casey leans forward to examine the picture. "Just look at the colors and the shading." His gaze returns to my shoulder. He trails a finger from my collar bone, down my arm. "It would look beautiful on you."

A shiver passes through my body. I swallow and look at the poster again. An intoxicating rush of adrenaline swirls through me.

I don't like needles. They remind me of too much. But a small voice inside me says, *It's time to let that go.*

I take a deep breath and turn to Casey. "Okay. I'll do it." Casey's face lights up. I lay a finger on his chest. "On one condition."

"And what's that?"

"You're getting one too."

Casey laces his fingers and stretches his arms out in front of him, like a pro card player who knows exactly what he's doing.

"You're on."

I recline in the black leather chair, licking my lips. "Is this going to hurt?" I ask, hating how nervous I sound.

This is a bad idea. A *really* bad idea. I don't handle pain well, and needles really do freak me out. I can't even go for blood work without nearly passing out.

"Relax," Casey says. "It's a bit like being pinched, but it isn't too bad. In fact, it can be a real rush. Ever wonder why people have so many tattoos?"

"No," I say, squeezing my eyes shut as the artist walks toward me with pots of color.

"They're addictive," Casey says. I feel my chest getting tight, and I work hard to control my breathing. "Nat, do you want to watch me get one first?" Casey asks.

I laugh. "Just like a kid watching their parents get a vaccine?"

"Exactly."

The artist sits down and wheels the chair closer to the table.

"Are you ready?" she asks with a kind smile.

This lady has pale pink hair, facial piercings, heavy black eyeliner, and a black dress covered in a neon green skull pattern. Her neck, chest, and arms are covered in beautiful black and white tattoos. Apparently she's what this crowd calls "psychobilly." Kind of a goth version of rockabilly. She's absolutely stunning, in a tough-as-nails way. I can't wimp out in front of her.

I nod. "Yes, I'm ready."

Casey squeezes my hand just as I feel the first prick of the needle.

CHAPTER 17

Rockabilly Boogie

"How's your arm feeling?" Casey asks.

I think it's about midnight; the last concert ended about an hour ago. We're eating ice cream, which is now my preferred way to end the day. Bubble lights are strung in a crisscross fashion above our heads between the vendor stalls, and romantic music is playing softly in the air.

In the end, I opted to get a single rose on my shoulder, rather than a half sleeve. Break myself in gently, you know. Casey got the same.

"It's a little sore, but fine," I say, rubbing the edges of my bandage. "It's kind of weird that we got matching tattoos."

He licks his ice cream cone. "It means we're soul mates. We should get married now."

"You're such a dork."

"Seriously, they have a chapel set up over there," he says, pointing ahead.

"Does it have an Elvis theme?" I ask, half joking.

"It does, in fact."

"Shut up!" I say. "That's hilarious."

"Us getting married is hilarious?" he asks.

"*Anyone* getting married in an Elvis chapel is hilarious," I say. "Although, it seems to fit in here."

"So that's a 'no,' then?" he says.

"That's a no," I say.

He stumbles backward, clutching his heart. "Flat out rejected," he says. "I'll cry into my pillow tonight." I can't help but giggle at him. He walks backward for a few paces and stumbles, falling with a dull thud on the ground.

I laugh at his cute spectacle (Goddamn, why does he have to be so adorable?) and then walk over to him.

"Casey, are you okay?" I ask.

He gives me a shy smile and dusts off his pants. "My arse hurts less than my pride, so I think I'll live."

We continue walking, the music becoming louder as we go along. We eventually come upon a black-and-white-tiled dance floor. A pergola-type structure is built above it, and fairy lights and gauzy fabric hang from above. Some couples merely sway from side to side, while others are flashy and colorful, performing dance moves I've only seen in movies. Their feet follow such a complicated pattern that it makes me dizzy.

"I've always wanted to dance like that," I say.

"Oh yeah?"

We sit on a picnic table set up at the far end of the dance floor. When a new song starts, Casey stands and holds out his hand. "Come on, then."

"I don't think so."

"Really?"

I look out at the dancers twirling and laughing on the dance floor. I tried to learn years ago, but I just couldn't get it. And the more the instructor tried to go over the same moves, the more flustered I got and the more impatient he got. I never went back.

I look up at Casey's warm brown eyes. I don't think I could live with him being disappointed in me too.

"Really," I say.

His outstretched hand flops back to his side. "All right, then."

He starts to turn away, but quickly whirls back and grabs me by the elbow. He expertly twirls me on the spot, and then puts me into one of those low dips, the kind you see in romantic Hollywood movies and never think are done in real life.

"Casey!" I half shout, half laugh. "What are you doing?"

He sets me upright and lays his hands on my shoulders. "I know you're just itching to get out here and join everyone else."

It's almost scary how well he can read me.

"Yeah, but…"

"No buts. Tonight is about having fun. Who cares if we make fools of ourselves?"

He positions us in a classic dance pose. I'm acutely aware of his large, firm hand on my lower back. I'm momentarily tempted to nerd out with a *Dirty Dancing* flashback and say, "No spaghetti arms!"

I swallow and look up at him. "Now what?"

"First, I'll teach you how to waltz. Then we'll move onto the fun stuff."

I try to follow along, and at first I'm so nervous that my palms start sweating. I hope he doesn't notice. But Casey is so patient, and he keeps making me laugh so that eventually I let go and start enjoying myself.

"See? You're a natural," Casey says.

I feel myself blush. "Thank you. Now teach me some cool stuff."

Casey smiles. "Yes, ma'am."

"Your Texan is showing," I say.

He grins. "It has its uses."

Casey shows me a few other dances, like the cha-cha and the bop. He teaches me how to jive and swing, breaking down the moves so they're simple.

"How did you learn to dance?" I ask, breathless.

"Well, you go to enough of these and you sort of pick it up," he says.

"I call bullshit," I say.

"Fine. My mom taught me how to dance."

"Aw, Casey loves his mommy," I coo.

He smiles, bringing out those killer dimples. "I just wanted to impress girls."

He whips me in a fast circle until I'm in fits of giggles. This boy can dance. *Really* dance.

I'm still red faced and hanging onto his arms when the music stops and the lead singer asks for everyone to quiet down.

"Ladies and gentlemen, thanks for coming out tonight. You've been great. As y'all know, it's open mike night, so if any of you want to sing a song or show us your skills on the guitar, please come on up."

A buzz rips through the crowd. I bet a lot of musical people are here.

Someone at the front shouts, "I nominate Casey Nolan!"

Casey spins away from the crowd and then spins back, a sweet, bashful smile on his face. A lock of hair drips down over his forehead. I have to resist the urge to sweep it back.

"No, you guys, let someone else play," he says. "I'm teaching my friend here how to dance."

"Oh, come on honey! Let the man play!" someone shouts at me.

The crowd starts cheering and calling out Casey's name.

"You have quite the reputation, Mr. Nolan," I say with a laugh.

"So it would seem."

The crowd is getting louder, encouraging him to perform. Casey throws his hands up in the air and takes an exaggerated bow.

"Oh, all right, if my public insists." He jumps up on stage, borrows a guitar, and adjusts the mike. "How y'all doing tonight?" he drawls.

The crowd cheers back in response, especially the group of young women near the stage. A really pretty blonde in a red and white polka dot dress and curly ponytail is jumping up and down on the spot directly in front of him.

I imagine he'll notice her. Put a pretty woman with bouncing boobs in front of a man and he's bound to look.

He grins and looks down at his guitar, tuning the strings a little. I can't help but notice how his forearms flex with the movement. His broad chest strains appreciatively against his light blue shirt and suspenders. And when he turns to the band to discuss which songs he's going to sing, I notice that a trail of sweat has darkened the back of his shirt.

In a weird way, it's kind of sexy.

At first, Casey sings upbeat dance songs, like "Rave On" or "Long Tall Sally." Not only does he sing and play them well, but with his deep voice, he makes each song his own.

A couple of men offer to dance with me, and I figure I might as well. They aren't very smooth dancers, and I find it hard to remember the steps with them. It isn't nearly as much fun as dancing with Casey.

After a few songs, I feel someone nudge my ribs.

"Millie!" I exclaim. "Where have you been all day?"

"Oh, here and there," she says, smiling coquettishly. "Looks like you've had some fun today."

She points at my shoulder bandage.

"Casey and I got matching tattoos." I pull my bandage down a little so she can peek. "Roses."

She raises her eyebrows, looking amused. "Okaaay then."

"You had to be there."

Suddenly, the mood of the crowd shifts and everyone gets really quiet. The music has stopped, and Casey is standing in front of the mike.

"I'd like to dedicate this last song to my dear friend Natalie."

My heart leaps. I swallow hard, wondering what he's going to play for me.

Casey starts to strum his guitar, while the rest of the band takes a break. He starts singing a darker, slower version of "Take Good Care of My Baby," by Bobby Vee. I'm sure I've heard Casey sing this in his truck before, though it wasn't nearly so dark and sensual.

When Casey starts to sing the last verse *a cappella*, the crowd goes nuts. Especially the women near the stage.

I nudge Millie. "Geez, you'd think they were going to throw their underwear on stage."

She snorts. "They probably will."

Casey bows and then jumps off the stage. When he reaches me, he's a big, sweaty ball of excitement. "So, what'd you think?" he asks, hands on his hips and puffing hard.

"I think you might need to rest a bit, rock star," I say, laughing. "You were fantastic, by the way."

He puffs up his chest. "Oh, I know."

I playfully smack his chest. "Humble, too. Why did you dedicate that last song to me?"

He shrugs. "I wanted to do something nice for you," he says. "Plus, I thought you'd like the song."

"It sounded so different that I hardly recognized it," I admit. "You did a good job. A really good job."

He gives me a boyish, sideways grin that emphasizes his dimples. It's a smile that gets my heart beating a whole lot faster.

We're young. We're obviously attracted to one another. We have fun together. Why am I making this more complicated than it has to be?

That's it. I'm telling him tonight just how I feel. Maybe I'll make the first move.

While images of me leaning up on tip-toe to kiss Casey dance around my head, Millie starts filling us in on what she did all day. Just then, the blonde in the polka dot dress shows up.

She carefully slides around me and stands in front of Casey.

"You were really great up there," she says.

Casey nods. "Thank you."

She offers her hand. "I'm Lacey."

"I'm Casey. Hey, that rhymes," he says.

She giggles again, and I roll my eyes. Lacey takes another step toward him and places a hand on his chest. "I was just about to walk back to my trailer, but I don't really want to go alone in the dark. Would you mind walking with me?"

Casey offers his elbow. "It'd be my pleasure, ma'am."

"Your Texan is showing again," I mutter.

"You don't mind, do you, Nat?" he asks.

Images of me kissing those full, beautiful lips dissolve into the night.

"No, not at all."

Casey tips an imaginary hat toward Millie and me. "Evening, ladies."

Millie and I stand beside each other and watch Casey and Lacey and her swishy polka dot dress walk into the dark night, toward a field of trailers and dim orange campfires.

"Do you think he'll sleep with her tonight?" I ask.

Millie bobs her head from side to side, an evaluative gesture. "Probably."

My beating heart locks up and turns to ice.

Damn it. I should known better. He isn't interested in me. He doesn't feel the same way.

I sigh, feeling the ice spread out to my veins. I wrap my arms around my torso, feeling the bandage tug on my arm. "Good. I'm happy for him."

I barely sleep that night. My stupid brain won't shut off. And my stupid heart won't stop breaking.

CHAPTER 18

In the Still of the Night

It's a muggy Saturday night, and we're winding down from our second day at Rockabilly Riot. Casey, Millie, and I went to all of the main events together.

We wandered through the show-and-shine, where people show off their vintage cars and flashy paint jobs. We met some new people and sat around their trailers, drinking cold beers in the August heat. They were all very friendly, sharing their drinks. It was really hard to turn one down. I could almost taste it. I usually don't miss it, but sometimes I do miss the casualness of being able to have just one drink with a group of friends.

In the afternoon, we even went to a burlesque show. My dirty mind couldn't help but wonder if Casey had a boner through the whole thing. I'd be surprised if he didn't. Even I got a bit excited. Not that I'd tell him that.

The main concert of the weekend kicked off at about six, and my god, it was good. Despite only getting about two hours of sleep the night before, I managed to pull it together and have fun anyway.

Once the concert died down, everyone was invited to drive their vehicles to the other side of the field for the movie. Casey nods in the direction of his truck.

"Want to go to the drive-in with me?"

My stomach flip flops deliciously.

"Sure, so long as you don't try to cop a feel."

He snaps his fingers. "You take the fun out of everything."

Ha. If he only knew the sort of "fun" I'd like to have with him.

I laugh at him, and we start walking toward his truck. "What about Millie?"

He cranes his head round. "Oh, I think she'll be all right."

I turn around and, sure enough, I see Millie ambling along with a group of people. She seems to make friends easily anywhere we go.

Sooo. Casey and I will have the night all alone together? At a drive in-movie? I'm suddenly very aware of his every move. Will this mean anything to him?

If it does, it doesn't show. He doesn't seem particularly nervous or excited. Just his usual calm and happy self. A stark contrast to sweaty-palmed, dry-mouthed me.

We follow a long line of dusty vehicles, tires crunching over the dry grass, and park in a wide field where an enormous white screen is set up. The air is filled with noise: frogs singing, car doors opening and slamming shut, the metallic clang of beer cans popping, and folding chairs snapping open. This feels like the best camping trip I've ever been on.

Casey unlocks his truck and starts hauling out sleeping bags and pillows from the cab. He throws them into the truck box and arranges them into a squishy, cozy little nest. He climbs in and offers me a hand up. As I take his hand, I lock eyes with him for a moment, and he smiles at me. A blaze of excited nervousness ripples through me. My joints feel loose and wobbly, so when I step onto the rear bumper, my feet slip.

Just as my chin is about to smash onto the tailgate, I feel Casey's hands slide down my arms and clamp around my rib cage. His forearms tense as he effortlessly hauls me up so that we're chest to chest, our faces only a breath away from each other.

"Jaysus," he chuckles. "Are you all right?"

I can feel his deep, gravelly voice reverberating from his chest into mine.

I nod, too preoccupied with our bodies pressed together to feel embarrassed about my slipping and nearly knocking my teeth out in front of the hottest guy ever.

After a few seconds, my lungs remind me that breathing is kind of important, and I try to take a breath. Casey's eyes widen, and he realizes that he's still squeezing me.

"Oh, shit, sorry," he says, releasing me. "I didn't mean to grab you so hard."

I feel lightheaded, drunk on the rush of being in his arms.

After making sure that my clumsy ass is definitely not going to tumble out, he crawls to the far side of the truck bed, leans back and smiles, and pats the space beside him.

Wow. This is really happening. I'm going to be snuggled up with this man for the next few hours. I feel an excitement that borders on nausea.

Shit shit shit. I'm done for.

"Do you know what's playing?" I ask, trying to distract myself as I settle in beside him on the pile of sleeping bags.

"It's a double feature. *Cry Baby* and *Grease.*"

I fluff my pillow and lean back. I stare ahead at the screen, forcing myself to breathe evenly, forcing myself to relax. *It's just Casey,* I scold myself.

"Hmm. Never heard of the first one," I say. The intro music starts. "Wow, it's Johnny Depp. He's really young in this."

About half an hour into *Cry Baby*, I start to cringe. "Oh my god, this is so cheesy!"

"I know. Isn't it great?" Casey replies.

Voices from the vehicles around us rise as they sing along with the music and shout things at the screen. They even bring out props for certain scenes.

"This is so weird. It's like going to see the *Rocky Horror Picture Show*," I say.

"You've seen it?"

"Not for years," I say. "My ex and I used to go out on Halloween to this local theater." I smile, revisiting the few positive memories I have of that time in my life. "We really got into it. I'd dress up like Magenta, and he'd dress up like Riff Raff, and we'd throw toast. It was awesome."

He replies with a good-natured "Hmm," and we watch the rest of the movie. The plot and dialogue are so cheesy that it's awesome. If that makes any sense.

When the credits start to roll, I sit up and yawn. "What time is it?"

Casey looks at his watch. "Just about two in the morning."

"And we're going to watch another movie?" I say.

"Yep."

I yawn again. I can't remember the last time I stayed up this late.

"So, home tomorrow," he says during a slower scene in *Grease.*

"Back to reality." I feel my mood dip somewhat.

"Any word on your Facebook post thing?"

"Not sure," I say. "I can't get WiFi out here."

I can feel him nodding above my head. "Right, right."

"I'm not sure if this wild goose chase is going to work out or not, but I'm grateful for your help," I say. I look up at the stars. The night sky is never this clear in the city. I'm suddenly filled with a sense of gratitude. "Thanks for this weekend too. I needed it."

He lets out a low sound, something like a hum. "Any time, darl."

"Darl. Such a strange word."

"My dad used to say it a lot."

"To your mom?" I ask.

"My mum, the grocery store lady, my girlfriends, basically any woman. He was a real flirt."

"You come by it honestly, then," I tease.

Casey sits up a bit and he points at the screen. "This is my favorite song." He starts bobbing his head along with the music and singing the words.

"You know all of the words to 'Greased Lightning'?" I ask. He responds only by singing louder. "You like *Grease*, then?"

"Love it. I've only seen it, like, fifty million times."

"You're so weird."

"Yeah, and you love it," he says, winking at me.

My stomach flutters, and I force myself to look back at the big screen.

"I always liked Frenchy," I say, searching for a way to redirect the conversation. "She was so sweet."

"I always liked Eugene," Casey says. "The world needs more nice guys like that."

"Nerdy guys like Eugene would be considered cool hipsters today. Just look at those glasses," I muse.

"Frenchy would be cool today too," Casey says. "Look at that pink hair!"

We're both quiet until the high school dance scene, when Rizzo and Kenickie start grinding and dancing suggestively.

"You know, I've always had a thing for Rizzo," he says.

I laugh, but think to myself, *I used to be like Rizzo.*

Hickies. Pregnancy scares. Sleeping with boys who didn't really love me.

It's so weird. When I look back now, I feel oddly detached. Like those things happened to someone else.

As Casey and I continue to watch the high school dance scene, I'm reminded of the dance from yesterday night.

"So...did you hook up with Lacey?"

I catch myself holding my breath; I'm not sure if I'm going to like the answer.

He pops a potato chip into his mouth. "Lacey who?"

Has he forgotten her name already? Maybe Casey "walks" more women home at night than I thought.

"Pretty blonde on the dance floor? Red dress?"

"No idea."

"Bouncy ponytail?"

"Nope."

"Enormous boobs?"

His eyes light with recognition. "Oh, her!"

I roll my eyes. "Yes, her."

A breeze picks up and a chill settles around me. I pull my knees to my chest and pull the blanket tighter. Casey looks at me from the corner of his eye, and after a beat, he lifts up his arm.

"Come here."

I hesitate for a moment, noticing that my pulse has quickened.

"I know you're cold," he says. "You have goosebumps."

"Umm, yes," I say, feeling like my tongue is slow and awkward, stumbling over my words. My body feels jittery and cold, as if all the blood has rushed to my heart, and my flesh prickles with an intoxicating mixture of excitement and nervousness. There's no way I'm admitting that these goosebumps are from being around him.

He tilts his head to the side, inviting me in once more. A shiver passes through me. Probably half from the cold, half from adrenaline. I'm not sure if this is a good idea, but I'm freezing my ass off. I slide over and let him wrap his arm around my body. He pulls the blanket up higher with his free hand and tucks it around us.

"There. Snug as a bug in a rug," he says.

Casey's body is incredibly warm. Solid. Reassuring. I catch myself thinking that I wouldn't mind staying right here for the rest of the night.

"So, did you sleep with her?" I ask casually after my raging hormones have calmed down a little.

"With who?" he asks, sounding genuinely confused.

"Ginormous boobs."

He laughs. "No, I didn't. I just walked her back to her trailer and said good night."

"No good-night kiss?"

"No. She smelled like cigarettes. Yuck."

It feels like a weight has been lifted off my chest and I can breathe again. The cool night breeze picks up and I shiver. Casey tightens his hold of me.

"Wish I'd brought another blanket," he mutters.

"I'm glad you didn't," I say without thinking.

"Why?" he guffaws.

My heart throbs a quick, panicked pulse. Crap! He can't know how I feel about him! How can I fix this?

"Oh you know," I say, my voice sounding high and tinny. "You uh, wouldn't want to over pack."

He grunts, sounding amused. "Okay then…"

As he adjusts the blankets with his free hand, I look down at the arm he still has wrapped around me. Slivers of ridged scar tissue shine in the moonlight, peeking through gaps in the blue and green ink of his arm.

"Casey?"

"Yeah?" he says, distracted by rearranging our blankets.

"Do you mind if I ask you about your arm?"

He freezes. "Okay."

"What happened to you?"

His mouth twitches. "It was a horrible tooth brushing accident."

Tooth brushing?

It takes me a minute to realize that he's trying to keep a straight face, but a smile is breaking through.

"I'm serious," I say, trying not to laugh. "What really happened to your arm, Casey?"

He pauses for a moment. "A fire."

"Oh."

And we leave it at that.

I feel myself getting sleepy. I imagine it's almost four a.m. I can see a faint pink light emerging just above the treeline. I don't even remember the movie ending.

All I know is that while I snuggled in closer and felt Casey rest his head on top of mine, I realized I was falling for my best friend.

CHAPTER 19

Candy Man

Breathe. Just breathe. It's just one little date.

So, I let myself get a little too comfortable around Casey and I started to panic. What if I let myself get too attached? What if my little crush leads to somehow being naked in his bed and voila, I'm the hot Irish firefighter's flavor of the week?

I couldn't let that happen.

And so, as soon as I got home from the festival, I called my mom and told her that I'd meet Martin the accountant.

So what if this is my first real date in a couple of years? My parents wouldn't lead me astray. I'm sure Martin will be lovely. They wouldn't set me up with a complete weirdo, would they?

Anyway, it was probably the easiest date I've ever set up. I asked Mom for Martin's number. She texted it to me. I texted Martin. He texted me. We set up a date. And that was that. Not the most romantic "how we met" story, but whatever. With any luck I can start thinking about someone other than Casey. Or about something other than Casey's dimples. Or the feel of Casey's warm, muscular arms wrapped around me.

Ugh. Just stop it.

It's a beautiful summer afternoon. Martin picked a trendy, busy bar downtown. The sun is shining bright, the streets bursting with people eager to eat and drink after a long work week.

Each step I take, I allow myself to get a little more excited. Not that I really know what I'm in for. I don't exactly know what Martin looks like. All I know is that he's tall, has dark hair, and wears glasses. And is passionate about accounting.

God, who could be passionate about accounting?

Anyway, never mind. I'm sure Martin the accountant will be lovely.

Oops. I'd better stop calling him that in my head. *Just Martin. Martin. Martin.*

I scan the patio of the bar and note two dark-haired men sitting at separate tables. It's hard to tell if they're tall since they're both sitting. Not sure what to do, I decide to approach the guy closest to me. He's reading a menu and not paying the faintest attention to his surroundings. I cross my arms and bend sideways, trying to look him in the eye.

"Hello," I say, smiling. "Are you Martin?"

He shakes his head. "No."

The man behind him turns in his seat. "I'm Martin."

My eyes alight on a thirty-something man with dark hair, glasses, a superhero-square jaw, and stunning green eyes. For a split second, I envision him ducking into a phone booth and emerging all buff and encased in spandex, cape billowing out behind him, his glasses abandoned.

Wow. Good job, Mom. Maybe I should let her set me up more often.

I mutter a quick sorry to the first guy and stretch out my hand to Martin. "Hi, I'm Natalie."

That still sometimes feels weird to say, like it isn't really my name. Sometimes, when I look at my reflection, I can't really connect the name "Natalie" with the person in the mirror. It makes me wonder if I had a different name at birth.

Martin shoots upright, and his long legs bang the table, threatening to spill the glasses of water. His hands dart out to steady them, but he ends up knocking them over.

"Dang it," he mutters while dabbing at the table-top puddle. After containing the spill, he wipes his hands on his dress pants and finally shakes my hand.

When he stands, I notice that his dress pants are about two inches too short for him.

I give Martin a bright smile and take a seat. "Sorry that I'm a bit late," I say. "I had trouble finding a parking spot."

"You should take the bus. It's more economical. And better for the environment. Public transportation reduces greenhouse gas emissions," he says.

"Erm, right. Absolutely," I say while picking up a menu. "So, what are you having?"

Martin frowns. "Not sure," he says. "I haven't ascertained the cleanliness of the kitchen yet."

I blink. "Right. So…you haven't been here before?"

"No," he admits. "A colleague of mine suggested it. He said it was good for dates." Martin sets his menu down. "I don't, umm, do this very often."

My eyes are glued to Martin's hands. He's rearranging everything on the table so they're at right angles. Well, I shouldn't be too judgmental. Everyone has their quirks, right? Maybe we're kindred spirits. Maybe we'll connect on some deep level.

A waitress wanders by with a pitcher of water and refills our glasses. Just as I'm about to take a sip, Martin takes a small white packet out of his pocket.

"Alcohol swab?" he asks, offering it in my direction.

"Umm, no, I'm good, thanks."

He shrugs, rips the alcohol swab out of its packet, and wipes it around the rim of his water glass. "It's not sterile unless you scrub for at least sixty seconds," he explains.

I nod, my eyes never leaving his hands.

After he's done his cleaning ritual, he leans toward me and says, "So…"

You know, he really is attractive. And cares about the environment and is obviously smart. Maybe this won't be such a bad date after all.

Aside from the weird cleanliness thing.

"Are you prepared for the robot uprising?"

I blink. "I beg your pardon?"

Okay. Maybe he's joking. Maybe he's just nervous and this is his way of breaking the ice.

"Do you have an action plan?" he asks.

"Action plan?"

Martin nods, pupils dilated. "You know, for how you're going to survive once the world is swarming with cyborgs?"

"Umm, no…"

He slaps the table and smiles, making me jolt upright. "Have I got the book for you." Martin reaches down to his bag, which resembles a woman's overnight bag more than a briefcase, and brings out a dog-eared, weather-beaten book. The title reads *The Robot Uprising Survival Guide.* He hands it to me, and out of morbid curiosity I accept it. I thumb through the various sections:

What to do if you're attacked by robotic frogs. The difference between a humanoid walker and a cyborg. How to treat ray gun injuries. Never approach an unfamiliar robot in a rebel zone, and other basic tips.

He shifts his chair a bit closer to mine. "Fascinating, isn't it?" His phone lights up and starts buzzing. "Just a text from Mother. She likes to check in."

I somehow manage to get through twenty minutes of robot war tactics and back-and-forth texting between mother and son before our food (thankfully) arrives.

"How was your weekend?" Martin asks while I dive into my potato skins.

"It was great!" I say, relieved that he's finally asked a normal question.

I fill him in on the things Casey, Millie, and I did at the festival. I tell him about the bands and the car show, about Casey teaching me how to dance and Millie dressing me up.

Martin snorts. "Sounds imbecilic. Reminds me of those ridiculous people who re-enact the Civil War or dress up for Renaissance fairs. But, to each their own, I guess." He lowers his fork, and gives me some intense eye contact. "You don't plan to dress up all of the time, do you?"

Ha. This coming from the guy who role plays robot-attack survival scenarios with friends in his basement.

"Well, no," I admit. "It was fun for a weekend, though."

Martin smacks his lips. "Glad to hear it."

I pause. "How was your weekend?" I ask, feeling a sudden, awful sense that I've invited myself into another discussion about items that should or shouldn't be in a robot uprising survival kit.

Oh god. I just had the most terrible, creepy thought. This feels eerily like I'm having dinner with my dad. Change the topic from "robots" to "zombies" and it'd be the same. I already have enough problems worrying about the romantic feelings that I've developed for my philandering best friend. I don't need to add weird daddy issues to the mix.

In fact, Martin's response is rather boring. He fills me in on the details of some conference he went to. I nod and smile at all the appropriate times, but I honestly couldn't tell you what the conference was about. Financial something or other.

Turns out that my mom was right. Martin really *is* passionate about accounting.

After a while, an awkward lull settles over the conversation. When replacement drinks arrive, we lean forward and smile, relieved to have something else to focus on. I'm slowly becoming hypnotized by the swirl of ice in my glass when a voice calls out my name.

"Natalie?"

The golden evening light is at such an angle between the downtown buildings that all I can see is a silhouette. But I'd know that accent anywhere.

Martin turns around just as Casey approaches our table.

"I thought that was you," Casey says. He pulls up a chair and spreads out his legs as far as they can go. He grins, munching away on something green and rope-like.

I flash him an amused smile. "What are you eating?"

"Green apple licorice." Casey plops a bag of green licorice on our table. "Want some?" he asks, offering the bag to both of us.

I laugh. What a goofball. "I'll pass. Martin, this is Casey. Casey, this is Martin the...umm, the guy my parents set me up with."

Casey raises his eyebrows, and a sly smile spreads over his lips. After a moment, he sticks out his hand. "Nice to meet you, Marty."

They shake hands. Martin is sitting ramrod straight and jutting his chin out. "It's Martin."

Casey delivers a charming smile. "Oh, sorry mate. My bad. How's the tattoo holding up, Nat?"

Martin's eyes widen. "Tattoo?"

I slip the cardigan off my shoulders. The more I've looked at it, the more I've fallen in love with it. "See? I just got it."

Martin looks up at me, forehead creased. "You got a tattoo at this event?"

"We both did," Casey says, while pulling up his T-shirt sleeve to show his.

"You were outside? The risk for contamination would've been incredibly high. Did you confirm that they used sterilized instruments?"

I blink at him. "Well no," I say slowly, baffled. "But it all looked clean and professional."

Martin looks down at the table, shaking his head. After a moment, he forces a smile. "At least it's in an area where you can cover it up."

Casey clears his throat. "Hear anything new on the search for Nancy and the missing photo album?"

I smirk at him. "That sounds like a lesser-known Nancy Drew mystery."

He smirks back.

"Who's Nancy?" Martin asks.

Whoa. What a loaded question. Do I really want to get into all of this on my date? If that's what you would call this.

"Just a friend I'm looking for," I reply gently. "No, I haven't heard anything yet," I say, returning my attention to Casey.

Casey nods. At the restaurant next door, a group of women sit outside at the patio. It looks like a fun place, with exotic tapas and modern, beachy-looking furniture. The ladies keep sneaking furtive glances at Casey, smiling and pointing at him when they think he isn't looking.

He notices them – of course he does – and waves.

"So, Casey. What do you do?" Martin asks, emphasizing the word "do."

"I'm a firefighter," Casey replies.

"Do you need much schooling for that?"

I fidget with the hem of my shirt, feeling twitchy and awkward. This conversation feels more like an interrogation than anything else.

Casey shrugs, unperturbed as ever. "The course is only a few months long." He smiles and laces his fingers behind his head, his forearms and biceps bulging. "I love my job, though. I'm always happy to go to work."

"How much money do you make?" Martin asks.

I laugh uncomfortably. "I don't think that's really appropriate–"

"I make a decent wage," Casey replies. "It's enough that I can pay my bills and do the things I want to do." He picks up another piece of licorice and rips off a huge chunk with his teeth. He munches away for a bit, then leans his forearms onto the table. "So, Marty. What do you do?"

I kick Casey under the table, and he shoots me an innocent expression.

Martin crosses his arms. "I'm an accountant."

Casey asks a few polite questions about Martin's job, which Martin interprets as an invitation to describe taxes or mutual funds or something.

Note to self: Mom clearly has strange taste in men. Must avoid all her future attempts to "set me up."

I haven't a clue what they're saying to each other, but the one thing I do notice is the women at the bar next door. They're still casting furtive glances at Casey and smiling when they catch his eye. Every once in a while, in between replies to Martin, Casey's bright brown eyes crinkle up and he smiles back at them.

My chest tightens and my neck starts to feel hot. I decide that I probably should re-enter the conversation.

"So is that why you became an accountant?" Casey asks.

Martin shrugs. "More or less. What about you? Why'd you become a firefighter?"

Casey winks at a woman next door and bites off another chunk of licorice. "To pick up chicks." He pulls aviator sunglasses down over his eyes and grins at us, perfectly framing his white teeth. "Well, I'm off. Nice meeting you, Marty," he says. When he looks at me, I glare at him for purposely trying to wind Martin up, which he merely laughs at. "I'll see you later."

Casey affectionately squeezes my shoulder as he passes behind my chair, and my entire body feels warm, as though I'm swimming in honey. He saunters over to the table of ladies next door, pulls up a free chair, and starts talking to them. It looks as though they're old friends picking up where they left off. For all I know, they are.

I hold in a big sigh and watch with a sinking heart. I don't want to like Casey. But it's impossible not to. I just wish he weren't so...*available* to other women. Maybe if I could know for sure that he wasn't interested in anyone else. For all I know, he might be. He hasn't had a girlfriend around. None that I've noticed, anyway.

Maybe if...

Oops. And there goes that thought. He's got his arm around one lady, and another is practically sitting in his lap.

"He makes himself comfortable, doesn't he?" Martin says.

I smile, painfully. "He sure does."

"Is he your ex or something?" he asks.

"No, not at all. Why?'

"Just making sure."

I raise an eyebrow, but purposely don't ask anything.

"I think he's a bad influence on you."

I laugh. "What are you talking about?"

"Well, he clearly pressured you into getting a tattoo," he says.

I shake my head. "He really didn't."

"And he offered you candy. Candy!" he says, clearly flustered. "It's like a gateway drug, Natalie. First, you take an innocent bite. No harm done. The next thing you know, you start craving it."

"The horror," I say.

His eyes brighten. "And then before you know it, you start eating white bread–"

I fake a gasp. "Not the white bread," I say in my best gingerbread-man voice.

"Yes!" he says, stretching his arms outward. "It's a slippery slope."

Shit. He looks a bit scary, actually. Way too pumped up about this subject.

"When the robot uprising comes," he says, "there won't be any sugar, or any luxuries at all. It's time to prepare our bodies now."

I pick up my phone from my purse. "Well, look at that. My vet just texted me. I have to run. My pet's surgery didn't go well, and he needs an, umm…emergency tracheotomy."

Martin scrubs each finger vigorously with a wipe he's brought out of his bag. "Sorry to hear that. What kind of pet do you have?"

Oh shit. "Erm…a gerbil."

Martin nods solemnly. He's using a new wet nap for each finger. "Did you know that having a rodent as a pet is a sign of high intelligence?"

I pick up my purse and start backing away. "Wow, that's so interesting. Anyway, got to run."

"I'll call you!" he says.

I'll change my number, I think to myself.

I've barely turned away from him before he has his phone pressed against his ear. "Hello, Mother," he says. "Yes, I think it went really well."

We part ways, and just as I'm about to round the corner onto the next street, I hear Casey's distinct guffaw mingling with several women's laughs.

For a moment, I consider joining them. I could march right back there, sit at their table, and make new friends. But on second thought, we just spent the weekend together. Maybe he'd like some space. I'm glad he's having fun, too. Even if it does make me wonder what they're laughing about.

CHAPTER 20

Baby, Let's Play House

I've decided to act on Casey's suggestions:

1) Address Karl in his first language. (I've decided to learn "grandpa," which is *dziadek* in Polish.)

2) Sing "You Are My Sunshine."

I hope I pronounce *dziadek* right. I looked it up on Google Translate and listened to the audio clip over and over. Even with all that practice, I still feel like I'm saying "your dick."

Saying "your dick" to an elderly male patient might not go over so well. Or, depending on how pervy he is, it might go over *really* well. Which would be so bad.

Not much is happening on the long-term care unit on this quiet Saturday morning. I'm keeping busy by folding linen.

Eventually, I arrive at Karl's room. I'm already tense. I don't know what it is about me that makes him cry, but he can be happy and smiling one moment, and then the next he bursts into tears.

So, as per our usual routine, his eyes narrow and his chin wobbles as soon as he sees me. Was he hurt by a nurse who looked like me? I can't make sense out of it.

Well, here goes nothing.

"Dzien dobry, dziadek," I say brightly, which means, "Good morning, grandfather."

Good lord. It sounds like I just said, "your dick." Actually, "Jean dough bray, your dick," to be precise. I'm sure my accent is terrible.

Surprisingly, the waterworks he was gearing up for stop instantly. At first, it looks like he's surprised that I've addressed him in his native tongue. He stares at me for a moment and then claps his hands and prattles on excitedly in a strange mixture of Polish and English. I catch only the odd word, but I get the sense that he's telling me a story.

His smile is infectious, and I finally understand how the other nurses and nurses' aides have found him to be such a pleasant man.

At the end of my shift, I drive home hopeful that I've made a patient happy and my work life less stressful. If a few Polish words garnered a reaction like that, what will happen if I sing to him?

After I've finished my shift at the hospital, I go to Casey's house to put some finishing touches on the office. Hanging pictures and curtains, arranging furniture. That sort of thing.

I dance through his house, after letting myself in the front door, and skip into the kitchen, where I find Casey washing dishes. Hmm. But don't his forearms look lovely. All shiny and soapy.

I plop myself down at the kitchen table. "Hello, dahling," I chirp.

Casey raises an eyebrow, offering a bemused smile. "You seem happy."

I lean back in my chair, arms crossed behind my head. "Karl. I followed your advice and learned a few Polish words. He doesn't cry around me anymore."

"What'd you say to him?"

"Dzien dobry, dziadek," I reply.

"It sounds like you're saying, 'your dick.'"

I laugh. "That's exactly what I thought!"

"I'm glad it helped," he replies. Casey pours us coffee and we pick at some muffins he made.

"These are amazing," I say, taking another bite.

"Thank you. I made them this morning," he says, "I love having home-baked stuff. Reminds me of home."

"Shit, you'd make a great house wife," I say, and he laughs. "Where do you find the time?"

He shrugs. "Wasn't a big deal. Decided to make them before my shower this morning. I stripped off and whipped these up quick so I could eat them after my shower was done." He swipes a few crumbs off the table. "It was a real time-saver."

"You were cooking nude?"

He picks up his ratty old apron from the counter. "Well, technically, no. I had this on."

Good god. Casey wearing nothing but his birthday suit and a threadbare apron. What a sight that would be. That broad muscled back, toned buttocks peeking through, the strings tied loosely at the curve of his spine...

"Natalie?"

"Yeah?"

"You spilled," he says.

I look down at the puddle of coffee on the table in front of me.

"Sorry."

He waves my comment away and mops the coffee up with a dry cloth.

"Do you ever have pictures of firefighters cooking? In your calendars, I mean?" I ask, still staring distractedly at the apron, which is in a rumpled ball beside the sink.

He laughs. "Sometimes. We have a new calendar coming out around Christmas, actually. Why do you ask?"

"Just wondering."

And bingo. I know what I want for Christmas.

We share a moment of content quiet, the warm late summer sun spilling into the kitchen. It highlights the crumbs on the floor, the coffee stains on the table, and Casey's stubble. It couldn't be more perfect.

After we've finished our snack, Casey and I head up to his office. It's coming along quite nicely.

"See?" I say, standing back proudly. "What'd I tell ya? A hot pink feature wall looks fabulous in here."

"Totally fabulous," he says in his most gruff voice.

"Do you actually like it?" I ask, feeling another spasm of self-doubt set in. "I think the light in here is great with this color, but it's just one wall. We can easily change it."

"You should decorate the rest of the house."

I snort. "I can't do that."

"Why not?"

"Because it'll look like you have a woman living here."

"So?"

"So…your lady friends might not like that."

"I don't have lady friends," he says.

"What, just boyfriends now?"

He swallows and clears his throat. "Natalie. I've been meaning to say…"

"Yes?"

He opens his mouth to say something, but then reels it back in. "I just wanted to say that I really like the feature wall. Hot pink is definitely my color."

An awkward pause settles over us, and I feel like the room is thick with things unsaid.

"So. That was interesting, running in to you and Martin the other day," he continues.

"I think he nearly had a stroke when you offered him candy."

Casey rubs his fingers over his lips, eyeing me steadily. "Are you seeing him again?"

"Not if I can help it."

"Don't write him off so quickly. He might be your soul mate."

I roll my eyes and playfully elbow him in the ribs.

"Your alcohol-swabbing, robot-fighting, finance-loving soul mate," he says dreamily. "It's like a fairy tale."

My eyes squint up with pleasure. "You're terrible."

But what I really mean is, "You're wonderful." I love being teased like this. Nothing makes me feel more comfortable.

"What are you doing tomorrow?" he asks.

"Shopping for a birthday gift for Laura," I say. "It's coming up."

"Know what you're getting her?"

"Not a clue."

"What's she into?"

"Food, mostly," I say. "She loves the Food Network, food blogs, food trucks…"

"So buy her a recipe book or a new kitchen gadget."

"Or a dirty fireman kitchen calendar," I say, and then slap my mouth when I realize what I've said out loud.

Casey smiles suggestively. "Sounds great."

I busy myself with collecting paintbrushes and paint trays, my hands shaky, my chest feeling warm and flushed.

"What about you?" I ask. "What have you got planned for the week?"

He politely follows my lead to change the subject. "Plotting revenge on the rookie," he says. "He messed with my gear." Casey picks up a paint roller and sets it down with the other painting supplies with a satisfying clunk. "And that little gobshite has to pay."

"What's a gobshite?" I ask.

"Sorry, it's a word my dad used to use a lot." Casey leans back a little and screws his face up. "Ah, Jaysus, dat bay is a right fecking gobshite, he is. D'ya know what I mean, like?" he says in the thickest Irish accent I've ever heard.

"Talk more Irish to me. I like it."

"Oh. I know exactly what you'd like," he says, his eyes twinkling with mischief.

"You're shameless," I giggle. "Do you ever stop flirting?"

"Not if I can help it. Okay, how about this," he says, getting into it now. "Jaysus, lawd, my friend was with Molly from up the road last night, and well, she'd lay down in the nettles for it. Mad for the knob, she is."

"Does that mean what I think it does?"

"Probably."

"It seems that plotting revenge brings out your Irish side." His eyes widen and he nods eagerly. "You seem a little too excited about this," I comment.

"You never mess with a man's gear."

I can't help it. "What if I messed with your gear?" I ask, suggestively cocking up an eyebrow.

Casey's mouth hangs open for a moment, but it snaps shut quickly. "Depends on what gear you're talking about."

I laugh. "Okay. What did the big bad rookie do?"

He leans toward me with wide, animated eyes, arms out in full hand-talking mode. "So, every guy sets their coats and boots and stuff up in their own way. And if you mess with it, they lose time getting geared up. Or they might not gear up properly, and it's unsafe," he explains. "Anyway, this idiot moved my shit around and made a big deal about how funny it was. We're built on teamwork and partnerships, and to put one of your buddies at risk is one hell of a no-no."

I pause. "Can't you just talk to him first?"

Casey's mouth opens, but then nothing comes out. It almost looks like he's never considered this option. After a moment, he says, "But my way is much more fun." I lift my eyebrows, and he laughs. "He's had it coming for a while, anyway."

"Oh yeah?"

Casey nods. "Yeah, he's a know-it-all. A real cowboy, thinks he's riding in to save the day singlehanded."

"So, what are you going to do to him?"

"Nothing too bad," Casey says. "He's already been disciplined by our fire chief, so there's not much more I can do." A mischievous glint lights his eyes. "But I can still feck with the little maggot."

At the end of our visit, Casey walks me out to my car. On my way there, I see the orange cat wandering through the yard again.

I squat down beside the cat, scratching his back. "Hello again."

Casey leans against my car. "I never see that cat around unless you're here."

I scratch Kitty behind the ears. "Maybe you just never look."

"Did you have pets growing up?"

"No," I say. "Matthew was allergic to pet dander. Patrick and I were so pissed."

Casey laughs. "I had a dog. A big black Labrador named Luther." He crouches alongside me. "What pet would you have wanted?" he asks as the cat rubs along his pant leg. "The pet of your dreams."

"An orange stripey cat," I reply.

"That is the most boring dream pet ever."

"Hey, don't mock my dream pet," I say, laughing. "I don't know; I've always had a thing for orange cats. They just seem familiar and comforting."

We stand and brush orange cat hair off our hands. "Get out of here, you weirdo," he says to me.

"Don't be too mean to the rookie," I call over my shoulder.

"No promises," he calls back.

CHAPTER 21

Hey, Good Lookin'

"So what are you looking for, exactly?" Millie asks.

"A birthday gift for my friend Laura." I half-heartedly pick up a French recipe book on display outside of Chapters. "She already has this."

I take out a list of potential gift items: mortar and pestle; garlic press; madeleine pan. All of which are crossed off because, through some very stealthy questioning, I've found out that she already has them. There are only two stores left in the mall that I haven't been to. They both have sporting goods, camping gear, and work boots – that sort of thing.

"She likes camping," I say, desperately looking for a loophole. "Maybe I'll find some weird camping food-prep tool she hasn't heard of."

We walk into the store together, meandering through aisles of running shoes, golf clubs, and athletic wear.

I'm really starting to like Millie. She's fun to work with, and she shares her comfort food – a huge sign of friendship, if I ever saw one. That, and she tells horrible stories of what it's like to navigate the scary dating world as a single mom. Very entertaining.

I nudge Millie's shoulder and point out a cute guy with a military haircut, a wide chest, and no wedding band sifting through a rack of board shorts. A little boy in a Ninja Turtles shirt tags along behind him, mimicking the man's every move.

"Check it out. Hot single dad at ten o'clock," I whisper.

Millie flips through some neon running shirts. "I've come to the conclusion that hot single dads are mythical creatures. They don't exist."

I blink. "But I can see one. He's right over there. And he's rocking the military look you're into."

She tilts her head to the side, as if evaluating him. "Correction. Normal ones don't exist. Otherwise they wouldn't be single."

"And you're basing this theory on…?"

"Experience. They're either hung up on an ex or into kinky sex. The bad kind," she amends. "Or, they have massive credit card debt or a semi-incestuous relationship with their mother. I'm telling you, the *normal* hot single dad is an extinct species."

"Makes you wish someone would've raised awareness about ten years ago," I say.

"They could've done infomercials." She adopts a faux reporter's voice. "For one dollar a day, you could adopt this hot, normal single dad."

"With your donation," I continue, "we can keep this rare species alive."

We laugh to ourselves and walk toward the camping gear section.

"Any ideas yet?" Millie asks while running her hand over a buff mannequin's arms.

I fold my arms while looking at a display case of freeze-dried camping meals. A row of lumpy green packages advertises, "Chicken casserole in a bag. Just add hot water."

"Not really," I say, and move on to the gadget areas.

What the hell…a hand-crank blender? A camp stove with a charging station? An air mattress with speakers? A porta-potty that attaches to your bumper?

"Is it weird that I'm intensely attracted to this mannequin?" Millie blurts.

"What?" I say, distracted by these bizarre camping gadgets.

"He's just so hot," she says adoringly while rubbing the mannequin's broad chest.

"There's probably a medical term for that fetish."

She continues stroking the mannequin's chest. "Maybe I just need to get laid."

"Well, if this guy does it for you, there's always blow-up dolls," I say, struggling to keep a straight face.

Her face lights up. "Really? Do you think they make boy ones? I always thought that they only made female blow-up dolls."

"Not sure. We can Google it later."

She whips out her phone. "Already on it."

I'm just about to move onto camping recipe books with titles like *Bannock over the Campfire* and *Eating off the Land* when I see Casey walk past us. "Hey, stranger," I say.

He stops and hooks his thumbs through his belt loops. "Hey, ladies. What are you up to?"

"Looking for a present," I say. "Remember, my friend–"

"Laura," he says.

"Right," I say, feeling oddly pleased that he remembered. "What about you?"

He holds up a blue long-sleeved shirt. "Winter is coming."

I laugh. "Okay, Ned Stark."

He grins. "Thought I could use a new long-sleeve to layer up." He cranes his neck, looking over the clothing racks. "Looks like the fitting room is a bit busy right now." I look behind me and see a long line of people, mostly moms with small children, waiting to try things on. There must be a good sale on or something.

Casey's mouth pulls to the side and he looks at Millie for a second. She's absorbed in her phone, probably still giggling over dollies with inflatable, erm…accessories.

He looks back at the packed change room and mutters, "Ah, fuck it."

With a swift movement, he shrugs off his old shirt and tries the new one on, right in the middle of the store.

Millie gapes at him and I laugh. From all of the tight T-shirts he's worn, she must've had an idea of what Casey's chest might look like. But sweet Jesus…let's just say the real thing is better. *Waaay* better.

He stretches his arms and moves around a bit, getting a feel for the shirt. "Yeah, I think this'll do," he says.

Casey whips off the new shirt and is topless for a few moments while he turns his old shirt right side out. A lady walking by pushing a stroller stops mid-stride and stares at him. I swear she's about two seconds away from pulling her phone out and snapping a picture.

"I got some good news," he says, his voice muffled as he pulls the shirt over his head.

"Oh yeah?" I say, still feeling a bit dazed.

"My little brother, Liam, is coming up to see me in a few weeks."

"I remember you mentioning that," I say. "For how long?"

"Five days. I've got time off work and everything. You should meet him."

I smile, feeling excited by the prospect. "I'd love to."

Millie shoves her phone in my face. "They do make boy ones!"

"Do they come with wieners?" I ask.

Casey's eyebrows shoot up. "Wieners?"

"Some, but not all," she explains. "I don't understand the ones *without* wieners. I mean, they're a sex toy, right? Why would they bother making a male sex toy without a dong?"

Casey jerks his head up, eyes wide with shock. "*Sex toy?* What are you looking at?"

"Sex dolls," Millie explains.

I dig out my phone. I've been doing a little research of my own. "I was right!" I declare. "There is a name for your condition. According to Wikipedia, agalmatophilia is a paraphilia involving sexual attraction to a statue, doll, mannequin, or other similar figurative object." I look up from my phone and gesture to the tall, buff, dark-gray mannequin standing beside me. "Basically, it means that you'd like to get it on with this guy."

Millie lovingly strokes the mannequin's arm. "The heart wants what the heart wants."

Casey shakes his head. "There's something seriously wrong with you two." A moment later he adds, "Must be why I like you."

A pleasurable, warm sensation blooms in my chest. Casey likes me. Does he mean as a friend, or as something more? Although, maybe he meant that he liked Millie and me? I circle around these questions for a while until Millie interrupts my thoughts.

"Natalie?" Millie says, eyes glued to her phone. "I think we should stop at the Love Boutique before we go home."

"Have you figured out what to get Laura yet?" Casey asks me.

"Not yet," I admit. "At this point, I'm willing to take my chances at the Love Boutique."

"I'm in," Casey says, wrapping his arm around me and leading me out of the store.

I laugh and take a step backward, my face flushed by the idea. I intuitively know that sex toy stores plus Casey plus me equals trouble. Fun trouble, I imagine. But trouble, nonetheless.

"Joking, just joking," I say.

"I wasn't," Casey and Millie say in unison. After realizing what they've just said, they look at each other and burst out laughing. Both of them have a loud, infectious, guffawing sort of laugh. It suddenly strikes me that they'd make a great couple. Both of them are fun, charismatic types. Both love the same retro, rockabilly scene. They both obviously have dirty minds.

Are they attracted to one another? I'd be surprised if they hadn't thought about it.

A deeply uncomfortable feeling settles in my gut. I really need to distract myself.

Okay. Think about Laura. Birthdays. Perfect gifts. Anything other than what Casey and Millie might get up to at the Love Boutique.

I run my tongue over my teeth, thinking. I am officially out of gift ideas. The woman is single and makes oodles of money. If she wants something, she just buys it.

Maybe I don't have to find a physical gift. Maybe I can do something for her.

Okay. Let's brainstorm. Laura likes food. Homemade food, preferably. And people, since her job is in human resources. Hmm. People and food. Food and people.

"I've got it," I say, feeling like a weight has been lifted off my shoulders.

Casey and Millie raise their eyebrows. "What is it?" he asks.

I playfully push past him and scamper to the exit. "I'm going to throw Laura a party," I call over my shoulder. "A dinner party, to be exact."

I walk backwards out of the store, brimming with my own brilliance. So what if I've never thrown a fancy-schmancy dinner party before? There are several badly neglected cookbooks in my kitchen. You just follow the recipe, right?

Easy peasy.

CHAPTER 22

It's My Party
(And I'll Cry If I Want To)

Ugh. Easy peasy, my ass.

The dinner party is tonight. I've selected recipes way beyond my skill level, the house is a mess, I have flat hair and no idea of what to wear, and I'm cooking dinner for eight.

All on my own.

Okay. Deep breath. It's all going to be okay. It's just friends coming over. Millie, Laura, and a few of her work colleagues and close friends. It's not like I have to impress them. I mean, it's just a birthday party.

Just my best friend's milestone, monumental, kind-of-a-big-deal thirtieth birthday party.

I stand in front of my closet in just my underwear, piles of cast-offs on either side of me. Must find something that says "elegant hostess" or similar.

As I go through the classically elegant items that now dominate my wardrobe, I find myself longing for the colorful, flirty dresses the ladies were wearing at the Rockabilly Riot. Even though the entire get-up of teased hair, heavy makeup, and seamed stockings felt a bit costumey for my taste, I did enjoy the clothes. I pull out the navy fifties-style dress I wore on the first night of the festival, the one I found with the letters to Nancy.

Did Nancy wear this? Was it special to her?

The Facebook post has been out for a while now. I've been constantly checking my email in case someone responded. Apart from a few weirdos who have posted some nasty comments, I haven't received zip.

I throw the dress onto the bed. I can't think about her. Not tonight.

As I dig through the closet, I spot a box sitting in the bottom. It's just a plain old shoe box, but it holds all of my memories from my early twenties. The good ones, anyway. I try not to dwell on the rest.

I remove the lid and am instantly hit with a wave of nostalgia. Postcards, movie stubs, a half-used tube of my favorite lip gloss. At the bottom, I find a stack of pictures. The top one is of Kelly and me.

I pick up the stack of pictures, my fingers hovering over the faces.

We both look so young. Me with an extreme push-up bra and caked-on makeup. Him with spiky hair, a too-tight T-shirt, and bloodshot eyes. Our evenings were usually spent at sweaty night clubs, drinking cheap beer and expensive shots. It always started out well but usually ended with a dramatic fight in the parking lot or me crying in some bathroom stall because he left with another girl.

I look at my younger self, smiling in the picture, and feel strangely detached. As if my memories aren't really mine, like that chapter never happened. It's like I'm a stranger to myself.

I don't recognize who she is. Maybe I don't want to.

I set the photo down on the bed and look around my modern, muted, copied-and-pasted-from-a-decor-magazine bedroom. I look at my closet, a sea of neutrals. And I'm startled by the same sense of detachment.

Is *this* really who I am?

I eventually close the closet door and wander back to the kitchen.

I'll figure out my outfit later.

Let's think dinner party menu.

Laura has reassured me that she just wants a small get-together. Nothing fancy; just a fun birthday dinner among friends. Although, as the day goes on and I get closer and closer to the party, I feel this sort of pressure settle on my chest, around my stomach, and in my thoughts; squeezing the joy out of me. It reminds me that I've never entertained this many people at once. It reminds me that my carpet hasn't been vacuumed in a while. Guests will surely notice.

It reminds me that I've put on about five pounds in the past year, and my face has a few new spots on it, and my hair looks greasy, and there are piles of laundry sitting on my bedroom floor, and that I didn't check if any of my guests have food allergies or restrictions, and...

I suddenly realize that my body has been swirling around the house, much like my chaotic thoughts.

I remember what my counselor said and close my eyes and stop to take a deep breath.

It doesn't have to be perfect. It doesn't have to be perfect.

I repeat this in my head until I believe it.

When I reopen my eyes, I decide that the most important thing right now is food, and I should invest my energy into preparing food for my guests. It doesn't have to be perfect, but that doesn't mean I can't try some new recipes, right?

I admit, I might have got a little carried away with the menu. But best friends don't turn thirty every day, and I want to make it special for her. So I may or may not know what a parsnip is. Not a problem. So what if I don't exactly know what "deglazing" a pan means? I'm sure I'll figure it out.

Time to start the first course: Swirled Cream of Carrot Soup.

Step one: Simmer beets on medium-low heat until tender, and then puree with a food processor.

Beets? That can't be right...

I pick up the recipe book, eyes raking over the ingredient list. I flip through a few pages and see what the recipe is supposed to look like.

A pristine white bowl is divided between two vibrant colors: one side is bright orange, while the other is a deep burgundy. The colors are delicately swirled together and garnished with a dollop of crème fraiche and sprig of rosemary.

Beets. Huh.

Well, here goes nothing.

It takes several minutes of desperate searching, but I finally find it: my dusty, forlorn food processor, forgotten on a top shelf in a corner cupboard. And, since my kitchen island is a chaotic slew of cookbooks, spatulas, and ingredients (and there aren't any more free power outlets), I'm forced to plunk the machine onto a teeny, tiny sliver of counter space on the far side of my kitchen.

I pulverize the freshly cooked beets and swirl a spoon through the beet mush, admiring the dark ruby color. Even it if it looks and tastes like baby food, the color is quite pretty.

I walk across the room, the heat of the beets radiating through the thick plastic bowl.

"Ouch, that's a bit hot yet," I mutter.

A few steps more.

"Ouch!" I hiss.

Almost there. Damn this huge modern kitchen.

One more step.

I nearly reach the island when my fingers can no longer stand the heat and I drop the bowl. It's like I'm watching in slow motion.

Beet puree sprays out in all directions, crimson lines streaking down my white cupboard doors, puddling on the light gray hardwood floors.

"*Fuuuck!*" I screech.

I close my eyes for a moment and take a deep breath.

Okay. It's probably not as bad as I think it is.

I peek with one eye open.

Oh fuck. It's just as bad as I thought it would be.

My eyes follow a thick red trail up the wall. It continues up toward the ceiling and culminates in a huge red spatter. It looks a bit like a grisly, upside-down exclamation mark.

Oddly, a manic gurgle of laughter bubbles in my throat. I murmur a stream of swear words, twirling on the spot and noticing even more red spatters on the other side of the kitchen. All of my self-soothing talk about letting go of perfectionism is promptly forgotten, and all I can do is focus on what a shit show this has turned into. I wonder if this is what a panic attack feels like.

Just then, my phone rings.

"Hey, Thrift Shop Girl. What are you up to?"

"I'm up to my neck in beet puree."

"Sounds kinky," he says. "Tell Mr. Fireman what happened."

"I dropped a huge fucking bowl of fucking pureed beets, and…"

I lean against the fridge and look around the room. My back suddenly feels warm and wet. I glance over my shoulder. Blood red splotches are spreading across my T-shirt.

"I just…I just wanted to try cooking something new," I explain, feeling my voice wobble and hating myself for it. I hate it when I cry. "And I've got people coming over for Laura's birthday in a few hours, and I have this whole kitchen to clean. Well, whole house, really–"

I look around the beet murder scene, overwhelmed by a sensation that I'm drowning; not in water, but in details. Expectations. An ideal that I could never possibly live up to, no matter how much I try.

"This was such a bad idea. I have absolutely no experience being a hostess, or cook, or anything. God, what was I thinking?"

"I'm coming over."

The decisiveness of his tone makes me take pause.

"Why?" I ask.

"To help you, silly."

About twenty minutes later, Casey knocks on the front door.

"What in God's name are you wearing?" he asks, shrugging off his coat.

I lift up the hem of my frilly apron. "An apron. Not unlike the one you wear."

His lips twitch.

We walk into the kitchen, where I've been trying to clean up. I've more or less succeeded in smearing everything around.

He whistles. "It looks like a murder scene in here."

"And the best part is," I say, showing him an area that I've already tried scouring, "it stains."

"Never underestimate the power of bleach."

"And what about the ceiling?" I ask. "Should I just leave it for now?"

Casey crosses his arms, his eyes trained on the blobby amoeba-like splotch looming above. "Do you have any white paint lying around?"

My memory scans the stuff in the supply closet. I usually keep small cans around for touch-ups. "Yes, I think so."

"Go get it. And a small paint brush too."

While I go about bleaching every surface in the kitchen, Casey stands on a chair and carefully dabs at the ceiling, removing as much of the beet puree as he can without smearing it around.

"Fuck me, this stuff really does stain, doesn't it?" he says.

"Don't remind me," I say, half laughing, half crying. "I still have so much to do, and here I am."

Disappointment settles over me like a heavy quilt. I flop my bleach-soaked rag into the sink and take off my cleaning gloves. "I just wanted it to be perfect, you know? And now..." I look up at Casey. "And now, all I've got is a big mess."

I go to rub my hands on my T-shirt and realize about two seconds too late that I've just smeared around a few purple stains I hadn't noticed. I laugh, plucking my wet T-shirt away from my body. "Who am I kidding? *I'm* a mess!"

Casey goes silent for a moment, his eyes fixed on a particularly bad spot on the ceiling. "Messes are okay," he says. "You don't have to be perfect."

Something inside me goes numb. That makes sense to me; going numb often happens when you hit a nerve.

He wipes the brush onto a rag and smiles at me. "Your friends won't care. They'll love you anyway."

I laugh, though it sounds hollow and disbelieving. "And my mess?"

He smiles softly. "Especially your mess." He gets down from the chair and stands a few inches away from me. "Natalie, I–"

It's as if someone has hit a panic button inside my chest. I back away, my cheeks flushed.

"I appreciate you coming over to help," I say quickly. "Thank you."

He sighs deeply, his expression looking somewhat wilted. "Anytime."

We go about our work silently. Casey steps down from the chair a few minutes later, paint brush in hand.

"That oughta do it," he says.

"Wow," I say. "You can barely notice it."

"There's a slight pink tinge yet, so you might want to put another coat on tomorrow."

I nod and look at the clock. How is it four o'clock already?

"I am royally screwed," I say, glancing at my long, complicated menu.

"What's left to make?" he asks.

"Everything. Beet puree was the first thing on the list," I say.

He picks up the list and whistles. "Quite the line-up," he says. "Who decided on the menu?"

"I did."

Casey raises his eyebrows.

I playfully snatch the menu out of his hand. "What? I was having a Martha Stewart moment."

"Do you have any more beets?"

"Not unless we use what we scraped off the floor."

"Economical, but nasty."

I look wistfully at the cookbook propped on the counter. A glossy photo of orange and purple soup shines under my skylight.

"I'm running out of time."

Casey nods once, as if coming to a conclusion, and then crosses the room.

"Come on, we're going out."

"Where?"

"To the grocery store."

Casey and I scramble down the produce aisle, searching for beets. In the interest of saving time, he's made a few suggestions on our shopping list that'll be "shortcuts" for tonight's menu.

"But the idea is that I'm supposed to make it all," I protest.

"And you will, darling," he says while tossing a box into our cart. "With the help of your dear friend Betty Crocker. Is Millie coming tonight?" he asks. "Maybe she can help us catch up."

He's asking about her? Hmm. I wonder if he does like her. I thought I noticed a connection between them at the mall, when the Love Boutique came up. Or perhaps he's simply curious.

I nod, trying to keep my thoughts from wandering. "I thought about that, too. She is coming but can't leave any earlier than six, when her babysitter arrives."

Casey clicks his tongue. "Gotcha."

We wander through the store, laughing and joking around, and I almost forget why we're out shopping.

"I need to make one stop before we go," he says, dragging me toward the bakery.

On top of the bakery counter sits an enormous stack of fresh chocolate chip cookies piled high on a plate. He picks up two and takes a big bite out of one.

"Those are for little kids, you know," I tease. "So they behave for their mommies at the store."

"I'm a child at heart," he mumbles through a mouthful of cookie, "so it's okay."

He hands me the other cookie. I hesitate, my hand hovering above his. I probably don't need it. And it is getting pretty close to supper time...

Casey waves the cookie under my nose. "Last chance."

I can smell the sugar. The fragrant vanilla. The gooey, warm chocolate.

"Oh, fuck it," I say, and snatch it from his hand.

Casey smiles and takes another big bite. "Atta girl."

At the checkout, a little boy sits in a shopping cart while his mother loads groceries onto the conveyer belt. He's happily kicking his feet and munching on a cookie.

Casey bends down a little so he and the boy are eye to eye. "These are good, eh? I had a cookie too so I'd be good for my mommy."

I elbow him in the ribs.

The little boy tucks his chin to his chest and gives us a shy smile.

"Did your mom buy you anything nice?" Casey asks. "Cake? Candy? Pop?"

"She got me gummies," the little boy says proudly.

Casey smiles. "Oh, gummies are my favorite."

He seems to really be in his element, teasing this little guy.

The boy takes another bite of cookie and cocks his head to the side. "What happened to your arm?" he asks.

Casey sticks out his left arm, the blue and green swirling under the fluorescent lights. "It's called a tattoo."

The boy narrows his eyes, looking puzzled. "Why's your skin funny?"

Casey's smile never falters, but some of the mirth goes out from his eyes.

"You be a good little boy for your mum, eh?" Casey says, and winks at him.

The boy's mom pulls the shopping cart toward her and looks shyly up at Casey. He gives her a wink too.

I roll my eyes and plop a bag of beets on the conveyer. "Come on, lover boy. We have a dinner to make."

After we've loaded the groceries into Casey's rusty old truck, we climb in and hurtle down the highway toward home.

"I'm sorry about your arm," I murmur, secretly hoping he'll tell me more about it.

Casey continues to look out the window, tapping the steering wheel and singing along with his cassette tapes.

And just when I think he really didn't hear me, he quietly says, "It's okay."

I nod, and look out of the window. "Will you tell me about it someday?"

He turns up the radio. "Someday."

CHAPTER 23

Another Saturday Night

"Well, that ought to do it," Casey says as he takes the rosemary roasted chicken out of the oven.

"Casey, you're brilliant," I say. The kitchen is bursting with delicious smells, and the house is spic and span. "I don't know what I would've done without you."

"I don't know what you would've done either."

I playfully elbow him, and he elbows me back.

"Well, I'd better get dressed. You'll be okay out here?"

Casey folds his arms and leans against the counter. "Oh, I'm sure mischief will find me, one way or another."

I smile at him and skip down the hall to the bedroom. This is going way better than I expected. Casey really is skilled in the kitchen. Of course I knew that from the muffins he's baked for me, but I really had no idea that he was so…domestic. He'd make a lovely house husband.

Now, time to find a perfect, elegant hostess outfit. I have to look the part, after all.

I select a white button-down shirt. It fits my shoulders well but strains against my bust. I tug at the fabric, trying to adjust the button holes so they don't gape.

No luck.

Okay, this is fine. I can just wear a camisole underneath and undo a few buttons. No big deal. I do that, and shimmy into a silk skirt.

Oh god. This is a lot tighter than I thought it would be. Although, to be fair, I never did try it on in the store…

All right. Mind over matter. Just throw on a few pairs of Spanx, suck in your gut, and pull up the zipper before it has a chance to know what's going on.

I manage to pull up the zipper and let out the breath I've been holding.

"Yeeeuuugh!" I shout.

Casey's voice carries down the hall. "You okay in there?"

"Fine!" I wheeze.

I smooth down my skirt, turning from side to side in front of my mirror. My muffin top is barely noticeable so long as I hold my breath and stand perfectly straight. Maybe I can somehow get through dinner without actually sitting down.

I touch up my makeup and hair and toddle back to the kitchen.

"What do you think?" I ask, raising my hands up and twirling (erm, waddling) in a circle. If I move too quickly, I'm sure I'll burst a seam.

He pauses for a moment. "You look like the bored secretary at my dentist's office."

I smile. "Perfect."

He gives me an odd look and I shuffle away toward the dining room. I set out a few wine glasses and straighten out the cutlery. "What else do we have left to do in here?"

Casey follows me, hands shoved deep into his jean pockets. "Not much. The wine and appetizers are ready. I'll put them out before I go."

"Go? But you can't go! You've helped me so much today," I protest.

Casey shrugs. "No biggie. I was happy to help."

"Please stay. It wouldn't be fair to have you cook and clean all afternoon and not reap the benefits. Besides, it'll be nice to have someone to talk to."

He frowns. "You don't know who's coming to the party?"

"Millie is coming," I say while I adjust the flower arrangement on the table. "And I've invited some of Laura's friends and a few people she likes from work. They're just more Laura's friends than mine."

Casey nods. "Well, if you're sure…"

"Of course I'm sure."

"Well. All right then."

"Hello," a woman's voice calls out, followed by a giggle.

I round the corner and see a teeny, tiny woman with short brown hair and small, pointy features. She's wearing an understated yet stylish outfit. The picture of sophisticated chic.

"Hi, Elle," I say, hoping desperately that she doesn't take Instagram pictures of every course.

"Hello," she says breezily while taking her coat off and holding it out to me. I think she expects me to hang it in the closet for her. Not knowing what else to do, I accept it and hang it up. "Laura and I drove together."

"Where is she?" I ask.

"Finding somewhere to park, I think," Elle replies breezily. Her eyes do a head-to-toe sweep of my body, and I resist the urge to adjust my tight waistband. I've worn this get-up for twenty minutes and I'm already dying. Where are my tights and tunics? If I ever throw a dinner party that's just for me, it'll have a "lounge wear only" dress code. Yoga pants and hoodies are a must.

I bend over slightly when I pull out a chair for Elle, and the waistband cuts deeply into my stomach. I can't do this for another three, four hours.

"Please, have a seat," I say. "I'll just be a minute."

As I retreat to the bedroom, someone knocks on the front door.

"Casey, can you get that?" I say over my shoulder.

"Anything for you, darl," he says from the kitchen. He steps into the hallway, holding a dish towel and drying his hands, and opens the door. Laura's standing there in a flattering floral-print summer dress.

"Hi, I'm Casey," he says, extending his hand. "You must be the birthday girl?"

Laura's eyes widen, and her mouth forms an *O* shape. "Y-yes," she says.

Casey grins and leans past her to close the door.

Once his back turns, her face scrunches and she mouths *Oh my god!* I shoot her a smile that says *Told you so,* and retreat to my bedroom.

From inside the bedroom, I hear a pile of guests pouring into my house. It's a joyous cacophony of "Happy birthday!" and shuffling shoes trying to negotiate my narrow entryway. Above it all, I can hear Casey welcoming everyone and introducing himself.

I unbutton my shirt, unzip my agonizingly tight pencil skirt, and throw them across the room. I hate that dreadful thing, I've decided. I wonder if I'll ever feel comfortable in grown-up clothes. I've just finished undressing when the bedroom door creaks open.

Casey peeks his head through the door. "Hey Nata– Whoa. Nice knickers."

"Casey!" I fling my quilt over my body. "Just a last-minute wardrobe change."

"Just thought I'd let you know that everyone has arrived."

I nod. "Okay, I'll be right out."

"Sounds good," he says. Just as he's about to close the door, he pops his head back in. "Did you know that I love it when women wear black lingerie?"

Despite my best efforts, a smile breaks through. I point a smarmy finger at the door.

"Go. Entertain my guests."

He bows. "Straight away, madam," he says in a posh English accent, which makes me laugh.

As soon as he's gone, the enormity of the situation hits me, and my mind races through the following thoughts:

1) Shit shit crappity shit. The hottest guy I've never met has seen me in my underwear.

2) Praise GOD in heaven that I was wearing my nice stuff today. Although, maybe he noticed that the elastic on my underwear is going a little, and there's pilling along the seams. On second thought, maybe it *isn't* all that nice.

3) I totally need new lingerie.

4) Did he see the stretch marks on my thighs that I'm so self-conscious about? What did he think of seeing me in my skivvies? Did he like how I look? Well. Not that I care, really…

5) And…finally. My guests are waiting, and I seriously need to find a new outfit.

I return my attention to the closet. I close my eyes for a minute and think about what I really feel good in. And it isn't blazers or dress shirts or long skirts.

I select the blue halter dress. It's feminine and comfortable. Perfect. My version of it, anyway.

I accessorize it with some pearl earrings and a cream cardigan and walk back to the dining room, prepared to fulfill my role of hostess. I'll be demure and polite. I'll say witty things and win everyone over. And...try not to think about Casey seeing me in my underwear.

"Everyone ready for the first course?" I ask, taking my seat at the table.

A moment later, Elle leans over (of course she had to sit near me) and stage-whispers that my cardigan is inside out.

We've made it through the appetizer, soup, and salad courses, and now we're onto the main dish. To my complete and utter relief, everyone comments on how good the food is. Even Elle.

I wonder what she and Laura would do if they found out Casey made me use a boxed cake mix.

I'm seated between Casey and Millie, with Laura at the head of the table like the guest of honor that she is. Elle is sitting opposite me, asking friendly, if somewhat probing, questions. I really don't know her that well, so I end up talking about the most neutral topic I can think of: my soon-to-be-finished green dress.

"You should wear it to the foodie fest on New Year's," Laura says. "We're having it at some fancy ballroom downtown."

Laura and I have gone to this party a few times together. They award local restaurants for best appetizer and food bloggers for most intriguing posts, that sort of thing. It's always a good time.

"It sounds lovely," Elle says. "Is it custom made?"

I hesitate. "Umm, yes. I'm having my seamstress make it for me."

"How nice. Seamstresses can be so dreadfully expensive, though."

Not going to bother mentioning that my mother is the seamstress and she's doing it for free.

"So, Casey. What do you do?" Elle asks, obviously done talking to me.

"I'm a firefighter," he says.

Her eyes light up. "Don't be surprised if I set my house on fire in the next few weeks, huh?" She winks. "Just teasing. Well, not really."

Casey gives her a polite smile. When she looks away, he rolls his eyes at me.

"I imagine that being a firefighter is really stressful," she asks, and he answers with a noncommittal, "Hmm." She taps her fork on her lips, clearly looking for another way to keep the conversation going. "So, why'd you become a firefighter?" she prompts.

"For the chili cook-offs," he says without missing a beat.

Elle's fork hovers midway between the plate and her mouth. After a moment, she switches back to bubbly mode. "Lovely."

Casey leans toward me and whispers, "Just going to check on the dessert."

I nod. "Thank you."

"Anyway, your dress sounds lovely," Elle says, her eyes glued to Casey's retreating backside. "Wish we all could afford such luxury," she continues, her voice dripping with faux sweetness. She turns to me and pouts her bottom lip. "I don't imagine you could pay for it all, with your salary. What is it you do again, dear? Home care or something?"

"I manage a second-hand store," I say. "We accept donations and run programs for the disabled. It's basically a charity."

She nods vaguely. "How nice. We need people like you," she says. "Though, sifting through other people's cast-offs all day. I can't imagine how dirty it must be under your finger nails."

It feels like the conversations around us pause and all eyes sweep to my hands. They're long and graceful, and the nails are clean and cut short. I always thought my hands were one of my best features, but across from Elle's smooth, unblemished fingers and long manicured nails, I feel like a field hand.

I smile nervously and tuck my hands under the table.

"This is delicious, by the way," Laura says, taking a delicate bite of chicken.

Elle's eyes light up. "Did you stuff the catering bags away somewhere? Come on, you can tell us."

"Actually, Casey made most of it."

"The Scottish firefighter? Oh my. Handsome, and he knows his way around a kitchen," she muses. "Do you know if he's single?"

"He's originally from Ireland, actually," I say.

If she wants to know if he's single, she can ask him herself.

"Interesting," she says in a distracted way while swirling her wine glass. "Where did he get to?"

"Good question. I'll go find him," I say.

As soon as I'm away from the table, it feels like I can breathe again. I look in the kitchen first. No Casey.

Perhaps he's in the bathroom. I wait for a few minutes in the kitchen for him to return. Still no Casey.

"Casey?" I quietly call out. Either he's having the longest pee in history or he's snooping. I walk into the hallway and look both ways.

Or perhaps…oh shit. Maybe history is repeating itself. Maybe he's hit it off with one of Laura's friends and is ravishing her senseless somewhere in my house.

"Casey?" I hiss, louder this time. "I swear, if you're boinking someone in my house, I'll…"

A muffled, slightly amused *Oh my god* comes from down the hall. Did…did that sound come from my bedroom?

Checking over my shoulder to make sure that no one else is around, I quickly tiptoe down the hall. I discover Casey standing by my bed, holding a photograph.

My chest feels as if a swarm of bees is trapped inside.

I forgot to put away my old box of treasures.

"What are you doing in here?" I hiss.

"I got lost," he says distractedly, and then holds up the picture. "Is this *you*?"

It was taken about three years ago at a party I went to with Kelly. It's just of me, though. I don't where Kelly was at the time. Taking the picture, maybe. I'm wearing a shiny black mini skirt, a sequined top, and heavy eyeliner. My hair is dark and wild, and I'm sticking my tongue out.

"You have a tongue piercing? Come on, let's see it," he says, bending toward me.

I remember that night. Well, bits of it, anyway. I mostly remember the wicked hangover I had the next day.

"I took it out years ago."

Casey's eyes sweep over the new me, cardigan and all. He glances down at the photo again and runs a finger over it. "Damn. It's like Rizzo trying to be Sandra Dee. What happened?"

"Straight men shouldn't know *Grease* this well," I say.

He clutches my photo to his chest and starts singing, "Look at Me, I'm Sandra Dee." Before I know it, he's dancing around the room with my photo, singing every line perfectly.

"Give it back," I demand, trying to frown. A traitorous smile breaks through anyway.

"No way," he says, clearly delighted. "I'm keeping this."

I follow him around the room. "Casey. Cut the shit, I don't have time for this."

He continues singing and dancing away from me, always just beyond my grasp. At one point he leaps onto the bed and gives me a challenging look.

A look that says, I bet you won't follow me up here.

I'm not one to back down from a challenge.

I jump up, the mattress dipping noticeably in the middle with us both standing up there. Casey and I look at each other for a moment, and I try my best again to look serious.

We stare at one another, hoping that the other will crack first.

A snort of laughter rips through Casey's chest, and I follow right along with him. We giggle and pant, our faces turning red. The mattress shifts under my feet and I lose my balance.

Casey's arms reach out and wrap around my waist. Our eyes meet again, locked in a stare.

Casey licks his lips and takes in a deep breath. "Seriously. What happened?"

I stand still for a moment. "Nobody liked that girl. So I changed."

His face grows serious. "I like her."

I swallow hard.

Casey tightens his arms around me, pressing his body against mine. "Natalie," he says, his voice low, almost breathless, "I've always liked you."

My heart is about to beat its way out of my chest.

His left arm trails up my spine, and he winds his fingers through my hair, supporting the back of my head. He slowly, deliberately moves his lips toward mine. I arch into him, lifting my chin. Our lips touch.

I never really understood how a kiss could be hot until now.

Sure, I've enjoyed kissing before. But those kisses were usually with drunk guys who used too much tongue, or gentlemanly types with cold, chapped lips.

But these lips, oh god…Casey's lips. They feel like they're on fire. He darts out his tongue ever so slightly, barely hovering over my bottom lip. I've never felt heat like this in my whole life. I feel like he's branding me.

Maybe those romance novels weren't lying after all.

Just as I'm about to deepen our kiss, I hear the floorboards by the bedroom door creak. My heart jumps into my throat and I leap off the bed. Casey steps down after me and stands beside me.

"Oh hey, Millie," I say, stepping away from him. "I was just showing Casey some old pictures of me, and…"

Millie smirks at us and clears her throat. "I just thought I'd tell you that everyone's ready for dessert."

I run a hand over my face, lifting my bangs away from my sweaty forehead.

"Yes, yes of course," I say.

I smooth my hair and skirt and walk into the hallway. Just as I round the corner, I look back and see Casey tuck the old photo of me into one of his back pockets.

CHAPTER 24

Crazy Arms

Everyone has gone but Casey, and all that's left is a collection of empty wine bottles and a sink full of dirty dishes. Not that I'm even thinking about cleaning the kitchen right now.

How could I, when he's looking at me like that?

Casey takes slow, purposeful steps toward me. My heart is beating wildly. Without thinking, I take a step backwards.

He grins, knowing that he *so* has me.

He takes one long step toward me and wraps me in his arms. And then he leans down and presses his lips to mine. Our kiss starts out sweet and slow, but it doesn't stay that way. It morphs into this powerful, passionate, *Oh my god, take me against the wall now* sort of kiss.

With our lips locked, he walks me backward with slow, staggering steps until my back hits the counter top. He slides his hands up my back and slowly pulls the zipper of my dress down, running his hands over my skin. He slides the straps over my shoulders, revealing my black lacy bra.

He groans appreciatively. "You have the most beautiful breasts."

I thrill at his words.

He deftly tugs my left breast out of my bra cup and bends down. A shiver of anticipation ripples through me. With him so close, I can smell the cologne on his shirt and see the cowlicks through his hair line. He grabs my hips, pulling me closer.

"Oh god…Casey…"

A car alarm screeches across the street, distracting me. I try to stay in the moment, focusing on how it feels to have his mouth on my body.

But the sound gets louder.

Beep. Beep. BEEP. BEEP!

The smell of his cologne, the feel of his hands, the dirty kitchen, all slowly fade away, like an ancient photograph disintegrating before me, and I open my eyes.

I'm lying naked in my bed, sunlight peeking through my curtains. I stab the silence button on my alarm clock, flop back onto my pillow, and rub the sleep away from my eyes.

I just had a dream about Casey.

My eyes open wide.

Damn. I had a *sexy* dream about Casey.

You're not supposed to have dirty dreams about your friends. And I know he's totally going to be able to tell. It's like he has "that woman is fantasizing about me" radar, or something.

I just need to avoid him for a few days and maybe then I'll feel less weird around him.

I manage to successfully stay away from Casey for about a week, dodging his requests to hang out and making sure I stay busy, until one day, as I walk out of the library, my carrier bag loaded with an assortment of books and CDs, I get a text from him.

My hands feel sweaty and jumpy. I bite my lip, feeling unsettled.

Casey: What are you doing today?

Avoiding you, I feel like replying. I still can't believe we kissed. And, if my dreams are any indication, my subconscious would like to do a whole lot more than kiss.

Me: Nothing much. Cleaning up my house, that's about it.

Casey: Do you want to meet my little brother?

Me: Sure! He's here already?

And just like that, my plans to avoid Casey until I feel less like jumping his bones and more like being his friend are completely abandoned.

Casey: He just arrived. Thought we could have lunch. You game?

Me: Sure. Can I pick up anything?

Casey: Thanks, but we're covered. But if you absolutely have to pick up something, we could use some Doritos and juice boxes.

Me: Can do. Btw, you have the culinary tastes of a fourth grader.

He texts back lightning fast.

Casey: Proud of it. Don't forget to throw a toy in my happy meal.

About half an hour later, I walk into Casey's house holding Safeway bags full of chips and other goodies.

"Lucy, I'm home!" I sing while kicking off my tall leather boots. It's getting colder outside. I've had to scrape frost off my windows the past couple of mornings, and I've noticed flocks of geese flying south. I imagine we'll get snow soon.

Casey steps into the hallway. For a moment, all I can think is, *You kissed me,* and wonder if he's going to do it again.

He smiles. "Looks like more than just Doritos and juice."

We carry the grocery bags into the kitchen together. "I figured junk food was the way to win a boy's heart."

"Smart woman."

"So, where's Liam?"

"Just getting settled in," he says. "You wouldn't believe how picky he is about making the bed."

"What, your bed-making skills aren't up to his standards?"

Casey shakes his head. "He stripped the bed and put his own sheets on from home."

I laugh. "He brought his own sheets?"

"They're good ones too," he says. "Captain America. I might have to get some for my bed."

I snort. "That'll impress the ladies."

Casey merely waggles his eyebrows and pops a chip into his mouth. His perfect, beautiful, searing-hot mouth. We need to talk about that kiss.

I clear my throat. "Hey, so about last week–"

"Are those Cool Ranch?" a young boy's voice says from behind me.

I turn around, smiling. In my mind, I had pictured Liam as a smaller, younger version of Casey. And he is, kind of.

The first thing I notice about Liam, after his big smile and mischievous brown eyes (just like his big brother has), is his neck. And the right side of his face. And his right arm.

They're all covered in burn scars.

Casey picks up the bag of chips and throws it at Liam. "All yours, buddy."

Liam smiles shyly. "Won't these ruin my lunch?"

"This is lunch," Casey says, sitting at the table beside me and winking.

We never get a chance to talk about our kiss.

I can't decide if I'm relieved or terribly disappointed.

A couple of days later, I'm having lunch with Millie and her kids at my house when Casey calls me on my phone.

"Can you watch Liam for me this afternoon?"

I excuse myself from the table and walk into the hallway.

"Umm, I guess I could. But I thought you booked time off work."

"I did, but a few of the guys are off sick, and they're desperate."

"Sure, no problem," I say. "Hey Casey?"

"Yeah?"

"How do I entertain an eleven-year-old boy? I mean, what do eleven-year-old boys like?"

"Oh, if memory serves correct, my eleven-year-old self liked action movies. And pizza."

"Hmm, okay," I say.

"And boobies. Or even better, action movies with boobies."

"Not happening."

Casey grunts disapprovingly. "Spoilsport. My buddies and I had a theory about movies when we were growing up."

"And that is?"

"Movie without boobs, bad. Movie with boobs, good."

"Why? It's not like boobs are anything special."

"I respectfully disagree."

"What if I graded movies based on how much dong I saw?"

"I'd be into it," Casey says, laughing. "We should have a dirty movie date sometime."

Ha. And risk my dirty thoughts leaking out into the real world?

Not a chance.

"Never mind. What time do you start work?"

"Three."

"All right, see you later," I say.

I end the call and turn around. Millie is standing there, a puzzled look on her face. "Who was that on the phone?"

"Oh, umm, my mom."

Millie raises an eyebrow. "You talk to your mom about boobs? And dong?"

"Yes," I say, slowly drawing out the word. "She's, umm, always been very open about, umm…stuff."

As I walk up the driveway, a bag full of chips and DVDs swinging in my hand, my mind goes over the worst babysitting scenarios I can come up with. I like kids. Love kids, actually. But I haven't babysat anyone in years. Well, not that I'd technically call this babysitting. More like hanging out. But still. What are we supposed to do for the next eight hours, while Casey's at work?

The door swings open before I have a chance to knock.

"You're early," Casey comments.

I pull the movies out of the carrier bag.

"I wasn't sure what Liam would like, so I picked up these two," I say, handing them over to Casey.

"These are cartoons," Casey says with mock disgust, and then adds, "Ooh, I really wanted to watch this one."

I shrug. "He's eleven."

"I doubt there'll be much action in these," he says. "Or boobs, for that matter."

Casey playfully bats the tops of my head with a DVD case. "And besides, I don't have a DVD player."

"What?" I say, feeling my heart sink ever so slightly.

"Just VHS. Remember?"

"Oh. Well, I knew you collected them, but I didn't think you had *only* tapes," I say, peeking round the corner into Casey's living room. "I'm sure we can just pick out something from your collection. Or go for a walk and find a park, or something…"

Shit. Well, this plan has backfired quite nicely.

Casey leans against the wall and gives me a rather heartbreaking, lopsided grin.

"Nat. I'm kidding."

I blink up at him. The cheeky bugger. I shove his chest and walk into the living room.

"You ass," I mutter. He follows, chuckling behind me. "You really are a kid in a man's body, aren't you?"

He opens the bag of chips and pops one into his mouth. After a moment, Casey shouts up the stairs. "Liam! Natalie's here."

Liam comes bounding down the steps and snatches the chip bag out of Casey's hands.

"What'd you bring over?" he asks, jumping onto the couch. The table beside him is littered with the various trappings of a young boy. Comic books. Some Nintendo-looking thingy. An open can of pop, probably with a dribble in the bottom that will inevitably tip over and stain the carpet.

It reminds me of growing up with my brothers. A sense of familiarity and calm settles over me. Why was I so worried? I know boys. I can handle this.

"These two," I say, while handing the cases over to Liam.

"Oh, I really wanted to watch this one," Liam says.

I smile. "Your brother said the same thing."

"You two have fun without me, while I go to slave for eight hours," he says, puffing out his chest.

I start to push him out the door. "Out, you big baby."

Once outside, Casey turns around. "Thanks for helping me out, Natalie."

I really do love the way his tongue rolls around my name.

"Anytime," I say.

"I'll have my phone on me all night," Casey says, "so if you need anything at all—"

"We'll be fine," I reassure him.

As Casey backs out of the driveway in his ancient blue truck, waves, and heads off to work, my chest fills with a sort of happy achiness. He's going to make someone really happy someday. And for the first time ever, I seriously entertain the idea that that someone might be me.

Damn it. I have one dirty dream about a guy and I'm hearing wedding bells. I seriously need to get laid.

We're one-and-a-half movies and two bags of chips into our evening when Liam starts getting chatty.

"So what do you do for a living?" he asks.

I stifle a laugh. "That seems like a pretty grown-up question for an eleven-year-old to ask."

He shrugs. "I'm mature for my age."

I settle deeper into the couch cushions, thoroughly enjoying myself. Who knew watching cartoons with kids could be so fun? I feel like I'm reliving my childhood.

"I work at a second-hand store," I say. "But before that, I used to work at the hospital. Kind of like a nurse's assistant."

"Did you get to touch blood and stuff?" he asks.

"Sometimes," I reply. "Among other things…"

"What other things?"

"You really don't want to know."

He nods. "Cool."

"What sort of job do you want someday?" I ask.

"I want to be a nurse," he says. "Or an EMT. I haven't really decided yet which one I like better."

"Oh yeah?"

"Yeah, the nurses were really great with me, when this all happened," he says, holding up his scarred right arm. "But the EMTs were also great about calming me down. And they said they get to go to car accidents and other crazy stuff all day." He licks the salt off his fingers, never taking his eyes off the TV. "I think I'd be really great at that."

I nod. "Right."

I glance over at Liam. The right arm and right side of his neck are a swirl of multicolored ridges, the skin tight and shiny. I can only imagine that the right side of his torso looks the same.

It reminds me of Casey's skin.

"Was it a fire?" I ask.

"Yep," he says, "I was four. Casey saved me."

Casey walks back into the house shortly before midnight. I look up from the couch, where I've been reading a book I brought along.

"Where's Liam?" he asks.

"He went to bed an hour ago. Said he wanted to get a full eight hours."

Casey shakes his head. "That kid is way more responsible than I ever was at that age."

"Even this age," I mutter jokingly. Casey sticks his tongue out at me and walks into the living room. "Good shift?" I ask.

Casey flops onto the chair opposite me. "Fantastic," he says. "I finally got my revenge on Justin."

"Justin?"

"The rookie who messed with my gear."

I set my book down and sit up. "What sort of tortures did you unleash on this poor guy?"

He laces his fingers behind his head. "Oh, we got really creative this time." He leans back in his chair, his accent thicker when he's in full story-telling mode. "We discovered that Justin's not that fond of clowns."

I'm about to ask how they discovered that bit of strange information when Casey shakes his head.

"You don't want to know," he says. "Anyway, so I found this creepy clown mask–"

"Oh no…"

"–and this plastic knife…"

I shake my head. "You're kind of a bastard, aren't you?" I say, laughing.

"It was so fun," he enthuses. "Did I mention that we also lit a few paper bags on fire and threw them under the bathroom stall when he was in there? And of course, we got it all on video too."

"You're incorrigible," I say.

He bows slightly. "Why, thank you."

Casey looks around at the littered living room.

"Sorry for leaving the mess." I start scooping up chip bags and empty pop cans.

Casey waves a hand. "Don't worry about it. I'll get it in the morning."

"No really, I don't mind," I say, still scrambling around.

I feel a warm, heavy hand gently touch my shoulder.

"Natalie," he says. "It's okay."

I reluctantly put my handful of garbage back down and clear my throat. "Liam and I had a good time."

"He's a great kid."

"He really is," I say. I pause for a moment. "He was really chatty tonight," I continue. "He started talking about what he wants to do for a living when he's an adult."

"Oh yeah?" Casey asks, a cheery smile on his face.

"He told me he wants to be a nurse or an EMT. Said they made quite an impression on him."

A flash of pain crosses Casey's face, and his ever-present smile falters.

"It was a fire…" he says. His voice is level, but I notice his Adam's apple bob up and down.

"Liam told me you saved him," I say gently.

"He was four. I was going on a camping trip with my buddies and thought it would be fun to take my little brother along." I nod, hoping he'll continue. "On our last day there, I left my cigarettes and lighter in the tent."

I frown. "But you don't smoke."

"Not anymore," he says. "Anyway, I didn't think much of it at the time. I'd stashed them there all weekend, no big deal, right? I left to take a leak, and the next thing I knew, I heard Liam screaming."

"Oh Casey…"

He blinks a couple of times. "By the time I got back, the tent, the sleeping bags, Liam… they were all covered in flames. My buddies said it only lasted for about thirty seconds, but to me it felt like forever."

He leans forward, eyes downward. I lay a hand over his and he looks up at me. For a minute, he looks so vulnerable that I want to scoop his huge, muscular body onto my lap and just hold him.

But a moment later, he scratches his nose, and the vulnerability is replaced by a practiced look of reassurance. A look that says, *I'm fine, I'm over it,* when really he's not.

"I'd asked my friends to watch him, and they didn't think anything of Liam going into the tent. They figured he was getting a toy or something," he says, casually waving a hand through the air. "He said he was just trying to be big, like me." He roughly scratches under his nose and sniffs. "It was so preventable. Totally my fault."

"Casey…"

"I'm surprised Mom still trusts me with him," he says, trying to cover his anguish with a laugh. "I don't think I could ever be a father."

My heart splinters. "Casey, you're great with kids. You'd make a great dad."

He sniffs. "Yeah, well. Once upon a time, I might've." He winks mischievously. "But now, I get to have all the fun I want."

"But, it was an accident," I say.

"Well, yes, in a way, you're right," he says, "but I'm still responsible for leaving my lighter out. I'm responsible for not making sure that I'd taught him about fire safety first. That's why I became a firefighter after all this shit went down. I love my job. I can educate others and help to prevent things like this from happening to other kids."

I squeeze his hand. "You're a good man, Casey Nolan."

He squeezes my hand back.

I'm silent for a moment, observing his heavy, muscular arm. The swirling blue and green waves have been strategically placed to flow with his scars, making them less visible.

"Why get a water tattoo? Flames would've made more sense," I muse.

Casey shrugs. "I guess it was my symbolic way of redeeming the situation," he explains. "Water puts out fire."

Eventually, Casey kicks the cartoon DVD case on the coffee table with his toe. "Was this any good?"

I laugh inwardly, noting that our heart-to-heart seems to be over. "Liam and I thought it was really funny. Do you want to watch it?"

Casey looks at the clock on the wall. "Bit late, don't you think?"

I pick up the case and walk over to the television. "I'm game if you are."

Casey picks up the last bag of chips. "Bring it on."

Throughout the entire movie, I remember what happened the last time we were alone and keep wondering if he's going to kiss me again. But he never does.

CHAPTER 25

Wild, Wild Women

I fire up my computer, cup of coffee in hand. I have about an hour to kill before I go to work, and I decide to check my email. At first glance, it's all fluffy junk mail. Penis enlargements and Rolex watches; local MILFs looking for hook-ups.

(Note to self: Why do I get this sort of junk mail? Is there something about my IP address that screams out "pervy middle-aged businessman"?)

I'm about to switch over to something more interesting when I see an unfamiliar email address near the bottom of the page.

From: firemancasey

To: nataliebishop

Hey Nats,

At my request, Oakes ran our dear friend "Rusty" (aka meth head camping out in the woods) through some national database. He's totally known to the community (I knew it!) and has a record about a mile long. Anyway, the best part is:

Rusty has a record from the early nineties that says he was in a "domestic dispute" with his girlfriend, "Nancy Lyckiss."

I realize that I've been holding my breath, and my lungs are starting to burn. It all comes out in a rush, and I read on.

Oakes says that if Nancy was hanging out with Rusty and people like him, she likely has a criminal record. And people with criminal records often have aliases. It's very possible that the name "Nancy Carlyle" is an alias. But, without any supporting information, we're basically guessing.

We looked for Nancy Lyckiss. Let me tell ya, this lady lived a rough life.

My heart is knocking hard and fast in my chest. I lean a bit closer to the computer screen, as if getting closer might reveal something more.

Aggravated assault, theft, fraud, DUI, drug trafficking. You name it, it's in here. There are other notes of petty complaints from neighbors about noisy parties.

A cold, hard rock forms in my throat. I struggle to swallow past it.

Oakes says that constables keep notebooks, and it's likely that someone has more information on her. But we'd need to find that constable's old notebook. So finding a noise complaint, for example, from 1991 wouldn't be impossible, but complicated.

At least now we have another name to look for. Oakes said he'll keep digging. I'm not sure if that's what you wanted, but I hope this small piece of information brings you peace.

I sit in my office chair, knees tucked up tight against my chest, and stare at the screen for a moment. A lot of feelings are swirling through my head right now. Peace isn't one of them.

PS – I've attached the most recent photo Oakes had of this Nancy Whatever-her-name-is. It's from 1992.

I click about fifteen times on the attachment.

The lady in the photo has heavily smudged black eyeliner and crispy blonde hair with dark brown roots. And yet, despite her tired, glazed eyes and the purple bruising along her jawline, you can tell that she once was a beautiful woman.

The thing I notice most of all is her nose. It's an elegant nose. Long and tapered, perfectly symmetrical. Nothing like mine.

I close my laptop, lean back in my chair, and stare up at the ceiling.

Theft. Assault. Drug trafficking.

It scares me to think what this stranger's life has been like. To think about what my life could have been like. I used to be headed down that road. All I know is that that life isn't for me.

I close my eyes and wrap my arms tightly around my chest, staring at the photo on my computer screen.

I don't recognize a single thing that might be like me in this picture.

Maybe I don't want to.

"I'm surprised you didn't email me back last night," Casey says.

We're having a burger and fries at Nifties. A Sam Cooke tribute singer is on stage, crooning, "You Send Me." The gentle, sweet song wraps around me like a fuzzy blanket, and I feel myself unwind. It strikes me that it's really difficult to feel sad here.

Or maybe's it's just that Casey makes easy company.

"It was a lot to take in," I admit. "I really wish we knew for sure what her real name was. Carlyle. Cox. For all we know, her first name might not even be Nancy."

Casey nods, licking ketchup off his lips. "How do you think they pronounce that last name? What was it, Likess? Lickins?"

"Lick kiss," I reply. "Nancy Lyckiss Cox," I say aloud.

And then smack my mouth. "Lyckiss Cox," I say slowly, enunciating every syllable.

Lick. His. Cocks.

Casey nearly chokes on his bite of burger.

"Well, I suppose things could be worse," he says, after taking a sip of water. "That could be your last name."

I throw a french fry at him, and he playfully catches it between his teeth.

I can't help but smile. "Good catch."

We settle into a companionable silence, while the singer on stage segues into "Another Saturday Night."

I stir my cherry Coke with a straw. "I'm kind of afraid to find her."

"Why?"

"Because…what if she is my mom?"

He raises an eyebrow. "Isn't that the point?"

I twist the napkin in my lap. "Maybe I won't like who she is, or she won't like me. And as for extended family…"

Casey just waits for me, patient as ever.

I finally just spit it out. My greatest fear.

"What if they're like her?"

I hate the wobble in my voice. I look down at my lap and try to calm my breathing.

Casey waits for me to look up at him.

"But Natalie," he says, "what if they're like you?"

CHAPTER 26

Maybe Baby

So, Casey and I went Christmas shopping together. The holidays are coming up soon, and I wanted to get an early start. While Casey puts his latest Christmas purchases away in his office closet, I sit in the spot I've claimed, admiring the hot pink feature wall.

"I think this is the sort of office Lucy would be proud of," he says.

I laugh. "Undoubtedly."

After I watch him cram several shopping bags of stuff into the closet, we wander down to the living room.

"Want to watch TV for a bit?" he asks.

"Sure."

He suggests some sort of "most dangerous jobs" show, and I suggest *Say Yes to the Dress*, but we meet in the middle with an old re-run of *Friends*.

"I think I'm a bit like Rachel," I say.

Casey laughs. "You are so not a Rachel. You're definitely a Phoebe."

I look down at my trendy outfit and play with my straight, shoulder-length hair. "Am not."

He laughs. "Yes, you are. You might not let your inner weirdo out very often, but you're a Phoebe on the inside."

I squirm in my seat. I don't want to be a Phoebe. "Who are you, then?"

"Oh, I'm definitely a Monica," he says. "I've got an apron and a killer scones recipe to prove it."

I smile and am about to sass some sort of smart-arse reply when a commercial comes on advertising upcoming Christmas movies.

"Ooh! *Love, Actually*!" I exclaim.

"Never heard of it."

"It's so good," I gush. "It's my favorite Christmas movie."

"I don't think anything could ever top *Rudolph the Red-Nosed Reindeer*. Or the Grinch."

I laugh. "I think you stopped maturing at around age eight."

He flexes a mighty bicep. "Oh, I've matured a bit since then," he says, and returns to flipping channels. "So what else is new with you?"

"Working. Volunteering at the hospital. I'm trying to come up with a new Christmas display for the store," I say. "We have all of these encyclopedias that no one wants, so I've thought about stacking them to look like Christmas trees and stringing them with lights. Or maybe ripping them up and creating some sort of paper display."

"Such a Phoebe thing to do."

After about twenty minutes of watching TV with Casey, I become increasingly aware of my tight bra cutting into my ribs. I wiggle a bit and try to subtly adjust it through my shirt.

Casey cocks an eyebrow. "You okay over there?"

I look over at him, weighing my options.

Option one: Pretend that I'm not in pain, and muscle through the next few hours.

Option two: Take my bra off (and shirt and everything else), give into my baser instincts, and let Casey act out the dirty dream I had.

Or, option three: Just take it off like it's no big deal. It's not like it's top secret knowledge that I have boobs. I suppose I could be honest.

"I might be ready for the braless phase of my life," I say.

Casey takes a swig of beer. "I fully support this new phase."

I slip a finger under the tight back strap. "The stupid thing costs a small fortune, and it still hurts."

"So take it off, then."

"You'd love that, wouldn't you?" I lean back into the cushions and exhale. I'm a proper adult now, with a proper house, proper job, and proper grown-up hobbies. I don't take my bra off around friends.

Ha. Anymore, that is.

"No, I probably shouldn't," I say.

Casey props his feet up on the coffee table and opens up another beer. "Sure you can."

I hesitate. "You're a total perv, aren't you?"

He lifts his beer can up in a salute. "Damn skippy."

I twist my torso in one last attempt to get comfy. The band tears into my ribs and makes the decision for me. I discreetly take it off and slip it out from under my shirt.

"Any other pervy facts I should know about?" I ask as I stuff my bra into my purse.

"I think pregnant chicks are hot," he says, without missing a beat.

My eyebrows shoot up. "Really?"

"Really really."

"Huh," I say. "You're getting as weird as Millie, what with her mannequin attraction."

He laughs. "What about you? Any pervy facts I should know about you?"

"None that I'm sharing. Speaking of pregnancy," I say, reaching for my phone, "my sister-in-law is pregnant again. Check out this picture."

Casey focuses on the photo and then whistles. "Never thought I'd see camo in a birth announcement before."

I laugh. "Yeah. My brother is one hundred percent redneck."

My brother Patrick and his wife, Tanis, have a three-year-old daughter named Sarah. They're expecting another baby girl in December. Tanis and Sarah are dressed in pale pink, their blonde hair plaited in matching milkmaid braids. They're smiling sweetly into the camera, all white teeth and sunlit backgrounds.

And then there's Patrick, three-day-old scruff on his face and camo from head to toe.

Casey smiles. "He looks fun."

"He is," I reply. "I'm the closest to him, out of my brothers."

"How many brothers do you have?"

"Two."

Casey nods knowingly. "No wonder you're so comfortable around men."

I shrug. "You eventually figure out that all men are about the same. Sure, they might look different or have different jobs or values, but at the end of the day, they all laugh at farts and love their penises."

Casey chokes on his sip of beer.

"What about you?" I ask. "Do you have sisters? You seem really comfortable around women."

Casey winks at me. "I've just had lots and *lots* of practice." I snort, and Casey gets up and wanders to the kitchen. "No sisters. Just Liam. Can I get you another drink?" he calls over his shoulder.

The clock on the wall says ten p.m. How did it get so late? "No, I should probably get going." I yawn and pick up my purse and coat. "This is twice now that we've watched movies late into the night. You're a bad influence on me, Mr. Casey Nolan."

He walks back into the living room and bows subtly. "Why, thank you."

I open the front door, and Casey walks me to my car. "What are you up to this week?"

"Sewing, mostly," I say. "The dress my mom and I have been working on is almost done."

I get into my car, and Casey leans on the driver's side, half hanging into the open window. "You're all kinds of domestic, aren't you?" he teases.

"I'm going to wear it at the New Year's festival Laura loves," I say with a yawn. "There's usually good food, a dance, and lots of speeches."

"Sounds like a bad wedding. If you get bored, just message me. I'll text you dirty jokes all night and keep you entertained."

I laugh. "Thanks. Any plans for Christmas?"

"I might go to Vancouver and visit my mom for a bit," he says. "You?"

"I'll probably just end up at my parent's place. Of course, Matthew and Patrick will have their annual Christmas fight. The rest of the family and I have started placing bets on what they'll fight about this year."

Casey sputters out a small laugh. "Speaking of family, have you found anything new?"

I lean on the steering wheel. "Not yet."

A heavy silence falls between us. It's the silence that scares me. It holds all of my fear.

What if I never find my mother?

What if I do, and I don't like her?

What if I'm destined to always feel like the bottom is about to drop out and everyone is going to leave me? If my own birth parents could reject me, then why wouldn't anyone else?

What if, what if, what if.

"Don't let it bother you," Casey says, breaking the spell. "We'll figure it out."

I smile at his use of "we."

"You're a good friend, Casey."

He winks at me and taps the hood of my car. "Get outta here, Thrift Shop Girl, before I throw you over my shoulder and take you back into the house."

I roll my eyes and wave at him as I drive away.

As my heart flutters and my mind entertains the delicious fantasy of being thrown over a fireman's shoulder, I remind myself that he's a flirt. Plain and simple. I mean, the guy throws kisses around like confetti. He probably doesn't mean half of the things he says.

CHAPTER 27

Blue Christmas

"Oh, Nat," Millie says. "This looks amazing."

We're standing outside of the thrift store looking at the display window. Someone dropped off a tangled mass of white Christmas lights today. They now hang in a romantic, ropey vine across the window, their soft light feathering out into the darkness. Powdery flakes of snow lazily drift around us.

If only I had a mug of cocoa and Bing Crosby playing in the background.

"Yeah, it turned out pretty good," I say.

"Good? Nat, this is beyond good," Millie marvels.

I blush. "Thanks."

Save for Casey and his weirdness, no one watches VHS tapes anymore, so no one has bought any at our store in a looong time. Or an encyclopedia. Who needs a heavy set of books when you can just Google stuff on your phone? So, being that we have a *ton* of these things and no one around to buy them, I decided to take a risk and destroy them. I call it creative chaos.

First, I spray painted the tapes white and stacked them into pointy mountain shapes. I ripped out pages of the encyclopedias (and I admit, my heart broke a little every time I did that) and rolled them into tubes. I eventually made enough to create a 3D Abominable Snowman.

To this vignette, I added a mini forest of Christmas trees, a cartoony Rudolph, a blond elf, and a collection of cast-off toys that no one wanted to buy this year.

I quickly snap a picture of the window display and text it to Casey.

Remind you of anything? ;)

"Only two weeks until Christmas," Millie says, rubbing her hands together to stay warm. "Do you have plans?"

"Just at my parent's place," I say, shifting side to side. Time to go home soon. "I'm going to stay for a few days, visit with my brothers. My brother and his wife just had a new baby, so that'll be fun. How about you?"

My phone buzzes in my pocket.

Casey: Hey! It looks like the claymation Rudolph! Did you make an island of misfit toys? Just for me?

Me: I might have ;)

Casey: Best. Christmas. Gift. Ever.

I smile and tuck my phone back into my coat.

"Same, I'll be at my mom's house," Millie says.

"Will the kids go to their dad's house at all?" I ask.

Millie exhales sharply. "Not this year."

Silence stretches between us, and I sense that the topic is closed. Millie rubs her eyes with one hand. "I'm getting cold, babe," she says. She smiles warmly and reaches her arms toward me. "I hope you have a great Christmas."

I hug her back. "You too."

The next couple of weeks pass by in a blur of navigating crowded shopping malls, drinking way too much cocoa, and sewing late into the night to finish my dress on time.

On Christmas Eve, just as I'm about to head out the door with my overnight bag, my phone buzzes with a text.

Casey: Merry Christmas, my dear.

I can't help but smile. How can a guy be a lothario and yet be sweet and polite and old-fashioned too? Casey doesn't seem to fit into any one category, and I can't wrap my head around it.

Me: Merry Christmas, Mr. Nolan ;)

Casey: Wink face? Are you flirting with me?

Me: Lol you wish. What are you doing for the holidays?

Casey: Flying out to Vancouver tonight, going to stay with my mom and step-dad. I'm excited to see Liam.

Me: Nice. When are you back?

Casey: I fly back on December 31. You?

Me: Staying at my parents' place. I'm driving there tonight.

Casey: Be careful, eh? Those roads are nasty.

I look out my window. Fat snowflakes are falling in a steady rhythm, coating the street in a thick white blanket.

Me: I will. See you in the New Year ;)

Casey: There's that wink face again. I swear, you want me.

Me: (rolls eyes) Everyone wants you.

Casey: Christmas on the West Coast is awesome. You don't freeze your ass off, you don't have to shovel through two feet of snow so guests can come in, you can still walk around outside in your hoodie. You should come with me sometime.

I laugh out loud, drop my bags, and lean against the front door.

Me: If you keep texting me, I'll never get out of here.

Casey: Ok. Fine. (crying on the inside) Be safe, ok? And Merry Christmas. Again.

Me: lol Merry Christmas (again)

And just, for good measure...

Me: ;)

And a few minutes later...

Casey: ;)

CHAPTER 28

Rock Around the Clock

Christmas dinner with my family was fun. No one had food poisoning, no one got any awkward gifts (note from the epic Christmas fail of 2013: never buy shake weights for pervy uncles), and there weren't any major fights.

I call it a stunning success.

Well, except for that one incident when Matthew decided that it was his personal mission to enlighten Patrick on the evils of carbs and gluten during Christmas dinner. Patrick took a big bite of white bread and told him to fuck off. Gotta love family get-togethers.

Anyway, I am so excited. Tonight is the foodie fest, the New Year's Eve party that Laura invited me to. It's being held in this ballroom downtown, its fanciest venue yet. Chandeliers, creamy carpets, and menu items I can't even pronounce.

I'm feeling a bit giddy, so I decide to calm my nerves with a glass of wine. There was still some left over from Laura's party.

I hesitate, however, before I take that first sip. Should I have a drink? I've been sober for years now. It's something I've been thinking about a lot lately, and you know what? I think I can handle it now. People change, right? People mature. I'm not the same person I used to be. And besides, alcohol was never really my "thing" anyway. So long as I don't touch, umm…other substances, I should be okay.

Maybe I'll just have one glass.

Hmm. My hands are still a bit shaky. I must be more nervous than I thought. Oh, let's just have another glass. Can't hurt, right?

Wow. When did this mirror get so wonky? I hold my angled eyeliner brush, trying to decide how to line my eyes when I can't quite see them.

No worries. I've put on makeup drunk before. It should be like riding a bike, no?

I giggle and then hiccup, and my eyeliner brush jumps. A jagged black line runs up into my eyebrow.

"Oh shit," I say, laughing.

I dab at my eye, wondering if I can somehow smear it around enough to make it look like a new take on the smoky eye look. I'll call it "Cleopatra meets Bar Star."

I hurry my way through the other side of my face (God, I hope they match) and run over to my closet, knowing that if I don't get my shit together soon, I'll be late. Laura and I made plans to carpool, and she'll be here soon to pick me up. I slip into seamed stockings with Cuban heels. I've never worn these stockings before, and they make me feel instantly sexy. What is it about a line up the back of a woman's leg that is so alluring?

I put on my garter belt, my most expensive underwear, and a fitted, black corset bra. At this point, if I wore a paper bag over them, I'd still feel sexy. Never underestimate the power of good lingerie.

I lay my garment bag out on the bed and pull out the green dress. And even though I've looked at it at least three times a day since I've finished it, it still takes my breath away. The design reminds me of the dress Audrey Hepburn wore in the party scene in *Sabrina* – a strapless bodice, longish train, and asymmetrical hem that's shorter in the front, so it can show off my shoes. It fits me like a glove and flatters every curve. The rich emerald color makes my skin look flawless and my eyes look bright.

I step into the dress and feel like a fifties starlet ready for the red carpet. It has an elegant Sabrina neckline, a fitted waist, and a full skirt that stops just below the knee. The look is finished with a cute bow on the back.

This is probably the coolest thing I've ever worn, let alone made.

Laura still hasn't shown up yet. I wonder what's keeping her? There aren't any texts, and she isn't responding to my calls. Hmm.

So while I wait, I eat about half a loaf of bread to soak up the wine I drank earlier and watch *I Love Lucy* re-runs in my living room to kill time. During a particularly funny episode, I feel like calling Casey, and then I remember he's flying back home tonight. In fact, I think his plane landed about an hour ago. I imagine that he's tired and would rather catch up on sleep.

Just as I'm about to try calling Laura again (feeling rather worried about her now – she's so responsible, there's no way she'd just bail on plans), a text from her comes through.

Laura: I'm SO sorry, Nabalie, can't make it to the party. My appendix said, "Ha!. No party for yoooouuu." Surgery soon.

Wow. Either she's drunk or hopped on pain meds. I don't think I've ever seen her misspell anything, even in texts. I quickly tap a reply.

Me: That's awful! Are you okay?

Laura: Not bad. Really cute male nurse. Killer pain med. World seem fuzzy an awesum. I wish my appendix would've revolted years ago.

Me: Why stop there? Maybe you should fake a new illness every week.

Laura: Love it. They can call me Miss Munhawsen. Munschawsen. Aww, fug it.

Me: lol I believe it's "Munchausen"

Laura: Sorry to bail tonight.

Me: (dramatic sigh) Well, that was pretty selfish of you, getting appendicitis and all.

Laura: so soooo selfish

Me: I'll let you off the hook. Just this one time. And as payback, you must send me pictures of this cute nurse.

Laura: Done

My phone buzzes with several texts showing pictures of a guy in pale blue scrubs and wavy brown hair.

Laura: My McDreamy. MINE.

Me: How did you get so many pictures of him already?

Laura: Mighta been pretendingg to text while he was hanging IV meds. Thank you camera phone for making stalking so much easier.

Me: Behave yourself.

Laura: No promises. Not responsible for the next sevral hours. Blame the morphine. You still going 2 the party?

I'm about to text back, "Of course I am!" when I stop myself and consider whether I was looking forward to going to a fancy party with delicious food or just hanging out with my best friend.

Me: Nah, I don't think so. It wouldn't be the same without you there. Maybe I should just come see you instead!

Laura: Visiting hours over. Oh shit. Caught. he's walking over. Jig is up.

Me: Naughty girl. Maybe he'll spank you.

Laura: With IV tubing. Or his stethosoap. Stethoskop. Oh fuuuuuug, why won't autocorrect help me?

I laugh, envisioning my wonderful, weird, hopped-up-on-pain-meds friend being spanked by a hot nurse. It's a bit disconcerting, seeing her like this. Knowing Laura, I imagine she'll be embarrassed by this tomorrow. Though, in a weird way, it's almost a relief to know that she isn't perfect all of the time. Like I don't have to keep reaching for the same impossible standard.

Me: Talk to you later. I'll come see you tomorrow, ok? After you're out of surgery?

She doesn't reply.

CHAPTER 29

Then He Kissed Me

Well, either Laura is being spanked by a hot male nurse or she's simply turned her phone off. Although, I think she'd prefer the first option. A moment later, I realize that:

1) I'm really dressed up; and

2) I have no place to go.

And I'm in the mood to stay out late and get a little tipsy.

For a second, I consider calling Millie, but I immediately dismiss it. She has a date with a hot, single, normal dad tonight. Hurrah! The breed isn't extinct; only surprisingly rare. They're doing a "lets meet each other's kids and set off fireworks in the backyard for New Year's Eve" sort of thing. So, let's put cranky kids and stressed parents who are trying to impress each other together with fireworks. What could possibly go wrong?

I hope everything goes well for her. She's such a sweetheart.

I suppose I could go sit at Starbucks for a while and sip my way through a pumpkin spice latte (good Lord, I love those things), but how much time would that buy me? An hour, at most? And then what?

I pick up my phone and tap out a text.

Me: Hey Casey.

I imagine he's tired from his late flight and has passed out already. Or he made plans with some friends. I don't really expect a reply. And yet, my phone buzzes about five seconds later.

Casey: Geez, does the party suck already? Do you need me to entertain you with dirty jokes? Okay. A rabbi, a priest, and a minister walk into a bar...

A small laugh escapes my lips.

Me: My plans fell through. Laura's appendix decided to throw a party of its own.

Casey: Yikes. Is she okay?

Me: She's high on morphine and hitting on the nurses.

Casey: Sounds like a good time.

Me: I knew you'd say something like that! Anyway, I don't feel like going without Laura. Want to hang out instead? That is, if you're free.

Casey: I'm always up for hanging out with you. You're kind of my new best friend.

My heart pounds in my chest. Okay. Play it cool.

Me: You dork.

Another incoming text.

Casey: See? Only best friends can call each other dork and get away with it. Nifties? 20 min?

Me: Sounds perfect.

I stash a pair of black stilettos into my purse for later, slip on my bulky, horrible, unflattering snow boots (because let's face it, I'll be on my ass in about two seconds if I try to walk on icy sidewalks in high heels), and zip up my winter jacket. This may not be the night I had planned, but damn, I'm excited about it.

Somehow, I manage to shove my outrageously fluffy dress into my tiny car and drive over to Nifties. Casey is already there, casually leaning against the brick wall.

He whistles when he sees me. "Great dress."

This man loves me, I think to myself.

What? No. That's silly. Casey might like me. But Casey Nolan doesn't fall in love.

"Thanks," I say while twirling on the spot to show off the fruit of my (and my mother's) labor. "It's too bad Laura's in hospital, but I'm happy to be here too."

I take out my phone, and check if she's sent any new messages. She hasn't.

"I'm a little worried about her," I admit.

"Well, you've come to the right place," he says confidently.

"Oh yeah? Why's that?"

"Haven't you ever seen an episode of *Happy Days*?" Casey says. "Everything can be solved with a hamburger and a jukebox."

"You know something?" I say, my words muffled through a mouthful of food, "You're totally right."

Casey takes a big bite of hamburger. "Told ya."

We're sitting in our favorite booth, which is directly across from the stage. They've decorated it for New Year's Eve, with fairy lights and party hats galore. I look around at the people dancing and rubbing elbows all around me, noisily singing along with the band or having loud, animated conversations.

"How did you manage to get a table?" I ask.

He buffs his nails on his shirt. "You'll never know."

I feel my spirits lifting. Casey just seems to naturally bring that out in me. I don't think I've ever felt bad about myself around him. In fact, I always feel pumped up.

I wish it could be like this all of the time. You know, but with Casey and I kissing and riding off into the sunset and stuff. Call me old-fashioned, but I want a forever kind of love.

I just wish that's what he wanted too.

Casey dabs his mouth with a napkin and then throws it on his plate. "My place?"

I nod and follow him out of the restaurant.

"Whisky sour for the lady," Casey says, handing me a glass.

"Thank you," I say. When we got back to his place, he asked what I wanted and I said whisky. It took him a minute to realize that I wasn't joking. And like the good Irish boy that he is, he had a bottle in the pantry.

I regard the glass like it's an oasis in the desert. I haven't had one of these in years, and damn does it look good.

"Nice garnish," I say, smirking at the cherry and orange wedge speared onto a fake sword.

"Are you sure about this? I mean, I know you don't drink…"

Shame whispers in my ear. *He's right, you know.*

I ignore it. "You know, I think I'll be okay," I say, calmly. "I had a couple glasses of wine earlier, and I handled it all right."

Casey regards me seriously.

"I've been sober for years," I say, realizing that I should've told him a long time ago why I stopped drinking. "It wasn't really because alcohol was bad for me, but because it usually led to other things."

Casey perches on the edge of his chair, saying nothing.

"I'm not that person anymore," I say. I can feel the mood in the room dipping, and I so desperately want to get back to having fun. "I think I can have a drink now and be okay."

"Well, if you think you're okay..."

"I am."

After a few seconds, he raises his glass. "Here's to the new year. How are we going to ring it in?"

I down my glass and hold it out for a refill. "By getting drunk and watching Netflix, of course."

"Classy," he says, laughing.

While Casey turns the TV on, I wander around the living room. Casey has a few framed pictures up now.

The first I come across is a grainy photo of a couple with a little boy sitting between them. They're at the beach. The man has Casey's heavy eyebrows, while the woman has his deeply dimpled smile.

"Is this your mom and dad?" I ask.

"Yep," he says, smiling. "Easy to see where I get my good looks from."

"Just look at these outfits!"

"It was the eighties. Everyone had big hair and shorty shorts. I've still got those shorts somewhere, if you want me to put them on."

I laugh. "I'm good."

Casey snaps his fingers. "Damn. Maybe next time."

I move on, looking at the other photos. Teenage Casey hugging a big black dog. Casey holding baby Liam and feeding him a bottle. But the next one surprises me.

"Hey!" I exclaim. "You framed this?"

I hold up the frame and peer at it.

Casey chuckles. "I wondered when you were going to notice."

It's the photo Casey swiped from me at the dinner party.

"It's so weird to see a picture of me in your house," I say. "You clearly have issues."

He stands and looks at it from behind me. I can feel his body heat. "What? It's a good picture."

We study it together for a minute. Tongue piercing. Mini skirt. Heavy makeup.

"You don't even look like the same person," Casey says.

I laugh. "Good."

"What happened?" Casey asks.

I sigh. "It's so embarrassing."

"Try me."

I look up at the ceiling. "Okay. Where to begin." I suddenly realize that I've never talked to anyone about it. "You know how sometimes smart people can make stupid choices?"

Casey nods.

"Dating Kelly was my stupid choice. One of them, anyway. We met shortly after I'd moved into my place. It was the first time I'd ever lived on my own. I was a bit of a shit in my late teens," I say, and Casey laughs.

"I don't believe it," he says.

I raise my eyebrows. "Oh, trust me. I was. I was sleeping around, running away from home, stealing…" I shake my head and notice Casey's raised eyebrows. "Anyway, I got some help after I finished high school. Got some counseling, started making a life for myself. I had just started working at the hospital and was making decent money. I met Kelly one night in the emergency room. He'd been in a fight and had broken his hand. He was exciting."

I swallow hard. "I don't remember all of it. I try to put bits and pieces together, but there are still big, black gaps…" I take a deep breath. "We'd be madly in love one day, and screaming and throwing things at each other the next."

Casey nods.

I pull up my cardigan sleeve, revealing my pale forearm scattered with tiny, faded marks. "We did this together," I say, my voice wobbly, as if I might collapse from the inside out. Unable to make eye contact with him anymore, I drop my chin to my chest and self-consciously rub my runny nose. My hair falls forward, forming a curtain that hides my tears. "I'm so ashamed of myself."

"We all have scars, babe," he says, gesturing to his own arm. "Just some of us have ours on the outside."

Warmth pours over me, and I feel as if a small part of him understands. And it gives me the strength to tell the rest.

"We were on again, off again. So much drama," I say, shaking my head. "Around the time this picture was taken, we'd decided to give us one last shot. We had this sort of chemistry, you know? And even if life wasn't exactly stable, it was never, ever boring."

I blow out a long breath. "Anyway, a few weeks into our last attempt to 'see if it works out,' Kelly started talking about getting engaged. We looked at rings; it was all very romantic and exciting. And then, it all changed when my period was late."

I swallow. "I'm not really sure what happened. I was always very careful." Casey nods, looking at me intently. "Even though I hadn't really thought about having kids yet, I felt excited. I was about to get engaged. I thought Kelly would be happy."

"Long story short, he wasn't happy. He told me to get rid of it. He said that if I didn't, he'd be gone. I was so afraid I was going to lose him."

A tear rolls down my face. "And so, I did what I had to do to keep him."

"Nat, I'm so sorry…" Casey says.

I wave away his concern. "It's okay. I probably wouldn't have been a great mother. Not at that point in my life, anyway." I take a long drink. The whisky burns my throat. "We broke up soon after that. About six months later, I found out he'd gotten another girl pregnant. And they were planning a June wedding."

Casey sucks breath between his teeth. "Ouch."

I purse my lips. "Yep. So, rather than talk about it, I drank until I felt numb. I danced with some random guy I'd never met before. And eventually, he asked if I wanted to get out of there. I don't remember much after that. All I know is that the next day, I woke up in a stranger's bed with a bad hangover, no clothes, and no idea of where I was or how to get home." I rub my forehead. "I picked up some clothes off the floor, not caring whether they were mine or not, and left. I found a coffee shop down the street and decided to sober up first before I went home. I was checking my email on my phone when I saw this woman sitting at the other end of the room. Her hair was a mess, her skin looked gray, and she was missing an earring. I pitied her." I blink through a few tears. "It took me a few seconds to realize that there was a mirror at the end of the room, and that sad little woman was me."

Even though years have passed, and even though I'm not that person anymore, I can feel regret and self-loathing settle over me. Like an old, itchy sweater that's grown too tight. My chest tightens up, my breathing hitches. I'm so used to running away from these uncomfortable feelings that it's hard to sit still. I resist the urge to just get up and run.

"I sat in the coffee shop, staring at that mirror. I didn't want to be that partied-out person anymore. The person who slept with strangers. The person who stayed with an abusive partner just so she wouldn't be alone. And so, I decided to change my life. I threw everything out. My clubwear, my cheap makeup. I took out my piercings. I dyed my hair back to its natural color. I stopped hanging out with my old friends. I took over the mortgage on my house." I sip my drink. "I wanted to be a different person. A *better* person." I gesture to myself. "And so, here I am."

A long, quiet moment stretches between Casey and me. And in that long, quiet moment, a panic grows swiftly in my belly.

What have I just done? He'll never look at me the same way. He'll think I'm dirty. Tainted. Unlovable. He's going to up and run.

"I've never told anyone that before," I say. "Well, my mom knows bits and pieces. But I never told her about the baby."

Casey looks up and swallows. "I'm so sorry that all happened to you, Natalie. It means a lot that you'd open up to me like that."

He says it with the most kind, most sincere voice that I think to myself for the second time tonight, *This man loves me.*

Or maybe I'm just reading too much into it.

He leans back in his chair, eyeing me for a moment. "Have I ever told you that I'm glad we're friends?"

My heart flutters and soars. "I'm glad we're friends too."

Casey lifts his glass and drains it.

"Another?" he asks.

I nod and excuse my shaky, raw self to the bathroom.

I take a look at myself in the mirror. I look pretty good for someone who just spilled their guts out. My eyes are still a bit puffy from crying, but at least my makeup isn't running.

I walk back out to the living room and see that Casey has found a movie for us on Netflix. The opening scene of *Love, Actually* is paused on the TV screen.

"I love this movie!"

"I know you do."

I sit beside him and prop my feet up on the coffee table, feeling oddly relieved that he isn't acting differently around me now. "You remembered."

"Of course I did," he says. "I know all sorts of things about you."

I laugh. "Such as?"

"Well, for starters, you can't cook beets."

"I *can* cook them," I retort. "I just have a problem with carrying them."

He laughs. "Fine."

A moment later, he adds. "I know that you secretly want to dye your hair bright red so you can look like Lucille Ball."

"I've never once told you that," I reply.

"Ah, but it's still true, isn't it?"

A shy smile plays on my lips. "Perhaps."

"And now," he says, taking my empty glass from me, "I know that you like whisky sours."

"Are you trying to get me drunk, Casey Nolan?"

"That's the plan," he calls back.

A warm, fuzzy feeling settles over me. I've missed the casual friendliness of being able to share a drink with someone.

We sit through the movie while I provide a running commentary. "If I could rewrite this movie, I'd make Sarah and Carl end up together."

"Okay..."

"See, that's Carl," I explain, pointing at the screen "And he's really in love with Sarah, but she doesn't know it, and she's been pining for him for years."

"Fascinating."

"Right? And this part of the movie always pisses me off, because they're meant to be together and have crazy hot sex, but Sarah is too wrapped up in caring for her mentally ill brother…"

Casey smirks. "Uh huh."

I turn to him. "Are you just humoring me?"

"Maybe. But keep going."

"So, what'd you think?" I ask when the movie ends.

Casey stretches his arms over his head. "It was good. Funny."

"What? That's it? That's all you've got?"

He laughs mid-stretch. "Yep."

"It's almost midnight," I say, yawning.

Casey runs a hand over his mouth and chin, staring at me.

"What?" I say.

"It's a shame you didn't get to show off your fancy dress tonight," he says. "You would've been the belle of the ball."

I pick up the hem of the skirt and let it float back down. "Oh, this old thing?"

He stands in front of me. "Have you danced in it yet?"

"No," I say. "This is the first time I've worn it."

"Well, that settles it, then."

He picks up my hand and pulls me toward him, locking our arms into a dance frame

"What about the music?" I murmur.

"We'll make our own music."

Casey starts singing "Be My Baby" with gusto. He spins me and surprises me with new dance moves.

"Who sings that?" I ask, feeling breathless and giddy.

"The Ronettes," he says. "I love that song."

"Isn't that a sixties girl band?"

"Not doing it for you? Okay, how about this one."

He starts belting out "500 Miles" by The Proclaimers, his accent growing thicker and thicker.

"Ooh! I love that song!" I exclaim. "But it seems a bit modern for your taste," I tease.

"Did you know they were a Scottish band?" he asks, dipping me as the song ends.

My head is still dipped down, blood rushing through my ears. "No, I didn't," I rasp.

He stands me back up. My hairdo feels like it's falling apart, and my face is warm. He stares down at me for a moment.

"God, you're beautiful," he says.

My whisky-muddled brain decides to speak for me. "And you're gorgeous. The most handsome man I've ever seen, in fact."

His eyes widen, and even though we're still in a dance pose, our bodies stop moving. It's as if we're suspended in this moment. Then, the clock on the wall starts to chime.

"Twelve bells," I say. I look up and smile. "Happy new year, Casey."

He swallows and looks me in the eye. "Happy new year, Natalie."

Then, he kisses me.

And for one perfect moment I melt into his arms and feel as if I'm exactly where I should be. I snap out of it pretty quickly.

"Casey," I say, pushing away from him. "What are you doing?"

"Kissing you," he says, leaning toward me again.

"But we're just friends." I lean away from him.

He gently takes my hands and holds them to his chest. His chest feels warm and solid.

"I love you," he says quietly.

My chest tightens and I feel like I might explode.

"What?" I say, feeling as if the world has gone sideways. "But, you said you don't fall in love."

His hands trail up and down my arms.

"After the fire, Liam was in hospital for months. My mom fell apart. It was hard enough, knowing that Liam was hurt because of me. But seeing my mom so broken, so… "

He pauses for moment, and shakes his head. There's a distant look in his eyes. "I couldn't stop thinking about how she must've felt. It must've been devastating. I swore that I never wanted to set myself up for the same sort of pain," he says. Casey strokes my cheek with a warm, callused hand. "But when I'm with you, Natalie, suddenly I feel like it's a possibility. Like, even if it does open me up to pain, it'll still be worth it. Marriage, kids, the whole shebang."

He nervously licks his lips. "I love you, Natalie."

My heart hammers in my chest.

"I've loved you since the moment you woke me up out of a dead sleep to ask me about a box I took to the thrift store.

"I've loved you since you said that my office was ugly," he says, "And you were right. And I love what you've done with it. I love that godawful pink color in there because you're the one who chose it."

I swallow.

"I've loved you since you watched the entire first two seasons of *The Lucy Show* with me, just because you thought it might make me laugh. I loved you when you dropped a bowl full of beet puree in an all-white kitchen. I love that you snort when you laugh. I love your nose. It's so cute."

I reflexively lift my hands to cover my nose, stifling a nervous, unbelieving laugh. *Is this really happening?*

"I love how determined you are. That you're still trying to find whoever the photo album belongs to."

He spreads his arms out in a gesture of supplication.

"I just love you. Plain and simple."

I stand there, barely standing out of his arm's reach. My heart's beating out a rapid staccato. I feel simultaneously like running away and leaping into his arms.

A weak moment comes over me. And I decide to take the leap.

CHAPTER 30

Ring of Fire

I wake up to a dimly lit room.

There are only three things that I know:

1) I'm naked;

2) I'm drunk; and

3) I've just had wild, ecstatic sex with my best friend.

A thick, heavily tattooed forearm is draped across my chest. A memory of him appreciatively groaning over my black corset bra and garter belt runs through my mind. I rub a hand over my eyes and forehead.

Shit, shit, *shit*! How did I let this happen?

Damn it. I knew I shouldn't have started drinking. I always make bad decisions when I do. And now I've slept with my best friend and ruined everything. Oh god, this is a mess.

Casey's arm tightens around me, pulling me closer to his side, and I feel my heart melt ever so slightly.

Maybe…maybe this isn't so bad.

That thought creeps into my mind again.

This man loves me, it whispers.

He said it enough times tonight. Maybe he really does.

I know that I love him.

And then, his phone buzzes on the bedside table. It lights up the whole room with an eerie blue light. The sound disturbs Casey slightly, and he mumbles something incoherent and pulls me closer.

Hmm. I wonder who's texting him at this hour?

In his dark bedroom, I lay there, wrapped up in his arms, his breath warming my shoulder. Sleep is about to drag me under when his phone buzzes again.

I glance over, the light glaring offensively bright for a second and then dimming. There are two texts from someone named Sarah. Her picture comes up: a young, beautiful woman with dark curly hair, wearing firefighter gear.

Must be one of his co-workers. She looks sweet. But the texts are absolutely filthy. The second one ends with an invitation to join her at her place and ring in the new year.

I can feel my heart sink through the mattress and land with a dull thud on the floor.

Though I can't say I'm surprised.

Women are always texting him, and he's always very casual about it. As if having sex were no big deal, just a pleasurable way to waste time.

I cover up my face with my hands and will the mattress to swallow me whole. I wish I could disappear. My head feels like it has gone through a blender; it's difficult to think straight when one's thoughts have been chopped to bits and mixed together in a big, soupy mess.

I can't believe I slept with him. But, of course, I drank last night and broke sobriety, so that didn't help. No wonder I was weak. He was so convincing, though. Telling me that he loved me to get me in bed.

I can't be with another guy who doesn't really love me, I just can't. I have to protect myself. I have to get out of here.

As carefully as I can, I roll out from under his heavy arm, flop onto the floor, and quietly slip into the dress that was unceremoniously tossed into a corner just three short hours ago.

The bed creaks and the sheets rustle behind me. A lamp flicks on, flooding the room with soft light.

"Whatcha doing?" a dazed, sleepy voice asked me.

I turn around and am momentarily stunned by the most beautiful sight in the world. Casey is lying there, the sheet covering up only the most important bits. His torso is angled and reclined back on the pillows, as if he's in some Renaissance painting.

I can't quite believe that I've been with him.

Maybe I shouldn't be too hasty. Maybe I should stay and see where this thing goes. Maybe…

This was a mistake. You always make mistakes when you drink.

You aren't enough for him. He'll get bored of you in no time.

Shut up, insecure brain.

He doesn't really love you. He's just a good actor with a lot of past experience. He only said that to get in your pants.

He holds his arms out, smiling sleepily. "Come back to bed."

He knows everything about you now. He knows how broken you are. There's no way he'll stick around.

SHUT UP!

You're such a fuck up.

My heart is ripping apart.

"I should go," I whisper. "I should check on Laura, see how she's doing after surgery. I imagine she'll need someone to drive her home. So, yeah. Lots of stuff to do tomorrow." I glance at the clock. "Well, it's today now, technically."

He sits up and scoots to the edge of the bed. He reaches for my hands and runs his thumbs rhythmically over my fingers.

"Don't rush off. Maybe we can go see Laura together?" he asks, squeezing my hands.

Even though my heart is screaming out, Stay! Just stay, damn it! my mind whispers, You're so stupid. How could you do this to yourself?

If anything, life has told me that my heart is stupid. I should listen to my brain for once.

I pull my hands away. "This was a mistake," I say.

I look around the bedroom, the doorway, the lamp. Anywhere but Casey's crestfallen face. It feels like my insides are vibrating.

"I'm so sorry if I led you on," I say in a shaky voice as I walk toward his bedroom door. "Or made you think… Ugh. Sometimes when I drink, I do things I wouldn't normally do. I'm sorry."

"Do I really mean that little to you?" he asks quietly.

"Of course I care about you. But this was a mistake. Surely you can see that? And besides, it sounds like someone is eager to take my place," I say, trying to keep my tone light and calm, though I feel like a mess.

He blinks. "What are you talking about?"

"Check your phone," I say, feeling weary and just wanting to go home.

He retrieves his phone, eyebrows pressed together.

"Natalie, I have no idea why the fuck Charlie sent this, but I swear to God there's nothing…"

More lies. I can't go through this again. I just can't.

"I'm sorry," I say. "Let's just keep things casual, you know? I know that's how you want it, anyway."

I look at him. A piece of hair falls into his pained eyes.

"I could never be casual with you."

I feel simultaneously like laughing and bursting into tears. He really is good at this.

I practically run down the stairs and head for the front door. My booze-addled brain is frantically trying to remember where I've put my purse, shoes, and coat when I hear him stomp down the stairs behind me.

Thank god he's put on pants. I don't think I'd have enough resolve to leave if he fought with me naked.

"So that's it? You're just going to run away from me?" he asks.

"I'm not running. I'm doing damage control," I say while zipping up my winter coat. "We're best friends. Why ruin it with sex, you know?"

"We're more than friends," he says. "I thought for sure that you'd see that after that first time I kissed you."

"That was just a silly, one-time thing," I say, casually waving my hand through the air. "It didn't mean anything."

Casey's face crumples. "Do you make a habit of kissing all of your friends?"

I stare at him for a moment. "No."

He takes a step toward me. "I told you that I love you," he says. "And I meant it. Doesn't that mean anything to you?" He runs a hand through his hair. "Do you have any feelings for me at all?"

I want to tell him that my feelings for him scare me. That I'm afraid to love him. That I'm afraid that the bottom is always going to drop out.

So I lie.

"I care about you, Casey. But I'm not in love with you."

I sloppily slam my feet into my high heels, shuffle my half-drunk self through the front door, and nearly topple off the icy concrete steps.

"Shit," I mutter as I picture myself falling arse over tea kettle into the snow. I wish I hadn't left my winter boots in the car.

Just as I'm sure my butt bone is about to shatter on impact, two strong arms reach out to catch me.

"It's slippery," he says, holding my hands, helping me find balance. "I'll have to get some melting salt."

My mouth twists with a strange mixture of humor and anguish. I've just ripped this man's heart out, and he's talking about melting salt.

Maybe he'll be okay. Maybe I don't have to feel so cold, so heartless.

"Come on then," he says. "Let me drive you home."

I shake my head and the world moves a lazy second slower than my face. "I don't think that's a good idea," I say, a slight slur mushing up the consonants.

Casey looks at me levelly. "You're still drunk."

"So are you," I retort. "And, you're not wearing a coat."

He laughs and offers me his elbow. "I've only had one drink."

I ignore his elbow. I know if I touch him again, I'm done for. "I'll call a cab instead, thanks."

His mouth pulls into a tight, thin line. "The odds of you getting a taxi on New Year's Eve? You'll wait for another hour at least."

I look out at the street. Snow is softly falling in fluffy white flakes, illuminated by the street lamps. We'll probably wake up to another foot of snow tomorrow.

"Okay," I say, wishing I had any other option.

Casey nods, grabs a coat and set of keys from the house, and walks me to his garage.

The ride is beyond tense. The roads are icy and the snow is deep, and the drive takes twice as long as usual. I play with the hem of my dress so that the lining is twisted inside out. It reminds me of how I feel on the inside.

When we finally turn the corner and I see my place, I feel a rush of anguish and relief. My mind is a snow globe, pieces of thoughts swirling around, obscuring the view. I'd give anything to just see clearly.

"Thanks for the ride," I say quietly.

He's looking straight ahead, hands gripping the steering wheel, as if he's bracing against something. "You bet."

"Casey?" I say, licking my lips. My stomach twists with nausea and my pulse is thrumming in my ears. I really don't what to say it. But I must.

I'm really, *really*, going to miss him.

He looks at me from the driver's seat. "Yeah?"

"Casey," I say, while clearing my throat. "I really do appreciate the ride and all, but..." I take a deep breath. "Casey, we can't just be friends. We've crossed a line, and there's no way to go back from that. It'll always be an issue between us," I say, feeling helpless.

"And you honestly don't want more?" he asks quietly.

I could go back to his warm bed. He could help me nurse my hangover in the morning. We'd smile shyly over our cups of coffee, and then we could ravish one another on the kitchen table. And in the shower. And up against the pink wall in our office. Oops, I mean *his* office.

I could believe him when he says, "I love you." Maybe we could ride off into the sunset.

I feel like this "could" work. That he "could" be telling the truth.

But feelings aren't always the most reliable indicators. We need to use logic. And the logic of staying with a man who doesn't want to commit, who doesn't want children, a man who has told me that sex is just for fun, that he doesn't really believe in romantic love...well.

For the second time tonight, I lie to my best friend.

"I honestly don't." I open my door and get out. "I'm sorry. Good-bye, Casey."

I close the door with a satisfying click and run toward my house, wishing once again that I hadn't left my big, ugly snow boots in my car and praying the whole way, *Please God, don't let me slip in these damn stiletto heels.*

It isn't until I've locked the front door behind me that I realize my car is still at Casey's house and I'll have to find some way to pick it up tomorrow.

CHAPTER 31

I Fall to Pieces

Whoever said Valentine's Day is the most wonderful holiday ever is full of shit.

I do not feel wonderful. What I feel is miserable.

Even though I know I've made the right decision, I can't get Casey off my mind. I hang out with friends when I can, although Laura has been googly eyed over her hot nurse boyfriend (she asked him out when she was coming out of anesthetic), so she's been busy. Not that I can blame her.

Now I'm just going through the motions of my daily routine. My life B.C.: Before Casey. Work. Volunteering. Being alone on the weekends. More work. It strikes me how this routine never bothered me before, but now...

Anyway. Mind over matter. I will get over it.

My "getting over Casey" strategy for today is throwing myself into creating a Valentine's Day display for the thrift store. I've set up an old dress form and am draping it in my latest creation: a Victorian-inspired "Queen of Hearts" dress made out of playing cards all in the hearts suit. Very *Alice in Wonderland*. You know, without the beheadings.

Millie walks up. "Can I help?"

I hand her a pile of cards. "Sure, thanks." I show her how to punch holes in the corners and string them together.

"How do you come up with stuff like this?" she asks while fastening a banner of cards across the dress form.

I shrug. "Dunno. I saw something like it on Pinterest once, but it wasn't nearly as elaborate."

I lean back, admiring my work, looking for gaps and places I can add more detail. It's like something Marie Antoinette would've worn. Even Gladys surprised me by saying it looks nice. I wonder if she's hit her head recently.

"I haven't seen Casey in a while," Millie says, holding up a finished string of cards. "How's he doing?"

I clear my throat. "We uh…we don't really hang out anymore."

A handful of cards flutters to the floor. "What? But you two were inseparable!"

I still my hands. "He told me he loves me." A tingling sensation starts in my throat and works its way up to my eyes. I swallow it away. "But it wouldn't have worked out."

Millie stares at me for a moment and then refocuses on her string. After a minute, she looks back up at me. "Do you miss him?"

Every day.

I shrug. "It's not like I knew him for that long, anyway."

Millie clips off the end of a string and hands it to me. "How's the Nancy search going?"

"Oh, that," I say, equally grateful and discouraged that she's changed the subject. I feel like I'm dancing around the edge of that that familiar black pit. If I'm not careful, I might fall in. "That kind of fizzled out, too."

I clip off the end of a string with my teeth and turn away, pinning the new banner of cards onto the flowing train of the dress. "It was a long shot, anyway."

I stopped looking for the owner of the photo album and Nancy whoever-she-is after New Year's Eve. Once Casey wasn't around as my partner in crime and I hit one brick wall after another, I just let it go.

Millie looks at me oddly, as if I've just told her that someone died.

"What?" I ask.

She surprises me by leaning forward and wrapping her arms around me. "It just looks like you need a hug."

I try to hold them back, but the tears come anyway. And because lying to my friends is working out so well for me lately, I do it again.

"It's okay," I tell her. "Really, it's okay."

CHAPTER 32

Only Sixteen

That was perhaps the most awful, awkward date of my life.

In an effort get my mind off Casey, I accepted another invitation from Martin the accountant. First impressions aren't everything, right? And maybe he was nervous the first time we met and was weirder than usual. We all have off days. Anyway, I decided to give it another go.

Bad idea. Bad, terrible, awful idea.

It began with dinner. He wiped each piece of cutlery with a wet wipe before using it, and he had his mother on speaker phone.

The. Entire. Time.

After dinner was over, he smiled and said, rather seductively, "You know, you really remind me of my mother."

On the drive home, he told me that he prefers that women rinse their mouths with a disinfecting mouthwash before they kiss him. In turn, I told him about my recent trip to Asia, where I contracted a rare form of strep throat they haven't exactly found a cure for yet.

He couldn't wait to get me out of his car.

While I was unlocking my front door, I turned around to wave goodnight, only to see that Martin wasn't looking in my direction at all. No, he was too busy wiping the passenger side down with wet wipes.

So yeah. That happened.

It's the morning after and I'm sorting through a massive pile of laundry. Not particularly because I want to. I just really need to focus on *anything* other than how weird that date was. I'm on my second load when the phone rings.

"Hello? Is this Natalie?" a man's voice asks.

I adjust the phone between my ear and shoulder, while hauling another load of laundry through my bedroom door.

"Yes it is. Who is this?" I ask.

"My name's Curt. I'm a friend of Casey's."

My fingers spasm at the sound of his name, and the laundry basket drops and smashes my toes.

"Shit," I hiss.

"Umm…did I call at a bad time? I can call later."

"No, it's fine," I say as I hop around on one foot. "What can I do for you?"

"It's more what I can do for you," he says, laughing shakily. "It turns out I might be able to help you. I might know how to find Nancy."

My heart seems to freeze in my chest.

"Hello?" he says after a moment.

I shake my head, trying to focus. "Yes, I'm here."

Curt tells me that he's a social worker and is often at the police station to help out with some of the more difficult cases. He was doing a case conference with Constable Oakes one day when Casey happened to walk by.

"We got talking, and Casey told me all about your search," he says. "Oakes told me about the drug op you found out in the bush."

"Rusty," I say.

"Exactly," Curt says. "Do you remember a young girl there?"

I absently rub my forehead. "I think so. Skinny girl, long dark-blonde hair. She was passed out on a couch in the yard."

Curt sighs. "Sadie. That's a sad case. She's only fifteen. I've been working with her and her family for years." Curt tells me that after Casey and I found Rusty and his little shed and the head-lolling teenagers, Oakes followed up on it. "So get this," he adds. "Rusty isn't just some guy who sold Sadie drugs. He's an old family friend."

I snort. "Some friend."

"No kidding. Anyway, Sadie's mom has been talking about Rusty, ranting about the old days and wishing she'd never gotten in with him and his girlfriend, Nancy."

"Really," I say. Mostly because I can't think of anything else to say.

"Apparently they all used to be good friends," Curt says. "I'm doing a home visit tomorrow. It's kind of against the rules, but would you like to come along? See if you can find anything else?"

"But what are we going to say? They might be suspicious if I start asking the wrong kind of questions," I counter.

"We'll say you're in training and you're my helper for the day," Curt says.

We agree to meet for coffee tomorrow morning and drive out to Sadie's house afterward.

"I've gotta warn you," he says. "The house isn't exactly, well...you'll see when you get there. Just wear something dark, okay? I wouldn't want you to stain anything."

After we finish the call, I lie back on my bed and look up at the ceiling, nausea scrambling up my throat. I'm not sure if it's from fear or excitement.

It seems that the further I go down the rabbit hole, the stranger and darker it becomes.

Throughout the day, a dim, cavernous feeling settles over me, my mind swinging restlessly from thought to thought like a monkey swinging from one branch to the next.

The photo album. Nancy. My parents. What they'd think of this new twist.

As night settles and I lie alone in my bed in the dark, my thoughts turn to Casey. And after a while, it occurs to me that the cavernous feeling isn't loneliness.

It's homesickness.

I toss and turn, my mind racing. After a few hours, I get up and put away the basket of clean laundry I abandoned hours earlier. I feel strangely comforted that something so mundane can distract me from my troubled thoughts. As I put clothes away, I remember Curt's advice to wear something dark and I pull a plain black shift dress out of the closet. I usually reserve it for funerals. Perfect.

We drive. And drive. And drive.

"Where exactly are we going?" I ask.

"It's just a bit farther," Curt says.

I look out at the endless highway, the gray and brown fields, and the random rock piles. Out here, the world looks colorless. Neglected. Forgotten.

My hands are restless. It seems like I'm either biting my nails or rubbing my palms down my pant legs. I'm scared of what we might find.

Curt eventually slows the car, and we turn into a yard. Well, calling it a yard is a bit polite. It looks more like a landfill.

The driveway curves, and at the end of it stands a decrepit house. Garbage bags are piled up around the house, half of which are spilling open and being picked at by crows. Mismatched, weathered pieces of plywood cut at strange angles have been thrown together into a makeshift dog run that opens onto the saggy porch. Black sparkling eyes and wet noses peek through the cracks.

"Here we are," Curt says, parking the car.

A woman swings open the screen door and stands on the spongey front steps. She has large pendulous breasts and is wearing a grease-stained pink T-shirt with no bra. Her salt-and-pepper hair is combed back and held in place by a tight headband.

She toddles down the steps, waving wildly at us. I'm not sure who this is or what I should do exactly. So I smile and extend my hand.

"Nice to meet you," I say. "I'm Natalie."

She ignores my hand and wraps me up in a bear hug.

"Oh, I am so happy to meet you," she says. "I'm Lilah."

I can't help but notice that her hair smells like onions and sweat.

"Lilah, this is Natalie," Curt says warmly. "She's helping me out today."

Lilah waves us toward the house, talking non-stop and yelling at her dogs to keep quiet. She opens the front door, props it open with her foot, and leans over to let the dogs out of their pen. Two small creatures with matted fur race out, yapping and running in tight circles.

"In, in, come on, get in," she says to them.

Curt and I follow her into the house, and I'm immediately struck by the powerful stench of old urine. I'm about to take my shoes off when Curt whispers in my ear, "Just keep them on." I nod and notice that one of the dogs has squatted in the foyer and is peeing on the carpet.

"Oh, Missy," Lilah scolds. She looks up at us and smiles. "Don't mind the puppies, they seem to like going inside more than outside."

She shrugs and beckons us to follow her down the hall. Musty boxes, yellowed stacks of paper, plastic organizer bins, and all sorts of random things are lined up along the walls. It takes some clever footwork to follow her. She settles us into a small living room before scuttling off to the kitchen, mumbling something about a turkey. Somehow, five couches, seven chairs, and three coffee tables have been shoved in here. It's more storage room than living room. Hazy blue smoke fills the air, swirling lazily above the wilted house plants.

A deep, hacking smoker's cough sounds from the far side of the room. I see a small man leaning back in a recliner, the armrests black and greasy from years of use. The man is wrinkled and pinched-looking, a bored scowl permanently etched onto his face.

"Look, Mother," the man says while blowing out a stream of smoke. "His Majesty has decided to grace us with his presence. And he's brought a fancy little woman with him too."

The man gestures to an ancient burgundy velvet couch behind me.

"Well, aren't you going to sit down?" he demands. Curt and I sit. I wish I could disappear into the couch. "So who's this one?" the man asks, pointing his cigarette in my direction.

"This is Natalie," Curt replies easily, unperturbed by this man's aggressive energy. "She's a colleague. Natalie, this is Dan. Sadie's father."

Dan snorts a little, and his eyes slide back to the television.

"Where is Sadie?" Curt asks.

"Sadie!" Dan yells, which sets off a coughing fit. "Your fancy counselor man is here to see you."

Curt leans back, eyes observant, one hand covering his amused smile. I imagine he must see a lot of strange things.

"Guuuh-awwwed!" a sullen teenage voice calls. "I'll be right there."

One of the little dogs jumps onto the couch with us. Its fur is so matted and long that I have no idea what breed it is. It climbs onto my lap, happily panting.

"Hi baby," I say quietly, scratching its neck. The fur is stuck to the collar. I lift it up and notice several wet, open sores underneath. "And down you go," I say.

I glance at the table next to me – glass candy dishes, doilies, and mismatched picture frames, all of which are covered in an impenetrable layer of grease and dust. The photo closest to me is of a young soldier kneeling on the ground, his face shadowed by his helmet.

"That's me, when I was in the Persian Gulf War," Dan's gravelly voice croaks.

Sadie trudges into the room, rubbing her eyes, and sits down beside me.

"Really, Dad?" she says, yawning. "You're still going with that war story?"

Dan sits up straight and points a finger at her. "You'd do well to show a little more respect around here for the people who kept this country safe."

Sadie rises abruptly. "And on that note, I'm going outside for a walk."

The house is oppressively hot despite the several fans going. From the kitchen, we hear water running, pots banging, and the occasional "whoops."

"Curt?" Lilah calls from the kitchen. "Can I get a hand in here? This turkey is way too heavy for me."

Curt sighs. "I keep telling you, Lilah, you don't have to cook for me."

A loud, whirring noise, like from a blender or hand mixer, blasts from the kitchen.

"It's not for you today. It's Sadie's birthday, you see," she replies, yelling over the sound. "I wanted to do something special for her sweet sixteen."

Curt shrugs and walks toward her chattering voice. As I watch his retreating back, I feel like I've been left on a desert island and my rescue boat is going in the wrong direction. Dan leans back in his easy chair, lights up another cigarette, and relaxes into storytelling mode.

He waxes lyrical about life in the army, the ins and outs of being a soldier, and shares tidbits of what he calls "insider knowledge." From the way he talks, I gather that those were his glory days.

"And now," he says, concluding his story, "I'm old, cranky, and useless."

I pause, feeling awkward. "Oh, umm, I'm sure you're not useless." *Old and cranky is spot on*, I feel like adding.

Lilah pops her head around the corner. "Dinner's ready! And I've made something really special for our birthday girl."

We eat in the living room. Dan never gets up from his recliner.

"Sadie, you've barely touched your food," Lilah whines. Her large breasts stick out like a shelf and she's resting her plate on top. One of the little dogs perches on her shoulder, taking delicate nibbles off of Lilah's fork.

"I'm not hungry." Sadie stirs the food around her plate.

Lilah's face falls. "But these are your favorites."

Sadie lifts her upper lip in a half sneer. "When I was little." She adds quietly, "It's not even my birthday. It's next month."

Lilah's face screws up for a moment, pondering this idea. And then she lights up and turns to me. I'm amazed at how fast she can switch gears. "Sadie was such a cute little girl," she says. "Would you like to see some pictures?"

Maybe this is my in. Maybe if I can get Lilah talking about the old days, I can find out more about her connection with Nancy.

"Sure, that would be nice," I say.

Lilah abandons her plate, and about ten minutes later she returns with an armful of albums and framed photos. She hands me one of the frames. Sadie alternately rolls her eyes and stares holes in my head. We start flipping through pictures, with Lilah giving me an overly detailed account of their trip to southern Saskatchewan.

Once they've eaten, Curt takes out some paperwork and asks if he can talk to Sadie for a little while. They head into the adjoining kitchen, while Lilah and I sit in Dan's swirling cloud of smoke.

"So how's your training going?" Lilah asks.

I look up from the photo album in my lap. "Hmm?"

"You know. To be a social worker?"

I cough. "Oh yes, *that* training. Umm, it's going well. Curt is a great teacher."

I thank Lilah for showing me pictures of Sadie from when she was little, and hand them back to her. "Do you have any older photo albums?" I ask. I plaster on a smile, hoping that I don't seem too obvious. Hoping that she won't sense the fear that lurks just beneath. "I just love looking at people's pictures."

I don't even have to bother coming up with some plausible reason of why I'd like to see them. Lilah's wide smile breaks from ear to ear. "How many years back do you want to go?"

I almost didn't see her at first. It looks like it was taken at a house party, and there is a ton of people in the frame. She's standing toward the back, and I only see her profile.

But there she is.

A younger, less haggard-looking version of the mugshot I saw last fall. But it's definitely her.

"Who is this?" I ask.

Lilah squints. "Oh. That's Nancy." She flaps her hand dismissively. "We were friends. A long time ago."

The smoother, less ruffled Nancy looks more like me than the mugshot did. More like me than I care to admit. I shudder involuntarily.

"Are you cold, honey?" Lilah asks. "Do you want me to close the window?"

She rocks her body forward, propelling herself into a standing position.

"No!" I practically yell into the smoky haze. "No, I'm fine," I add gently. "Thank you, though."

Lilah looks at me strangely and then resettles beside me. She stares at the photo for a moment and then looks up at me, her eyes a well of pain and regret. "I imagine Curt has told you all about Rusty." I nod. She sighs heavily, her eyes fluttering shut. Her jovial attitude is gone, and all that's left is a woman who looks very, very tired.

"Did you know he was using Sadie out in the woods? You know. *Using* her?"

My throat feels thick. "No, I didn't," I say, my voice raspy with anguish. I lay my hand on Lilah's. "I'm so sorry."

She grips my hand tight and looks me in the eye. "You're a good girl. A good one, you know?"

Unsure of what to say, I simply smile and say nothing.

As she continues to look at me, her expression changes.

"You know, it's funny that you picked Nancy out of that picture," she says. "You look an awful lot like her."

I laugh nervously and feel like pulling my hand back. "Really?"

"Yeah," she says.

And for an excruciating moment, I think I'm caught.

But, to my relief, she shakes her head, releases my hand, and lights a cigarette.

"Well, they say we all have a twin somewhere," she says, and she blows out a stream of blue smoke. She shakes her head again, her eyes focused on the window. "When you're young, you have all these dreams and plans of how it's going to turn out." She closes her eyes, cigarette perched delicately between her fingers. "I'm not perfect. But I think I've done the best I could. But if I could change anything, I wish I wouldn't have ever met Rusty and that damn Natska." She turns to me. "I can't believe what that monster did to my baby."

"I'm so sorry, Lilah," I say again, knowing just how inadequate those words are.

My brain trips over the new name. "Sorry, what name was it you said?"

"Natska."

My brow furrows. "But, I thought you said her name was Nancy."

Lilah coughs several times and then says, "She changed it to Nancy Carlyle about a year after I met her. Her real name was Natska Czarnik."

Before I can think of anything else to ask, Curt walks in, saying that he has an afternoon appointment and we need to get going. Lilah walks us to the door, and I say goodbye to Dan.

"Nice meeting you," I say.

He doesn't acknowledge me. Instead, he stares at the hockey game on TV and turns up the volume.

Sadie stands with us by the door, pulling a pair of boots with broken zippers on. "Can I get a ride into town?" she asks.

Curt shoves his hands in his pockets. "That's kind of against the rules."

"Please," she begs. "I just need to get out of here. And besides, my mom says she needs stuff from the store." She holds up a crumpled up note with faint pencil writing on it. Curt crosses his arms, and Sadie shoves past him outside. "Fine, I'll just walk then."

Curt rolls his eyes and turns to leave. "Thanks for lunch, Lilah. I'll drop in again soon."

"Oh, before you go," Lilah yells over her shoulder as she bustles down the hall. She returns a moment later holding a gift bag. She walks outside with us and holds out the bag for Sadie. "I've put something together for you, sweetheart," Lilah says. "I can't believe you're already sweet sixteen."

Sadie shakes her eyes and looks heavenward, as if pleading with the universe. She reluctantly lifts the crumpled tissue paper off the top of the bag. I lean over to peek inside.

"It's all stuff from when you were little," Lilah says. "Pictures of you; that old scarf you liked, the one I knitted, don't you remember? Oh, and I put in some of your favorite Barbie dolls." The bag crackles as Sadie tilts it from side to side, looking at but not actually touching anything. "I know it's not much, but I thought with you having such a milestone birthday and all, you might want to reminisce," she says, smiling so wide that her gums show.

Sadie stares down at the bag. "Thanks," she says, in a quiet, flat voice.

Our departure is full of long, uncomfortable hugs and Lilah demanding that we visit more often, as if we were old friends. She stands in the yard and waves until we're out of sight.

Once we're on the highway, Sadie chucks the gift bag out of the window. I watch in my sideview mirror as it tumbles and eventually lands in a ditch.

CHAPTER 33

Hang On Sloopy

All the way home, I repeat the name in my head, like a song with only two words.

Natska Czarnik. Natska Czarnik. Natska Czarnik.

The drive back home is somehow faster than the drive out. Maybe because my mind is busy. Curt was nice enough to drop me off at home, and, to my surprise, Sadie climbs out of the car with me.

"Do you have a ride home?" I ask.

She shrugs, shifting her weight from one foot to the other. "I've got some friends I can call."

I look at this broken teenage girl, her lank greasy hair, her pale thin face. I reach out and wrap my arms around her. Her tiny body goes rigid.

"It won't be like this forever," I say quietly. "You have a choice in how your life goes."

She pulls back and looks at me. "You have no idea what it's like to be me."

I give her a sad smile. "I know more than you think."

I dig out a pen and paper and write down my cell number. "I want you to call me if you need to talk. Anytime."

Sadie shoves the scrap of paper into her back pocket. "All right," she says, eyeing me suspiciously. Her eyes flicker over me, as if she's seeing me for the first time. "I like your jacket," she says.

I smile. "Thanks. It got it from a thrift store that I work at."

She nods, but then looks down at her shoes. And for a moment, she reminds me of the teenager who came into the store with a snake around his neck. Our pasts might not be exactly the same, but something in me recognizes something in them. Something angry and broken.

I recognize that this girl needs to feel like she belongs somewhere. That she isn't helpless, that she doesn't have to be a victim. That she is more powerful than she realizes. That she can, in fact, help others. That she needs a place that makes her feel useful.

A series of thoughts jumble together, like puzzle pieces clicking into place.

"Hey, do you need a job?" I ask while adjusting my purse on my shoulder. "We're always looking for more volunteers."

She shrugs. "Anything to get me out of that hell hole for a few hours."

I nod. "It's a great place to work. And you get first dibs on any clothes that come into the store."

"Hmm. Cool," she mumbles, fingering the hole in her sweater.

I tell her to come in the next day to meet the store manager, and I have her promise to call me if she needs a ride home. As I walk up to my front door, my mind is buzzing with a slowly growing to-do list.

1) Call Cheryl and discuss expanding the Bright Futures program to include troubled youth.

2) Find out who Natska is.

3) Figure out how to spell that frigging name. Natska? Nattzka? Zarnick? Tsarnic?

I sit down at my kitchen table with my laptop. I've just got off the phone with my mom. I wanted to go over with her again any information she has on my birth. We know when I was born and how long I was in foster care before I was adopted (five days). We know which hospital I was born in. I bet that if I was born here, there's a chance my birth family was from here too.

With a shaky hand, I type "Czarnik" into Canada411.

A surprising amount of results come up, and I scan the list. My eyes alight on the top name. A. Czarnik, (780) 555-4172

I pick up the phone, my heart pounding.

"Here goes nothing."

CHAPTER 34

You Belong To Me

Two months later…

I sit in my car, a cloud of exhaust floating up into the gray April morning. It's been almost a year since I first found the album and letters. And now here I am.

My shaky hands grip the steering wheel, the knuckles turning white. I'm parked outside of an ordinary house on an ordinary street in an older neighborhood on the west side of the city. It doesn't look like a special day.

But it feels like one.

I look down at my outfit. It took me hours to pick it. You only get once chance to make a first impression on your birth family.

The first number I called was for A. Czarnik. Her name is Anna. When I told her I was looking for my birth family, she breathed out a single name.

Nancy.

It turns out that she has a sister named Natska, aka Nancy, who gave up a baby for adoption twenty-seven years ago. And now, here I am.

It's taken me two months to work up to this. Sometimes you don't know how scared of something you are until it's right in front of you.

Anna's invited me over to her house to meet the family. Afterward, she and I will have a chance to talk and hash out the finer details.

My parents offered to accompany me, but I said no; I felt like this was something I had to do on my own. Although, now that I'm here and scared shitless, I'm seriously wondering if I should just call them. I know they're waiting at home for updates, though.

I wish Casey were here, too. He'd make me laugh or tell me a good story or sing a song or simply hold my hand.

Anyway. No time to dwell on that.

I take my key out of the ignition and open the car door. My face hits the crisp spring air, and I wrap my arms around my ribs as I walk toward the house. I have a bag tucked under my arm containing the photo album, letters, and dresses. My brain is on a constant repeat: *This is it. This is it!*

I ring the doorbell. The door swings open. And then, the soundtrack in my brain stutters and stalls, like a record being ripped away from a record player.

"Karl?"

"Hello!" he says, his heavy accent pulling at the consonants.

"What are you doing here?"

A woman with short, dark-brown hair and crow's feet around her eyes appears at his side. She stretches out her hand. "You must be Natalie? I'm Anna. We spoke over the phone."

I laugh nervously and shake her hand.

As I walk into the living room, the first thing I see is a wall of pictures. A family wall, I guess. It's an eclectic mix of mismatched frames and random portraits and family photos from over the years. No one really looks all that familiar, but one. I walk up to it, willing the tears to stay in my eyes. She looks just like the woman from the photo album.

She looks a bit older in this picture. And it's in color too. But it's still her.

Karl points at me and then at the portrait on the wall, smiling and says something in his usual mishmash of English and Polish. Anna nods and replies back to him in Polish.

"He's saying that you look so much like my mother," Anna explains while Karl's red-rimmed, bright blue eyes stream with tears. "Your grandma."

She steps back and makes some room for me in the entryway.

"Come, come. Meet your family."

After the initial excitement of meeting my two other aunts, plus uncles and cousins, Anna leads me into her kitchen and tells me the whole story. About how her little sister gave up a baby years ago, and they'd always wondered where she was.

It seems that once she turned twelve, only her parents called her Natska anymore. Everyone else called her Nancy.

"But if her last name was Czarnik, where did Carlyle come from?" I ask. "Maybe it was my birth father's last name? Or the name of someone really significant to her?"

Anna shrugs and stirs her tea. "No idea. I think she changed her name to distance herself from what happened."

"What happened, exactly?" I ask, though I'm not sure if I'm ready for the answer.

"She was always a little wild," Anna says, looking thoughtful. "She started to rebel in her teens and, well...things just got crazy from there."

Recognition hits me like a hammer.

"She was involved with a teacher at school," Anna says after a pause. "We never knew which one. Natty wouldn't talk about it. She dropped out shortly after."

I grip my mug a bit tighter. "Right," I say, quietly.

It strikes me as odd only now that I've never wondered about my dad. It's so weird. I've never really thought about it before. And with this information, I'm not sure if I'd want to meet him anyway.

So. My mother is a high-school dropout who got knocked up by a teacher. Fantastic.

"You feeling okay?" Anna asks.

I look up from my tea. "I'm not sure yet," I answer honestly. "I've had so many questions." I wipe my eyes. "And now that they're being answered, I...I guess I never really thought about what it would feel like to learn the truth. I guess it's just a process, coming to grips with reality and letting go of what I thought."

Anna nods. There are no words. I'm glad she doesn't try to fill up the space with ones that don't quite measure up.

"Where exactly did you find these things?" she asks while flipping through the photo album.

"In a little old house, not too far from here," I say. I tell her the whole story, though I never refer directly to Casey. I feel like it would complicate things even more.

At the end of it, Anna shakes her head. "It's amazing to think that she was just a few blocks away. I never did find out where she was. I tried, but she always wanted to meet in public places. But, Mom must've known where she was all along."

"I wonder why she didn't tell anyone," I say.

"Who knows. It's hard to say now. Maybe she was afraid of dad finding out, and Nancy running farther away?"

She brings the album closer to her face and peers a bit closer at one photo. "It must've been a comfort to her, knowing that her daughter was close by."

"But why did Nancy have the photo album? And the dresses?" I ask.

"Our mother was really close to Natty. We used to tease her that she was the favorite," Anna says. "When Papa threw her out, I imagine she took whatever she could so she could feel close to her family." Anna pours us another mug of tea. "I know it grieves him now," she says quietly. "But people did things differently back then."

My mind whirs over the past few months. "I still don't know why we didn't figure it out sooner. Surely an aunt or someone would've noticed the resemblance?" I ask, gesturing to my face.

"We always came to visit during the week, after supper," she explains.

I raise my eyebrows in recognition. "And I volunteer at the hospital on weekends."

I look meditatively at the tea leaves. I still can't quite believe I'm here, visiting with my aunt in her yellow kitchen, trying to take it all in.

On the wall there are five different pictures of the Blessed Virgin holding a shining heart that has been pierced with a dagger. Anna must be Catholic. Were they raised Catholic? Did my mother have a rosary and go to confession? Would she have taken me to church? How would my life have been different if she had kept me?

So many questions.

My heart beats a bit faster when I think about the question I want to ask next.

"Do you know where Nancy is?"

Anna's eyes soften. "I'm sorry to tell you this, but Nancy died a few years ago."

And just like that, a chunk of my heart breaks off and shatters.

"We got a call from the police about five years ago. They informed us that Nancy had been out of the province and had died in a car accident. She was the passenger, but it sounds like alcohol was involved."

I nod, trying to process the new information, trying to handle it like an adult and not the lost little girl I feel like inside.

"I'm sorry," she says. "You've probably been dreaming about meeting your birth mom for years."

I smile through my tears, unable to speak. My eyes dart to my bag on the floor, and I see a sliver of blue peeking through the top.

"Oh, I almost forgot," I say. I pull the dress out and drape it across my arms. "I found this in the box, along with the photo album and letters. Does it mean anything to you?"

Anna's eyes light up. "Your mother loved that dress," she says. "You see, my mother, your grandmother, was a seamstress."

"Was she?" I ask, aiming for calm and polite, but sounding squeaky.

"Oh yes," she says, smiling, running her hand over the fabric. "We grew up with a parade of women coming through the house. 'Hem my bridesmaid dress, change this neckline.' Her sewing room was always a mess."

I feel as though my whole body is alert.

"Natska loved to watch her work," she says, looking across the kitchen but seeing only what's in her memory. "When she was little, she liked to lie under the dresses and watch Mom sew."

I swallow hard.

"This was the last project they worked on together," Anna murmurs.

I hold my arms out, offering it to her. Anna's fingers slide over the fine, slippery fabric, a distant smile on her face. "It was a bitch to sew. There was a lot of swearing."

I laugh and think to myself, Mom is never going to believe this.

After a moment, she hands it back and places one of her warm hands over mine.

"I think you should keep it."

I lie in my bed and stare at the ceiling, the duvet pulled tight under my chin. I know sleep won't come tonight. I find myself going over the new things I've learned today as if I'm studying for a test.

There were at least five other people in the room with noses like mine. They were loud and colorful. I look eerily like one of my cousins. And one of my aunts and I have practically the same laugh. It strikes me that you can wish for something your whole life without really knowing it.

Just as my eyes begin to feel heavy, my phone pings on the bedside table. It's an email from Anna. She's attached a picture.

From: annaczarnik

To: nataliebishop

I knew I would find it somewhere! Nancy bought it for you in the hospital gift shop, but for some reason it was left behind when your foster family came to pick you up. Let me know if you want it.

Love, Anna

I open the attachment, and a breath is trapped in my chest so tightly that I feel like I've been stabbed.

It's a picture of a plush toy. An orange cat with white stripes.

Tears cloud my eyes and my body shakes with adrenaline.

I type back a simple message.

Thank you! Yes, I want it. Would you believe me if I said I have a thing for orange cats?

CHAPTER 35

Sweet Love on My Mind

It's a hot afternoon in July and I'm sunbathing in the backyard. It's been a long week but a good one. The thrift store's Bright Futures program has been expanded to include at-risk youth, with me spearheading the new changes.

Everyone has been given training on how to care for these young people and how to create an atmosphere that they can grow in. There are still some details to iron out, and we don't have that many teenagers working with us yet, but I know this is going to be something worthwhile.

For the first time in my life, I feel completely like myself.

It's a combination of things. First off, I've been going for counseling again and talking to my sponsor. I was so afraid my counselor and my sponsor would judge me, but they've been there and know what it's like to feel that deep shame spiral that happens when someone relapses. They've helped put things in perspective. It's put the Casey situation in a whole new light, and I regret running out on him.

I've thought about calling him, but after so many months of not talking, it just feels awkward to bridge the gap.

I've also been getting to know my birth family, which I've found to be incredibly healing. I've heard stories about Nancy and my aunts and my grandma. I've seen dozens of photo albums and friended my cousins on Facebook. They've met my family too. Mom; Dad; my weird, totally opposite brothers.

Mom and Dad were absolutely thrilled that I dumped Martin the accountant. It turns out they don't really like him anymore. Well, Dad doesn't anyway. They had a massive disagreement. Martin was talking about the "robot overlords" and how he plans to become a human liaison for our metal masters when the uprising comes. Dad thought this plan was basically selling out the human race, called him a "robo-quisling" and a "species traitor," and stormed out of the office.

Poor Martin. I hope he finds someone. If my weirdo dad could, I know that Martin can.

Anyway, life is good. It's like everything has finally clicked. In a weird way, even though this began with me trying to find Nancy, I ended up finding myself.

But what about Casey?

My thoughts have been drifting to him more and more lately.

Especially since yesterday afternoon.

It wasn't a police check, but the fire department equivalent. Fire trucks were parked along the road, blocking a lane on either side. As soon as I saw the fire trucks, I started to panic.

I was both thankful and disappointed, however, when the person who approached my window was a young woman with dark, curly hair, dressed in firefighter gear.

She smiled and leaned down to look into my driver window. "Hi, I'm Sarah," she said.

I recognized her. Her picture had been on Casey's phone, on New Year's Eve. It had come up with her texts.

"The fire department is raising money for cystic fibrosis," she said, and handed me a pamphlet describing an upcoming fundraising carnival. "The fire chief's daughter has CF, so you know. We do what we can to help with research."

I felt tongue-tied, so I just nodded in reply.

"I hope you can join us," she says.

I did a sort of awkward salute with my pamphlet. "Thanks, I'll think about it."

Just as I was almost free from this woman, she leaned in a bit closer. "Hey, you're Casey's friend, aren't you?"

I froze. "Uh…Not, umm. Not really," I said. "Not anymore."

"Sorry to hear that," she said, her professional face back on. "Anyway, please, tell your friends and family to come check out our carnival. Have a nice day!"

I felt like this was my cue to go. I'd have loved more than anything to just drive away. But the words came tumbling out of me anyway. "So, are you dating Casey?"

Sarah wrinkled her nose. "No. Why?"

"I saw the text you sent him on New Year's," I said, my heart pounding. "I wondered if maybe you two had…"

I considered making an obscene gesture for a moment but then thought better of it. Probably best to keep what little dignity I had left.

Her eyes lit with recognition. "Oh. That," she said with a laugh.

I know I shouldn't have felt angry. But I did anyway. Her attitude seemed so…blasé.

"Let me explain," she said, nearly giggling. "Our whole crew went out for drinks on New Year's Eve. We were all having fun, and the guys started to drink a little too much. The next thing I know, they had stolen my phone and were sending drunk texts to my entire contact list."

She definitely had my attention. "Like, what?"

"Mostly dirty ones," she replied. "Things that would curl your grandma's hair."

So yeah. That was the bombshell that was dropped on me yesterday afternoon.

I ended our conversation with an apology (how Canadian of me) and drove home, feeling lost, embarrassed, and pissed off at myself. If what Sarah said was true, then I'd thrown away a man who'd loved me because of a prank text.

He'd said he didn't know anything about the texts Sarah had sent him.

He'd said that he wanted a wife, family, the whole shebang.

He'd said that he loved me.

And I'd refused to believe him.

I officially feel like the worst person ever.

I lean back in my chair in the back yard, my mind going round in circles. I pick up the newspaper, trying to figure out my next move.

Maybe I should go see him, but I can't just drop by his house unannounced. It would be weird, after all these months.

Although, now that I know what the texts on his phone were all about, I feel compelled to make things right with him.

A sensation of intense uncertainty pushes down on me. It's a lot like being lost on twisted back roads at night and feeling unsure of how to find your way home. It reminds me of how I felt in those profoundly scary moments when I was sitting in my car gearing up to meet my birth family. I'd wanted to know the truth so badly, but when it was right in front of me, I was scared of it.

I realize now that I feel the same way about Casey. I wanted him to love me, but I didn't think he'd ever feel the same way. So when he was right in front of me, saying that he loved me, I was too scared of my past to believe it.

Now that I believe him, can I get over that fear?

Still not sure of what to do or how I should even approach Casey, I absently flick through the newspaper pages, looking but not really seeing, when a small ad catches my eye.

ROCKABILLY ROCK OUT

CASEY NOLAN TO PLAY AT NIFTIES TONITE!

HALF-PRICE SANGRIA

TRY OUR NEW ELVIS BURGER: 5 OZ SIRLOIN TOPPED WITH BACON
AND PAN-FRIED BANANA, AND DRIZZLED WITH PEANUT BUTTER
AND HONEY

My heart starts to beat faster at the sight of his name. And damn, that burger sounds weird yet tantalizing.

Maybe I could drop by. Surprise him while he's on stage. Maybe I'll dress up, make myself look really good. First, I'll dye my hair Lucille Ball red, and then I'll wear my green Audrey Hepburn–inspired dress that he liked so much. The one he had so much fun taking off me.

I can picture it now. The crowd will part. I'll walk up to the stage. He'll have his eyes closed, and just as he finishes a song and looks down, he'll see me.

He'll lift me up on stage and kiss me. The crowd will roar. We'll celebrate with Elvis burgers all around. And we'll live happily ever after. Or something like that.

A bubble of excitement expands in my chest. Yes, I'm doing this. And it is going to be awesome.

Okay. This is *so* not awesome.

The hair dye I bought dyed my scalp bright red as well. I look like I have some sort of tropical rash.

I decided to plunge ahead anyway, and I took my time doing my hair and makeup. I put on my green dress and seamed stockings. I drove over to Nifties feeling excited. Hopeful.

Only to discover that Casey wasn't there.

"What do you mean he isn't here?" I ask.

The bartender shrugs. "He just didn't show up."

My mind whirrs with the possibilities. Maybe he's stuck in traffic or is sick in the hospital. Or maybe he was called into work.

"But he loves it here! Where would he have gone?" I say, feeling flummoxed.

"Don't know. He's been out of sorts lately. Said he felt 'scunnered,' whatever the hell that means."

Okay. Where would Casey go if he felt scunnered?

A distant memory flits through my mind.

Chinese restaurants. The kitchens, specifically.

After I call the fire hall (just to rule it out) and find that Casey isn't there, I do a quick search of all of the Chinese restaurants in the city (there are roughly a bazillion) and narrow my focus to ones by his house.

When I pull into the first parking lot, I start looking for signs that Casey might be around. His truck isn't there, but that might not mean anything. It's so close to his home that he might've walked.

I climb out of my car and trot up to a restaurant banner that says in bold red letters BINGS #1.

I'm briskly walking between the crowded tables, heading toward the kitchen, when a concerned-looking young man in a black apron stops me.

"Can I help you?" he asks, looking me up and down.

I must look a bit like a disgruntled high school grad, stomping around in her high heels and fancy dress.

"No, no," I say, craning my neck to look around him. "I'm fine. Just looking for a friend."

He nods. "Okay," he asks. "What does your friend look like?"

"Oh! You might know him, actually," I say. "Chinese restaurants are his thinking spot. I know, weird, right? I'm sure you've noticed him. Big guy? Weird Irish/Texan accent?" I say, while holding a hand high above my head to show how tall Casey is.

"Right," he says, drawing the word out slowly. "And are you the only one who can see this friend?"

"What? No!" I say.

I see a tall, shadowy figure dart past the kitchen and my heart begins to pound.

"Casey!" I shout, and I shove the waiter aside. I race past the swinging kitchen door, my head turning from side to side. I finally spot a tall man with dark hair and a brown jacket heading out a back entrance.

I pick up my skirts and dash toward him, and I narrowly avoid slamming into a waitress carrying two heavy trays of sticky food.

"Casey!" I shout again.

He stops.

This is it. My big, romantic reunion. Sure, I'm sweaty and we're standing in an alley beside a dumpster. But whatever. It's still romantic to me.

"I've been looking everywhere for you!"

He turns around, and I pause mid-step.

"Oh," I say. "You're not Casey." He gives me an odd little look. "Sorry," I say quietly.

He does an awkward little wave and leaves. I blow out a puff of air and dig my phone out of my purse. I pull up the list of local restaurants again.

"One down, six more to go," I say aloud.

CHAPTER 36

Searchin'

Hours later, I'm sitting dejectedly in my car, feeling tired, cranky, and more than a little ridiculous in my outfit. I've been in more restaurant kitchens than I ever thought I'd be in. And still, no Casey.

In the meantime, I've tried calling anyone who might know where Casey is. The fire hall (again). Nifties, in case he finally decided to show up. (He didn't.) Millie, to see if she's heard from him. (She hasn't.)

I've even tried calling Casey's cell, but it goes straight to voicemail. I've sent him a few casual texts, asking him how he is and what he's up to, but he hasn't replied.

My phone says it's nine p.m. Restaurants will be closing soon, so I decide to call it a night. My stomach grumbles and I remember that I haven't eaten anything in quite a while. I drive around, looking for a place to eat. I had kind of banked on eating those weird banana-and-peanut-butter Elvis burgers. I imagine Nifties will be open late tonight. They were supposed to have live entertainment, after all.

I drive around for a while and eventually pull into a mostly deserted parking lot with a hole-in-the-wall Chinese restaurant at the end of a strip mall. The orange neon sign in the window says CLOSED.

I'm about to drive away when something catches my eye. At the end of the parking lot, near some bushes, stands a shiny, old-fashioned truck.

But this couldn't possibly be Casey's truck. His isn't shiny. And yet I find myself parking beside it and getting out to inspect it.

It has the same shape as Casey's truck, I decide. But that's it. This vehicle is pristine. The body is a pale blue with discreet silver stripes down the side, and the cab is upholstered in black and white leather, with a shiny chrome steering wheel.

There's no way that this truck is Casey's. There aren't any dirty floor mats or discarded McDonald's wrappers. No tape collection perched on the middle seat. It probably belongs to some retired guy who only takes it out during summer months.

As a heavy, sinking feeling settles in my heart, I'm surprised to realize just how much I'd grown to love that ugly, dirty old truck.

I'm about to get into my car and drive back to Nifties to drown my sorrows in grease when I see it: the edge of a familiar ripped cardboard box sticking out from under the seat. A few cassette tapes are visible, organized in neat rows for once.

A bubble of excitement threatens to explode in my throat.

He's here. Somewhere.

I look around the quiet parking lot, which is surrounded by semi-abandoned strip malls that have seen better days. The only thing that's still open is a pet store.

A streak of anger runs through me.

A pet store?! You've been in a frigging pet store this whole time?

I spring toward the pet store and push the door open. It's a small, narrow place, but with lots of nooks and crannies. This time I'm not taking any chances. If he's here, I'm going to search everywhere. I rush around the front area, ducking my head into aisles and looking behind enormous stacks of dog food.

The cashier doesn't even look in my direction but continues to stare at her phone, feet propped up on a table. Maybe she's used to weirdos traipsing around the place.

Eventually I end up with nowhere else to look but the fish and lizard area at the back of the store. I'm not overly optimistic. I mean, wouldn't he want to look at the cute puppies? Maybe he isn't even in here at all. Maybe he washed up at the Chinese restaurant next door and then went for a walk when they closed. And I'm in here, ducking behind water bowls and plastic fish-tank plants, hissing his name.

"Casey? Are you in here?"

I'm just about to go back outside and wait by his truck when I see a tall silhouette near a shadowy corner. He's staring at a tank, and his face is cast in a bluish tinge.

"Finally!" I shout.

Casey startles and nearly knocks over an enormous (and probably expensive) tank.

"What are you doing here?" I ask. "Do you know how many Chinese men have thrown me out of their kitchens tonight?"

I'm about two seconds away from tapping my toe. How Lucy-esque of me. Then again, he'd probably like that.

He blinks at me. "This is the only place in town that has blue lobsters."

I blink back at him. "Blue lobsters?"

"See for yourself," he says, and he points to the tank he's been staring at.

I'm not really sure how to read his mood. I crouch down and look inside the tank. Sure enough, there are five teeny, tiny blue lobsters scuttling around the tank.

"Hmm. Weird," I say, because, honestly, I really don't know what else to say.

"What are you doing here?" he asks.

"Looking for you."

"Why?" he asks, bewildered. "And how did you find me?"

"Believe me, it hasn't been easy," I say, with a relieved laugh. I stand and look him in the eye. "Are you okay?"

"Well, I'm a bit worried that you might be a stalker. Although I've always suspected as much," he says, with the trace of a smirk. "Are you okay?"

"What? I'm fine."

He wipes his brow. "I was starting to wonder if you haven't taken this dress off since the night…well, you know. That night."

I laugh. "I hadn't considered that," I say. "Does seem a bit crazy."

He lifts his eyebrows and says "Mmm" in agreement.

"I wanted to see you," I say. "The paper said you were playing at Nifties tonight."

A troubled look comes over his face. "Yeah. I feel bad for blowing that off, but, ugh...I just couldn't." He shakes his head. "It doesn't matter."

I step closer to him. "I'm worried about you."

He snorts. "That's funny. I didn't think you thought about me at all."

"But I do!" I protest. "All of the time."

He turns to me, and all of the mirth has gone out of his eyes. He doesn't look angry. Just completely, utterly heartbroken.

"Then why haven't I heard from you?" he asks.

I bite my lip. "I was afraid," I say, and I'm immediately angry at how lame that sounds.

He gives a noncommittal grunt and looks away.

"Casey," I say, my mind scrambling for the right thing to say, "I've been running away from things my whole life. My feelings, my problems, my self. I even run away from the things I want most."

He looks up at me, cautious expectation on his face.

I hold my hands up, feeling vulnerable, as if I'm about to surrender. "I'm done with running."

I pause, waiting for him to say something.

He doesn't. Though his arms are still crossed, his eyes look hopeful.

I decide to press on, and I say the first thing that comes to mind. Anything that will bridge this awkward gap.

"I ran into Sarah, yesterday," I say. "She said that your drunk buddies had stolen her phone."

Casey sets his mouth into a thin, grim line.

"I'm sorry," I say, after a long, awkward pause. "I'm so sorry that I didn't believe you."

He nods and then looks back at the lobster tank. He's twitchy and rubbing at his eyes every few seconds. I sense that he might bolt if I don't keep the conversation going.

"I went on a date with Martin," I blurt.

"The accountant?"

I smile. "Yes. And it was our last." Casey raises an eyebrow. "He had his mother on speaker phone the entire time."

A ghost of a smile appears on his lips. "Shocker."

"Yeah. He said he hated Lucy," I say. "It was a deal breaker for me."

A surprised gust of laughter bursts out of Casey. "Well, that is a pretty serious thing to disagree on." He shakes his head and then looks over at me. "I didn't think I'd ever see you again."

"I didn't think you'd want to," I say. I try to take a lighter, teasing tone. "Besides, I haven't heard from you in months, either."

He whirls toward me, palms upward in supplication. "Because you said you didn't want to be friends anymore!" he shouts.

I'm about to reply when the cashier appears to our left. "Umm, hey," she says. "I need to start closing up, so…"

Casey sniffs and rubs his nose. "Right, right. Of course."

We walk outside, feeling a bit like chastised, unruly children being shooed out of a library or something.

"Good Lord," I mutter as we amble toward his truck. "I can't believe I was about to deliver my declaration-of-love speech in a pet store."

Casey stops walking. "Your what?"

"My declaration-of-love speech. I've been mentally rehearsing it all day."

"Oh yeah?" He leans against the truck and regards me for a moment. "Hypothetically speaking, how would this speech go?"

I take a step closer to him. "I love that I can be silly with you," I begin.

He seems to be watching me intently, and seconds pass.

"I could go on and on," I say, emphatically. My hands are jittery, and I feel breathless. An awkward pause threatens to drive a wedge in our delicate intimacy, and I feel just how important this moment is for both of us.

A smile twitches on his lips. "Go on."

"I love that you love Lucy just as much as I do," I say, the words rushing out of me, as if they've been waiting to be poured out. "And even though I think it's a bit weird, I still love that you collect VHS tapes. I love that you taught me how to dance. I love how you always made me feel at home. I've loved you since you first offered to help me find Nancy. Who I've found. Well, kind of."

His eyes light up. "Really?"

"Really. But I'll get to that later. I love that you're my partner in crime. I don't think anyone else could've convinced me to impersonate a police officer." He smirks. "I love that we have matching rose tattoos on our shoulders. I love that you helped me hide evidence of the beet massacre." He laughs. "I loved you even more when you finally told me about your scars, and why your job means so much to you."

His throat bobs up and down. I feel my eyes misting over, and my nose prickles.

"I even loved your ugly, rusty, falling-apart truck." I glide my hands over the smooth hood of the truck. "She looks beautiful."

"Yeah," he says. "I've had a lot of time on my hands over the past few months."

He doesn't say it in a mean or passive aggressive way. Just as a simple, heartbreaking fact.

My chest squeezes. "I'm sorry that I haven't got in touch sooner. I really wanted to, Casey, but I just didn't know if I should. I didn't know if you'd even want to see me."

Casey just looks at me intently. "Go on."

I tell him everything that I've been worried about. All of my insecurities wrapped up in a messy, tear-streaked package.

"I love how you love me and accept me for exactly who I am. And I love you, Casey Nolan, for exactly who you are."

I pause for a moment to catch my breath. Casey just stands there, hands shoved into his pockets.

I stretch my hands out and take a small bow. "So, umm. That's it. I just love you. And that's that."

Casey nods. "Okay."

I raise my hands in an evaluating gesture. "Okay?"

He nods. "Well, I'd have to be a special kind of asshole to refuse you after a speech like that," he says, laughing.

"Kind of like what I did to you," I say, embarrassment flaming my face. I pinch the bridge of my nose. "I've been such a complete shit."

He opens his arms and murmurs, "It's okay."

I rush toward him. "I've missed you."

He chuckles. "All the girls say that."

I poke him in the ribs. "No more girls," I say, mockingly.

He wraps me tighter and strokes my hair. "No. In fact, there hasn't been anyone else since last summer."

I look up at him. "You *did* bang the blonde from the concert, didn't you?"

"Maybe a little."

I try to wriggle away, and he folds me in even tighter. "No, Nat, there hasn't been anyone else but you. Not in a long time."

I smile up at him. He's so sweet. And thoughtful. And romantic…

"I'm getting serious blue balls," he says, deadpan.

And there goes the romance.

He laughs. "It's been six months. It's on my mind a lot."

I put a hand on the truck door. "Why don't we go back to your place, then?"

Casey freezes. "For real?"

I seductively drape myself against the truck door and play with a loose tendril of hair. "Well, if you're not that interested…"

Casey whips his keys out and has me inside the cab so fast you could call him Greased Lightning.

"I swear to God, Nat, if you're joking…" he says, smiling like an idiot.

"I'm not joking."

He turns the ignition. "Good."

The next morning, I'm cuddled up to Casey in bed and running my fingers through his chest hair.

"What are you doing?" he asks, tucking his chin down.

"Making patterns," I say. I've never played with chest hair before. I'm rather fascinated. "It reminds me of when I was a kid and I'd rake my fingers through the carpet."

He shakes his head. "You're so weird."

I smile and continue to swirl my fingers over his body. "Yeah, and you totally love it."

A strong, calloused hand reaches for my chin and tilts my face upward. He gives me a slow, scorching kiss. When we break apart, he smiles. "Yeah. I totally do."

He strokes the top of my head. "I'm really digging the new red hair."

"Knew you would," I say, feeling all warm and snuggly and romantic.

"Though your scalp looks like you baked in the sun too long."

And...there goes the romance.

We spend the entire day in bed. We eat muffins and decide to worry about the crumbs later. We cuddle and sip our coffee.

We do, umm, other things. Fun things.

But mostly, we talk.

I tell Casey about my new youth program at the thrift store (which he's totally thrilled about), and he fills me in on the antics the fire hall has been up to. He asks a lot of questions about my newfound family. I tell him about introducing my parents and brothers to my birth family, and how strange yet cool that's been.

"What are they like?" he asks. "Your new family, I guess. I don't know what else to call them."

"Weird. Loud. They eat a lot of butter and Polish things," I say. "Like nalysnyky or perishky."

"I love it when you talk Polish to me."

"Oh, and did I tell you that Karl turned out to be my grandpa?"

"What?"

I fill him in on the back story. When I'm done, Casey lays back on his pillow, fingers laced behind his head. "Wow. Truth is stranger than fiction," he says.

I snuggle up into his chest, my fingers still buried in his chest hair. I'm so glad my prince and my beast are the same person.

"You should read some of the adoption stories I found online," I reply. "Now those are some crazy reunion stories."

"So, did you learn much about Nancy?"

I fill him in on Nancy's history. What she was like, and the many information gaps I still have.

Casey gently squeezes me to his side. "Does it bug you? Still having so many unanswered questions?"

"I'm not sure yet," I answer truthfully. "But in the meantime, I have a wonderful family I can get to know. And they're enough." He kisses the top of my head. "I have one question for you, though," I say.

"What's that?"

"Oakes."

Casey's chest starts to quake with silent laughter.

"He's been overly helpful. Creepily helpful, some might say," I add. "He did the initial search for us and let you look at criminal databases. He even lent us police uniforms, knowing full well that we'd be impersonating cops!"

"Uh huh," Casey grunts.

"What gives? Do you have dirt on him or something?"

Casey pulls his mischievous mouth to the side. "Kinda."

I sit up and twist around to look at Casey. "Spill, Nolan."

He holds up his hands. "Okay. So, one night when I was at work, I heard some unusual noises coming from the showers."

I grimace. "If this gets weird, I don't want to hear it."

Casey sits up with me. "But that's the best part!" he protests. "Anyway, I wasn't sure if I wanted to go inside, but I knew for a fact that everyone else was in either the gym or the kitchen, so I started wondering who was in there."

I tuck my knees up to my chest. "Oh no..."

Casey's eyes glitter with mischief. "Oh yes. Turns out Oakes's wife has a firefighter fetish. They like to sneak in once in a while. He dresses up in some of our old gear and they play 'hide the fire hose.'"

"Ack!" I shriek. "Really?"

He laughs. "Really really."

"Maybe he should consider a career change," I say.

"Who knows? Maybe if he really were a fireman it would take some of the fantasy away." Casey waves a hand through the air. "Anyway, it's not my business. Oakes was more than a little surprised when I stumbled in. I was embarrassed, and he was scared that I'd rat him out. So we made a deal. I turn a blind eye, and he helps me out when I need it."

I blink at him a few times. "I figured it had to be something good."

Casey waggles his eyebrows. "Oh, doing a firefighter is always good."

I roll my eyes.

"Is that a challenge?" he says, grabbing me by the waist. "Or do I have to show you again?"

He pins me onto the mattress, while I laugh and giggle and half-heartedly try to get away.

"You ever been naked on a fire truck?" he asks, sounding breathless.

I give him a bewildered look. "Umm, no."

"Would you like to be?" he asks.

I laugh. "Where'd you get that? The firefighter's book of cheesy pickup lines?"

"Yes," he says. "They hand them out with basic training. Okay. How about this one: My smoke detector is going off like crazy, you're so smokin' hot!"

"Wow. That's like poetry. Take me now."

"There's lots more where that came from."

I look up at him for a moment. He smiles and looks down at me, his breath a little labored. "What?"

"I love you," I say. "So much."

He smiles back. "And I love you, Thrift Shop Girl."

And as I lay my head on Casey's chest once more, I reflect on the journey that he and I have been on. Even though it didn't work out the way I thought it would when it came to meeting my birth mom, it's all okay. Everything I need is right here.

I snuggle deeper into his arms, and it reminds me of being wrapped in my favorite blanket: warm, comforting, and familiar. It feels like coming home.

Acknowledgments

This book has been a long time coming! I started working on it in August of 2014. It has gone through several major redrafts, and at several points, I was tempted to just abandon it and move onto another project.

Thank you Jenny and Meghan, my absolutely wonderful editors at Tryst, for making this book even better! I loved your insightful comments, ideas on how to tweak scenes. It has been an absolute pleasure working with you both.

My husband Chad for (once again) reeling me back in when I felt like my writing was awful and I wanted to scrap the whole project. You're my own personal cheerleader, and I love you so very much.

My early readers, Selena, Amber, Mary, Steph (Australia Steph, to be specific. I know way too many Stephanies), Holly, and Marcus. I doubt this book would have seen the light of day were it not for you. Thank you for your support, encouragement, and general all-around awesomeness.

St. Andrew's Thrift Shop, thank you for allowing me to tour your facility (I'm still drooling over the racks and racks of clothing in your basement. I could literally spend days down there), and for explaining the ins and outs of how you run your store. A special thanks to the manager, Maureen. You are an amazing person, thank you for being so welcoming. (And for sharing the snake customer story with me! I've included it here, with a few minor changes.)

Ania, for clarifying Polish words.

RCMP, friends, and neighbors, for letting me pick your brains on investigations, missing people and what it's like to be a big, bad cop.

Joanna for inspiring the police officer impersonation scene in Chapter 8. (That is, by far, one of my most FAVORITE chapters in this whole book!)

And finally, to my creative, encouraging, absolutely wonderful Facebook community for answering questions on my author FB page. Thank you for helping me brainstorm when I ask you to help me name characters, share bad date stories, etc. A special shout out to Marcus and Rachel. You two have the best answers ever!

CPSIA information can be obtained
at www.ICGtesting.com
Printed in the USA
LVOW08s0150200517
535127LV00001B/26/P

9 781988 387048